D1536514

*Leaving Halberd Peak*

**ROWAN HELAINE**

ISBN: 978-1-7379671-4-9

eISBN: 978-1-7379671-3-2

*To my Stepmom Ellen.*
*You were right. Sometimes bored and horny*
*can be the start of something great.*

*Trigger Warning*

This book contains references to:

- Casual Drug Use
- Child Abandonment
- Consensual BDSM Themes Including Exhibitionism, Corporeal Punishment and Use of Restraints
- A Fuckton of Profanity

# Prologue

"Hey Trin, you here?" Sam called as he came through the kitchen door, swinging several bags of groceries onto the counter. There was no sound aside from the crooning of the winter wind against the side of the cabin, so he set about putting up the perishables and took out a beer. It was quiet. Usually, by this time, his brother Justin would be home and monopolizing the television with a video game controller in his hand.

He climbed the stairs to his loft, thinking she'd laid down with one of her headaches, but when he reached the top of the stairs, there was no one there. Her toothbrush was missing from the cup on the bathroom shelf, so was her glittery purple cosmetics bag and the flowered microfiber turban she twisted around her head after she washed her hair.

He frowned at the tulip-shaped Post-It stuck to the mirror above the bureau. Circling the corner of the unmade bed, he plucked the note off the glass. One short sentence was scrawled in Trinity's girlish, rounded handwriting: *This isn't working anymore.*

*Well, fuck...* Sam snorted softly, crumpling the Post-It in his fist. He probably should've been more surprised than he was, but things hadn't been great the last couple of months. Trinity seemed distracted and withdrawn, and he'd started questioning whether they were ready to move in together when her lease was up. He only wished it hadn't taken her two years to figure out that they were wasting each other's time.

Carrying his beer to the living room, he dropped onto the couch and froze, his hand hanging in a midair reach for the remote. Turning his head, he blinked at the empty cubby in the television stand. Justin's Xbox was gone.

Crossing to his brother's room, Sam gritted his teeth as he twisted the doorknob, bracing himself for what he might find. They'd spent a lifetime walking in on each other at awkward moments, enough to respect the closed-door policy around their shared home, but when he poked his head inside, he felt his stomach clench cruelly. There was nothing but cold, airy emptiness. A diagonal column of late evening sunlight streamed through the window, forming a sharply slanted rhomboid on the dusty floorboards where his brother's bed frame used to be.

Walking back to the living room, he flopped onto the sofa, his hand shaking as he lifted his beer to his lips. He swallowed, feeling an insidious numbness expanding in the hollow of his chest. Reaching for the remote again, he flicked the television on without paying attention. He just needed something to drown out the consuming silence that was threatening to swallow him whole.

"LET'S TAKE A LAP." Gretchen's work wife Jenny leaned over her cubicle wall, flipping her long russet ponytail over her shoulder. "Some sixty-year-old engineer just cornered me in the cafeteria and his opening line, I swear to god, was to tell me how unhealthy my turkey club wrap was. I was like, 'Thank you, Grandpa, as if you've been missing so many meals.'"

"Gotta keep it tight for the scabby old lech contingent." Gretchen pushed back her desk chair, fixing Jenny with a satirical grin. They'd known each other since the second grade, but it'd taken coming to work in the testosterone-drenched halls of Moxley Becker Engineering to make them friends. After a decade in the trenches of the good old boys' club, being called "sweetheart" and "honey" so many times that all the thinly veiled misogyny faded to white noise in the background, it often felt like her female colleagues were the only thing keeping her sane.

Exiting the door of the locked high-security area, they strolled down the third-floor hallway, enjoying the change of scenery for a few minutes. Catching sight of a band of bright-eyed boys coming from the opposite direction, Jenny leaned in, whispering. "Oh, *he's* cute."

*Which one?* Gretchen watched the approaching crowd of men, all sharing the inoffensive, perfectly homogenous good looks of catalog models. As they drew closer, she could make out a volley of "*dudes*" and "*bros*" peppered into the conversation, spoken with the same universal frat boy affectation. One broke rank, a predictably handsome guy with nut-brown hair and shy brown eyes, to step into her path. "Hey, I've seen you around a few times."

"That makes sense," Gretchen began, sliding a bored look in Jenny's direction. She should've been used to this by now, but somehow, she never got past the disagreeable feeling of having strange men pestering her at the office. "I work here."

"Ha, yeah." He laughed easily, tucking his hands into his pockets and looking down in a way that was, *damn him,* actually kind of sweet and self-effacing. Standing about ten feet behind him, his friends looked on with raised eyebrows, waiting to see how bad their comrade crashed and burned. He offered her his hand. "I'm Brian."

"Gretchen." She smiled tightly, ignoring Jenny's salacious smirk.

"Nice to meet you, Gretchen." Brian stepped to the side, running his hand over the back of his neck. "I guess I'll see you around."

"Well, hello, brown eyes!" Jenny giggled as soon as they were out of earshot. "You know what? You should totally invite him to come to the cabin in Bar Harbor this weekend!"

"I don't even *know* him." Gretchen sighed, shaking her head. It was tough enough running into her last three boyfriends in these halls at least once a week, and if she was being honest with herself, she was tiring of the endless date-breakup-repeat cycle. "Anyway, I'm off engineers."

"Your loss, honey," her friend said with a grin. Moxley Becker was a target-rich environment. In a place with such an unbalanced ratio of males to females, a girl only had to be single if she wanted to, and Jenny was *never* single for long. "Just be advised that there probably won't be many more weekends in Maine."

"Seth not working out?"

Jenny rolled her eyes at the name of her current boyfriend, the owner of the aforementioned vacation cabin. "We've been together for almost eight months, and he's still dragging his feet. You know?"

"I guess if it's not right, it's not right." Gretchen shrugged, squashing the instinct to point out that once Jenny got her dream wedding, she'd have to be, you know, *married*.

"That Brian guy's a cutie, though." Jenny brightened, giving her a playful nudge. "If you don't want him, I'll take him."

# CHAPTER
*One*

Gretchen cursed as an ominous shudder went through the front end of her car, loud enough to obscure the Japanese language lesson playing through the speakers. Sighting an exit sign, she sent up a silent word of thanks to the road gods and maneuvered across two empty lanes, approaching the stop sign at the end of the ramp just as a sharp *pop* split the air. The lesson cut off mid-sentence, and the engine sent out a long-suffering death rattle.

"Come on, baby. Don't do this to me." Reaching up, she turned the key again, forcing a tight hiss through her teeth as the engine failed to turn over. Sitting back, she began mentally calculating how much cash she had stuffed into the zippered bag under her seat. Rural tow truck drivers rarely took credit cards at the curb, and it was way too late to find an open bank.

She climbed out to roll the little hatchback onto to the shoulder, pushing with all her strength and steering one-handed. She reached in and grabbed her backpack out of the rear footwell, stuffed her money into her pocket, and slammed the door. Giving the front grill of the unresponsive car a mournful look, she slung her bag over her shoulder and started trudging along the densely forested road, following the bouncing globe of light emitted by her flashlight keychain.

Passing a faded sign that read, "Welcome to Halberd Peak, Home of the Fighting Fisher Cats," she exhaled a sigh of relief, happy that she was at least pointed toward civilization. Noticing a shimmer of neon peeking between the trees, she caught sight of what appeared to be a brightly lit twelve-foot-tall lumberjack standing next to a seedy Swiss chalet with gap-toothed gingerbread eaves. The flickering roof-mounted sign announced the bizarre structure as Rooster's Bill_ards & Mini Go_f in eye-watering electric green, but as she drew closer, she could see that the putt-putt course had become overgrown, the untended attractions marooned in a waist-high tangle of pricker bushes.

There was a moment of doubt as she navigated the unpaved parking lot, almost breaking an ankle when she stepped into a pothole and pitched forward. Glowering at the front of the building, she felt around for her keychain and brushed the pebbles and dirt off her skinned knees. Muffled strains of something raw and bluesy played through the walls as she stepped up onto the porch and yanked open the door, sending the rugged cadence of an twelve-bar riff spiraling out into the darkness.

Shoving her keys into the pocket of her shorts, she limped up to the bar and slid onto a stool, ignoring the curious stares of the handful of people milling around the room. Her eyes burned with exhaustion, and she laid her forehead down against the backs of her hands before she could stop to consider the questionable substances that might be smeared on the hideous beige laminate.

WELL, *this* was unexpected. A strange woman had just come stumbling in forty minutes before closing and now appeared to have fallen asleep facedown at the end of the counter, her dark hair forming a fluffy mound on the bar top. Folding his book closed, Sam hopped off the ledge in front of the bottle display and swept an amused glance around the room, approaching the slumbering creature. "Hey, sleeping beauty, you want to order something?"

"Yeah. I'll take a coffee with a handful of crushed caffeine pills around the rim," she mumbled, lifting her head and pushing an overgrown fringe of curly bangs out of her eyes. They were bloodshot and somewhat glazed, but extraordinary; one a warm brown, the other sea glass green. "Could I use your phone? I need to find a tow truck, but mine's dead."

Sam rocked back on his heels, shouting over his shoulder to one of the men clustered around the big screen television. "Hey, Charlie! Lady needs a tow!"

Charlie Scarver lumbered over and leaned one elbow on the counter, doing his best impression of a solicitous grin. Thankfully, his thick salt-and-pepper beard hid the worst of the damage to his teeth. "Whatcha need, little lady?"

"My car broke down at the end of the exit." She jabbed a thumb over her shoulder. "I pushed her off to the side but I'm not even sure if she's worth saving at this point."

"No worries. We can check it out tomorrow if you wanna give me the keys." Charlie shrugged, holding out one massive paw. "You need a ride into town?"

"I uh..." She looked circumspect, as if she was trying to gauge the wisdom in accepting. Sam forced down a smile. Anyone who'd been in Halberd Peak for five minutes had seen Charlie and his husband Frank pushing a cart through the aisles at Lundy's Grocery, bickering about whether they'd bought chunky or smooth peanut butter last time.

"Listen, I can take a look at it if you want to wait until after close," Sam offered. "But Charlie's the only tow in town."

"No, it's okay." She fished her keys out of her pocket and slapped them into the old mechanic's hand. "Is there a hotel nearby?"

"Not too far." Charlie bobbed his head. "Tell you what, you hang out here. I'll swing back and get you once I have the car hitched up. I can drop you at the Sugar Birch Motor Lodge on my way into town."

"Great, thanks." She pivoted back to the bar as Charlie left and gave Sam a weak smile. "And thank *you*, too."

"Not a problem." Sam reached for the coffee and hesitated, knowing that he'd be serving her the sludge at the bottom of the pot. "You sure I can't get you something else?"

"At this point, the caffeine'll get me back to normal until I can find a place to crash." She laughed unenthusiastically, her voice scratchy with exhaustion.

"Sounds like you know what you're doing." Sam emptied the pot into her cup, then he stood back against the bar and crossed his arms again. "I didn't want to say so while he was here, but you've got nothing to worry about with Charlie. He's a good guy."

"Thanks." She reached for a packet of sweetener and shook it into her cup.

"You just passing through, or staying in town for a while?"

"I'll be sticking around until I know what's up with the

car." Sipping her coffee, she winced and set it back down, her eyes flicking to his. "I guess I finally drove the doors off her."

"Well, if you need to make some cash in the meantime, I just lost a waitress," he suggested, then frowned at the impulse, because it wasn't like him to be helpful to strangers. Not anymore.

"Nah, I'm good." She tucked her hands between her knees, her smile becoming more genuine.

"Gotcha." Sam started toward the kitchen, where his grill person was already cleaning up for the night. One of the dishwashers quit last week, which meant he had another hour of work to look forward to, standing at the pot sink in a rubber apron. "Coffee's on the house."

"Thanks!" She beamed, displaying a slight gap between her two front teeth. Sam felt the urge to break a stein atop his head.

---

WAKING in her motel room just after eleven a.m., Gretchen curled her lip at the mysterious stains on the baby shit-green carpet, the peeling wallpaper, and the tatters of dusty cobwebs decorating the popcorn ceiling. She'd been too tired to care about how *disgusting* the place was the night before, reasoning that at least there were no signs of bedbugs or bullet holes. Still, looking around in the harsh light of day, she decided that if she was going to spend another night in Halberd Peak, she would have to find better accommodations.

The apathetic teenager in the office informed her that there were much nicer places downtown. It appeared

Gretchen had washed up in the low-rent fringe, while the fashionable elite dominated the center of town. All she had to do was follow the main road into the eye of the picturesque village and pick up a copy of the *Halberd Peak Statesman* to check the listings in the back.

Her first order of business was finding something to eat that didn't come from a vending machine. Wandering into a charmingly offbeat café, she ordered a cherry soda and grilled chicken pesto wrap from the kid at the counter and slid into a booth against the exposed brick wall. She was still staring up at the man-sized papier-mâché leopard frog squatting in one corner of the ceiling when a curvaceous beauty with a pixie cap of unicorn-dyed hair brought out her sandwich. Gretchen seized the opportunity to ask if there were any rooms available in town.

"There's the Quartz River Inn up the hill, but it's the busy season, so they're usually booked up." The woman paused to gnaw on a frosted pink lip, her high, graceful cheekbones and tawny skin suggesting a heritage somewhere in the Abenaki or Mohawk Nations. "And there are a bunch of PopCurb rentals, as long as you don't have any pets. That stupid app seems to have taken over the whole town if you want the truth."

*Ugh.* Gretchen wrinkled her nose at the notion. The last time she'd attempted a PopCurb, she'd shown up to find an air mattress on the floor of a strange man's walk-in closet and ended up camping out in her car for the night. Faced with spending another night at the motor lodge though, she was willing to reconsider her distaste for the app. Lifting half of her wrap out of its basket, she took a gigantic bite and chewed while she reviewed PopCurb's availability.

Wow. It really *was* the busy season.

Of the properties listed for short-term rental, there was a tent site at what looked to be a hippie encampment and a single room that appeared to be decked out in wall-to-wall chintz and required guests to share a bathroom with the residents and their four cats. Setting down her phone, she decided to concentrate on her food before she sank into desolation. The waitress approached again, and Gretchen stole a look at the name tag pinned to her apron: *Cricket*. "Anything?"

"Not unless I want to buy a tent." Gretchen sighed with dejection. "I guess I'm stuck at the motor lodge."

"Oh *god*." The waitress shook her head, giggling in horror. "That place should've been condemned years ago!"

"Tell me about it."

"Hold on." Cricket sat down opposite her and fished her phone out of her apron pocket. Tapping out a quick message, she gave Gretchen an encouraging smile. "Texting a friend. He might have a place you can use. He usually wouldn't rent it out, but maybe he's in a charitable mood."

Her phone pinged, and Cricket looked down, her brows gathering. She looked up again. "How long were you planning to be in town?"

"I don't really know." Gretchen shrugged. "My car's out of commission at the moment, and it's a cute area. I don't have anywhere to be right now; I could see staying for a month."

The girl nodded and started tapping a reply into her phone, nibbling her lower lip as she went. A moment went by, and Cricket gazed intently at the screen, waiting. The phone chirruped and Cricket's expression brightened. "He says you can take the house, but the month-to-month rate is pretty expensive."

Cricket turned her phone to show her the amount quoted, and Gretchen stifled a smile. It was several hundred dollars *less* than she'd paid for her old apartment, and that was with a year-long lease. Lifting her gaze to meet Cricket's, she nodded her approval. "I can handle that."

# CHAPTER
## *Two*

Cricket Bonhomme's fuchsia pink Volkswagen bug pulled into the parking lot. Sam stopped rolling cases of beer into the rear storeroom and swiped his forearm across his face, his breath catching at the sight of the girl climbing out of the passenger side.

*Fuck.* Sam looked away as she turned her back to the building and leaned into the open car window, the skirt of her moss green sundress hiking up against the backs of her rosy thighs. *It just* had *to be her.*

Halberd Peak's resident coffee pusher had contacted him earlier to ask if his old cabin at the top of the hill was still empty. Although the prospect of having a stranger living in the house he'd built with his own two hands didn't thrill him, Cricket was a friend, and he didn't have too many of those. Besides, he hadn't been able to bring himself to venture up there for two years, and Cricket's brother Murphy, one of his part-time employees, had already gone to the trouble of coming by to get the place ready.

He turned around as the wheels of Cricket's car

crunched over the uneven ground of the lot. She paused at the exit, blasted two short honks, and hooked a hairpin turn onto the road, speeding away. The girl turned and caught sight of him, shielding her prismatic eyes with one hand. "Oh, hey. It's you!"

Ambling to the end of the cement loading dock, he hopped down. "You're here for the house?"

"Yup! Gretchen Clarke." She took a step in his direction and offered him her hand. He didn't move to shake it, and she dropped it after a beat. Sam squelched the observation that she looked better now that she'd had a good night's rest and a shower. Standing there with sunlight glinting off her glossy chocolate-colored curls and neon pink Band-Aids on both her knees, she had an unexpected angelic quality about her that threw him off-balance.

He angled his chin toward the bar. "If you want to come inside and sign the rental agreement, I can get you the keys."

"Right…" She lifted her suitcase off the packed clay and followed him into the side door, squinting in the sudden darkness.

He'd already laid the paperwork out on the bar. Leaning against the edge of a nearby table, he waited for her to finish paging through the agreement. Despite his best efforts to avoid looking at her, he caught himself admiring the way the lightweight fabric of her dress skimmed her curves. As he watched, one thin spaghetti strap slipped off her shoulder and she reflexively slid it back up. He almost chuckled as she lifted one small foot and scratched the back of her leg with the toe of her blue low top sneaker, but caught himself and slapped on a fresh scowl.

STEALING another glance at the berserker standing behind her, Gretchen clicked the button on her pen a few times, shifting her weight from one foot to the other. She didn't know if he intended to make her nervous, but he was fucking *intense*. For one thing, Samuel Soren was tall. Like... crushed under a fallen *redwood* tall, with two full sleeves of intricate greyscale tattoos and the kind of thick, ropy muscles that made him appear to swell in her peripheral vision.

"All right, there you go." Folding the pages over, she turned to him, mustering up a breezy smile. "Nice and legal."

"Great," he grunted, maintaining his hard-bitten exterior at all costs.

"Oh, hey." She tilted her head to the side, gazing at his tattooed forearm. Her mouth fell open. "Wait...is that Godzilla?"

His lips twitched. "Yes."

"Ha!" She took a step toward him and bent to scan the movie monsters adorning his bicep. "Oh, far out! You've got 'em all, don't you? You know, that's what I call those really uncomfortable phone calls you get from your exes around the holidays? Kaiju attacks. Because they come on way too strong and they're a little scary."

Setting his mouth into a humorless straight line, he reached into his jeans pocket for the keys and tossed them to her underhand, like he was lobbing a softball. Pushing away from the table, he strode toward the swinging doors at the back of the hall, the overhead lights glinting off the top of his utilitarian shaved skull. "Follow the stairs behind the building. Can't miss it."

Gretchen stood for a moment, clasping the keys in one

outstretched hand, and blinked at the doors where he'd disappeared.

Lugging her suitcase out the door and up the hill as directed, she was pleasantly surprised to discover a cute single-dormer cabin perched at the top. Stepping inside, she lingered for a moment, admiring the cool blond wood, overstuffed sofa, and bank of empty bookcases against the opposite wall. There was a small but bright kitchen to the right, with white tile counters and beadboard cabinets, and to the left, an empty guest bedroom with a combination bath and laundry room. At the rear of the house, there was a wraparound deck looking out into the woods beyond, with a little stamped metal patio set. Everything was stripped down and compact, designed for optimal function, without an inch of wasted space.

Climbing the stairs, the glass brick wall of the master bath rose to the left, shielding the bed from the direct view of anyone standing below. The picture window on the far wall overlooked a sharp stone embankment, the land sloping downward at a deep seventy-degree incline and widening into a small valley traversed by a rocky tributary stream. Looking down, she caught sight of a band of fire-flies dancing above the water.

---

"Hey, Soren..." Sam was pouring a beer as Murphy slid past him, slapping his shoulder hard enough to make him slosh foam over the toes of his boots. Younger than Sam by almost fifteen years, Murphy still exhibited the youthful exuberance of a man who had yet to have his dreams yanked out of his ass and pissed on. "I heard you finally let the old cabin go. To that hot little brunette who's been hanging around my sister."

"Best to not get attached," Sam grumbled, sending a glare over his shoulder. Halberd Peak was a small town and there was a pronounced shortage of single women. The arrival of a toothsome creature like Gretchen Clarke was bound to make news, even if she was only temporary. "She's only renting for a month."

"I dunno, man." Murphy chuckled, displaying the same unsinkable optimism that drove all his personal choices. The kid was one short semester away from earning his teaching certificate for early childhood education, a fact that was equal parts touching and terrifying when one stopped to imagine him molding young minds. "Cricket says she could stick around for a while."

"Could happen." Sam slid the beer across the bar and pivoted to the kitchen window when the bell rang, signaling that someone's burger was up. He waved a waitress over to claim it and turned to take another drink order, working to push thoughts of his leggy renter out of his mind.

"So, what's she do?" Murphy asked, setting to work slicing oranges. "Must be making good money to afford what you're charging."

Sam's head shot up and he narrowed his eyes, a breath away from demanding how the hell anyone knew what he was charging her. Then he remembered that Cricket had been the one to broker the deal and swallowed the knee-jerk impulse to tell Murphy to mind his fucking business. "I don't know. Ask your sister."

"I *did*." Murphy jabbed his paring knife into the air, punctuating the statement. "She said she was a designer but wouldn't give me any more than that. I figured that you ran a background check when you rented her the place, so you might have a better idea."

"All I know is she doesn't have a criminal record, and she paid up-front. I never saw a pay stub." Sam shoved through the swinging doors and stepped out the back to hide in the protective blue glow of the bug zapper. As if his thoughts had summoned her out of thin air, he heard the soft clicking of an approaching ten-speed and turned just in time to see Gretchen walking a bicycle through the darkened parking lot.

He had to give her credit; she'd put together a very workable routine in a matter of a few short days. Someone already lent her a bike to get around until she got her car back, and he'd seen her down at the town flea market on Sunday, combing through the refurbished cast iron for a frying pan.

Sam pushed away from the wall when she came to the foot of the steps and bent to heft the bike over one shoulder. Did she really intend to carry that thing to the top of the stairs? Against his better judgment, he called out to her. "Hey!"

She spun to face him, only to get the railing wedged between the spokes of her rear wheel. The bike slipped off her shoulder and clattered to one side as she tripped backward and planted ass-first into a drift of dry pine needles. Sam hopped down and trotted over as she struggled to her feet, cursing softly. He choked back a snicker as she swatted the dirt and fallen leaves off the back of her cutoff jeans. "I was going to say you could lock that up down here. It won't get rained on."

"Oh, uh..." She glanced at the hollow under the bar's rear landing, then up at him, her cheeks flushing. "I guess if you don't mind. Thanks."

*Damn. I bet she blushes all over.* Sam took a giant step back and folded his arms, placing a physical barrier between their bodies. "I just don't need the lawsuit when you fall and break your neck trying to hump that thing up the stairs."

"Gee," she muttered, bending to turn the bike upright. "What a *prince*."

Her eyes went to his arms as she straightened. A light of recognition sparked in her gaze, and he heard her whisper to herself. "*Peer Gynt?*"

Sam glanced down at his arm, nonplussed. Anyone with the most basic knowledge of cult film could pick out the movie monsters adorning his left arm, but she was the first person to clock the scene on his right. Most people saw a brace of slavering, wild-haired trolls storming the gothic arches of a subterranean palace and asked if it was a *Lord of the Rings* reference. Shaking off his surprise, he dropped his arms to his sides.

"Hey, if you want to drag that thing up and down that hill all the time, be my guest." He stepped out of her way as she rolled the bike toward the pool hall. "At least you'll be able to stop after you get your car back."

"Car's dead." She bent to thread the locking cable through the latticework under the deck. Sam couldn't help but admire the way her denim shorts molded to the curve of her ass, quickly dragging his eyes away before she could catch him staring. She straightened, sighed with resignation, and pushed her bangs out of her face. They tumbled forward again, falling haphazard across one eye like a Friesian pony. "It was just her time."

"I'm sorry for your loss," he deadpanned, tracking her movement as she trotted past him, her hands smoothing over her hips as she went.

"Your sarcasm has been noted." She rolled her other-worldly eyes at him over her shoulder, favoring him with an indomitable smile. "But don't worry. I'm never down for long."

"I believe you," he murmured, watching her sashay up the stairs.

# CHAPTER
*Three*

Sitting in her regular booth at The Paper Frog Café, Gretchen scrolled through the morning's emails, noting any feedback on her latest concept. It was a damn good thing that Cricket offered free WIFI, because according to the cable company, by the time they could hook up internet service at the cabin, she'd be ready to pay another month's lease. The upside to living in a black hole was that she no longer worked in an isolated bubble. Cricket now expected to find Gretchen sitting on the stoop every morning when she came down to unlock the shop.

"You know, the WIFI reaches upstairs." Cricket appeared, leaning over the table to refill Gretchen's coffee cup. "Maybe you could use my apartment as an office during the day."

"I might take you up on that." She smiled, reaching for the creamer. "I do most of my concept and analysis work offline, but if I'm still here by the time we get to final development, I won't be able to go without."

"Well, let me know. I bet Barb would love the company." Cricket slid into the booth opposite her. "I'd let her come down here during the day, but some people are allergic to cats."

"Probably wise." Gretchen lifted her mug, savoring a sip of Cricket's freshly brewed extra dark roast Ethiopian Yirgacheffe. It was chocolaty and smooth, with almost no acidity at all. The woman had a serious gift for the roaster.

"So, now that you're done with work for the moment..." Cricket bent closer, dropping her voice to a conspiratorial whisper. "You should know, people have been asking about you. The guys, mostly."

"Men are like crows." Gretchen smirked. "They love anything shiny and new."

"So I should tell my little brother you're not available?" Cricket quirked an eyebrow.

"I'm not sure Murphy would be a good idea." Not that he wasn't *adorable,* with his satiny black hair bound up in a ski bro topknot, leather wrist cuffs, and easy smile. He was a little young, but under any other circumstances, she'd happily spread him on a cracker. "I feel like I'd break him."

"Yeah." Cricket giggled. "He has a lot of fuckboy tendencies to work through before he'll be ready for someone like you."

"Thank you? I think?"

"Oh, it's totally a compliment." Cricket reached across the table to pat her hand as she slid out of the booth. She picked up the coffee pot and carried it behind the counter, continuing to talk to her as she started a fresh pot. "Besides, you're not gonna be around long enough to get started with anyone, right?"

"No, at the moment I'm only good to hit it and quit it." Gretchen grinned, grateful that they were the only ones in the café. She gazed at her computer screen and started composing an email response, her thoughts going to the grim colossus who'd rented her the cabin up the mountain. He wasn't traditionally good-looking, yet there was something about him. Striking, she decided. He was more striking than handsome, with those severe eyebrows that formed two bold slashes above his tar-black eyes. "The only kind of romantic entanglements I can handle right now are the kind where I barely even *like* the guy. If I get hard up, I'll hit up the landlord."

"Wait, what?" Cricket came skidding to a stop next to her table, her cheerful mood replaced by abject horror. "Oh no. Oh, no-no-no-no-no-no *no*."

"Geez. Tell me what you really think." Gretchen frowned, feeling mildly insulted.

"No, it's not that..." Cricket crouched down next to the table, gazing up at her with huge, pleading brown eyes. "You can't mess with Soren. He got *brutally* fucked over a while ago. Like, in the worst way imaginable."

"You can't just drop a nugget like that and leave a person hanging."

"Okay..." Cricket sat down to face her again, folding her hands on the table like a newscaster announcing the death toll following a natural disaster. "A few years back, his fiancée left him. For his *little brother*."

Gretchen's mouth dropped open. "Wow. That is indeed brutal."

"I know! It's pretty baffling to think about, especially if you've ever met Justin." Cricket raked her fingers through her hair, making it stand out in all different directions. "My opinion? It was easier for Trinity to lead Justin around by his dick."

"I can see that. Soren seems a little too prickly for that kind of maneuvering."

"That's what I'm *saying*." Cricket gave her an urging

smile. "I know it feels personal, but you can't take it that way. He's just been in a *really* shitty mood for a few years."

---

Sam woke around noon most days after the rest of the town was already going about its business. Kicking off the sheets, he swung his legs over the side of the bed and sat for a few seconds, waiting for the lingering haze of sleep to clear. When he could stand upright without feeling like someone had hit him with a stun gun, he shuffled into the bathroom to piss, brush his teeth, and jump in the shower.

Stepping into the stall, he let the lukewarm water wash over his shoulders and ease some of the tension from his muscles. He ran a hand over his chest, casting around for something to occupy his thoughts outside of the little minx sleeping in his house; a task made more difficult by every guy at the bar keeping tabs on her activities with the voracious scrutiny of tabloid reporters.

The situation was further exacerbated when he'd caught sight of her pushing her bike through the parking lot for the second time that week. This time she'd been licking an ice cream cone and humming a cheerful tune, without a care in the world.

Of course, he'd pick that moment to take out the garbage. Nothing made a man feel quite so undeserving as standing next to a reeking Dumpster while watching a celestial creature like Gretchen Clarke glide by, working her tongue around a scoop of butter pecan. She'd bent down to secure her bike lock, holding her ice cream up out of the way, and giving him a perfect vantage point to see the shadows nestling between the two half-rounds of her tits. Then she'd bounced away, unaware of the man standing nearby, drowning in an undertow of sudden overpowering lust like he hadn't experienced in *years*.

Pressing one hand against the shower wall, he ran his palm along his erection from the root, thinking about her legs in that diabolical little green dress. He thought about the inviting way she'd smiled at him that first time, so open and warm, before he'd made a point of being an unmitigated *prick* to her. He thought about seeing her last night, alone in her own happy little universe, and the way he'd ached to reach out and take a piece of that serenity for himself.

*Jesus, fuck.* He snarled under his breath, tightening his grip. This needed to stop. The girl had been in town for two weeks and he couldn't stop thinking about her. Some nights, he'd be polishing glasses or taking an order and he'd *swear* he could hear her moan in his ear. A shudder would go through his body, and he'd feel her moving under him, her soft mouth crushed against his shoulder. It'd be all he could do to press his hands to the bar top and breathe through the wave of dizziness as all the blood in his head rushed south.

With that final thought, he came so hard that it almost brought him to his knees, his cock pulsing in his hand. He groaned at the release, relief washing over him. Perhaps now he could turn his thoughts to other things, rather than obsessing about a woman he couldn't even bring himself to be civil to. Turning off the water, he reached for a towel to dry himself and stepped out onto the ugly linoleum floor. Crossing into the tiny cubbyhole of his bedroom, he flopped back onto his bed to stare at the stained drop ceiling tiles overhead. He reminded himself that if he could just hold out for a little while longer, she'd be gone, and things could go back to normal.

"Vermont? What in the world are you doing in *Vermont*, Sweet Girl?" Gretchen's mother's concerned Connecticut nasality fed down the line, and she heard her hold the mouthpiece to her shoulder, shouting for her father to swap the laundry when the buzzer went off. "Why didn't you tell me you were planning such a radical move?"

"Because I really can't stress how *little* I planned it, Mom." Gretchen laughed, setting her speckled pothos plant under the kitchen faucet. "I got in the car and started driving."

"I don't understand. Did something happen, sweetie?"

"No, not really." To be honest, that was a big part of the problem. She felt like she'd wasted so many years in stasis, waiting for her life to start. Leaning one hip against the counter, she closed her eyes. "I just felt like I was going the same places and meeting the same people, over and over. I was living the definition of insanity."

She heard her mother take a deep, calming breath, in through her lips and out through her nose. Gretchen imagined her plopping down wherever she was and folding her legs into lotus position, breathing through her confusion. She was probably wearing a caftan, too. "I suppose I can understand that. Although if you'd told me you were leaving, I wouldn't have held your spot for the women's mindfulness seminar."

"Thank you." Gretchen let out a satirical laugh. "I crave your validation above all else, Mother."

"You know it's your good looks that save you, right? If you'd been an ugly baby, I would have left you for the coyotes," her mother returned. "And I suppose this *also* means you'll miss Great Aunt Lorraine's birthday? Your father was going to make his curried snapper."

"Unfortunately, yes." A happy bonus, considering she'd spent last year's gathering alternately dodging questions from inquisitive family members about why she hadn't gotten married and settled down yet and listening to her cantankerous old aunt criticize her mother about "*all that woo-woo hippie nonsense.*"

Her mother gave a long-suffering sigh, no doubt wishing she *too* could flee the state. "What about Japan? Have you heard back yet?"

"No." The Tokyo job was the carrot they'd dangled when she took the gig; the chance to act as project leader in a foreign country. "But we're supposed to find out soon."

Her mother was quiet for a long moment. Gretchen could picture the frown darkening her otherwise cheerful face. "This doesn't have anything to do with that little toad Brian, does it? I swear, I could put my foot straight up his ass, the way he thinks he can just pop in and stir the pot..."

"I blocked him, so you don't have to start planning the intervention quite yet." Gretchen grimaced at the mention of her ex-boyfriend's name. He wasn't *dangerous*; he just had an annoying habit of popping up at inconvenient times and making a heap of empty promises. The shitty part was that it had nothing to do with getting her *back*. He just derived a sadistic ego boost from damaging her calm. "New subject."

"New subject, new subject," her mother ruminated. "Did you find a nice place to stay? Are you being kind to yourself?"

"I am happy to report that I am not living out of a cardboard box." Gretchen peered out the window at the loud *beep-beep-beep* of a truck reversing. From this angle, she could just make out the white top of a box truck backing up to the rear of the pool hall. There was a fluttering of paper in the background.

"Do you realize I can't even find Halberd Peak on a map?" her mother asked, sounding befuddled.

"They have the money to stay small." Gretchen leaned away from the window and started pushing back her cuticles with a thumbnail, the way she did when she was thinking. "If you look it up online, we're *right* below the border."

"Oh wow, you're *way* up there."

"Yup. Almost made it to Montreal before the car died."

"Montreal is lovely," her mother mused, a sentimental note in her voice. "Your dad and I go there for that tantra workshop every year. Maybe this time we can stop and see you on the way!"

Gretchen gave a pained laugh, shaking her head at her mother's enthusiastic sexual practices. If anyone ever wondered at her choice of profession or general attitude, a brief introduction to her parents would clear up any confusion.

# CHAPTER
## Four

"Soren!" A vivacious feminine shriek rang out, and Gretchen turned to watch a nimble woman with lustrous deep copper skin and a fall of fine ombré braids vault over the bar, launching herself into the grouchy bartender's arms.

"Hey, Peanut!" Soren crowed, clapping his hands over the mysterious stranger's back and spinning, depositing the newcomer back on the ground with a deeply uncharacteristic belly laugh. Throwing his arm around the girl's shoulders, he reached across the counter to shake hands with the All-American wet dream of a man who'd just walked in. The golden boy laughed and set a silver trophy on the counter between them as the girl trotted around the end of the bar and tucked herself against Trophy Man's side.

"Dude," Gretchen murmured to Cricket, resting her pool cue against the toe of her sneaker. "Don't look now, but the world may be coming to an end."

"Oh, that's just Paige Batista." Cricket grinned, oozing nonchalance as she bent to line up a shot. "She's an absolute lunatic, but if *anyone* could get a smile out of Sourpuss Soren, it'd be her."

"And that tall drink of whole milk with her?"

"Ah, yes..." Cricket wriggled her eyebrows. "Dane Nilsson. There isn't a woman under seventy-five in this town that hasn't memorized the back pockets of those jeans, not that any of us ever got a chance. Those two have practically been together from *infancy*."

Her friend shot her a suggestive smirk from her stooped position over the table. "*You'll* appreciate this: Dane's bi and Paige likes to watch, so they occasionally pick up a little snack to share. To be a fly on the wall of *that* bedroom, am I right?"

"Usually, you have to pass out an anonymous questionnaire to get that kind of insight into the sex lives of strangers." Gretchen laughed, although the thought of watching a beautiful specimen of manhood like Dane with another man tweaked her inner voyeur.

"Yeah, well, I'm only telling you now because they're not at all secretive about it. It was weird for me because I've known them since preschool, but then I thought, whatever. They're happy." The balls clacked together, and Cricket straightened to study the table, calculating her next angle of attack. "The annoying part is they're both totally decent people. One time in high school, some asshole called me flat-chested, and Paige poured a tub of salad dressing down the back of his shirt."

"Sounds like a standup chick." Gretchen glanced back over her shoulder, taking in the bizarre scene unfolding nearby. "Speaking of weird, I'm not sure I can handle seeing Soren *emote* like that."

"Don't worry, you haven't stumbled into the *Twilight Zone*." Cricket scratched on her next shot and came to stand next to her. "He's been known to crack a smile from time to time."

"Could've fooled me," Gretchen murmured, mentally aligning balls with pockets.

"I guess you just bring the foul humor out in him." Cricket giggled, giving her a coltish hip bump.

"Seriously..." Gretchen slid a murderous glare in the other woman's direction. Ever since she'd admitted to having the *teeniest* bit of a thing for the surly pool hall owner, Cricket had teased her about it with the tenacity of a bull terrier. "Fuck all the way off."

"Cricket!" a voice trumpeted behind them, and both women turned in unison. Paige appeared, a broad smile on her face. "You look great! How's business?"

"Haven't gone bankrupt yet." Cricket laughed. "How's Boston?"

"*Crazy.*" Paige grinned, stuffing her hands into the pockets of her wide-leg jeans. "We just came by to settle a bet I lost to Soren last time we were in town. I have to let him put my old track and field trophy up above the bar."

Turning to Gretchen, Paige rocked back on her heels, the gold post in her eyebrow glittering as she gave her a welcoming once over. "I'm Paige. You must be new."

"Gretchen. My car broke down outside of town and Cricket's been kind enough to adopt me." Gretchen shook her hand, amused by Paige's directness. "What was the bet about?"

"We both had to strip naked and race down Main Street at two a.m." Paige tossed the heavy curtain of her golden-tipped hair, adding a rueful smirk. "I was banking on him chickening out and losing by default. How was I to know he'd actually drop trou?"

Cricket cackled like a mischievous sprite. "Dane was okay with this?"

"Dane was waving the flag." Soren appeared behind Paige, handing her a hard root beer and giving her shoulder a brotherly slap. "Don't tell me you're still narky about losing."

"I'm not narky!" she snapped with exaggerated indignity. "You just have freakishly long legs."

---

SAM WASN'T sure how he felt seeing Paige and Cricket chatting with Gretchen. It was an uncomfortable collision of worlds, watching two of his closest friends trading embarrassing anecdotes with the enigmatic siren who'd stalked his fantasies ever since she'd mounted his bar stool.

*Fuck. Don't think about mounting.* Retreating behind the bar, Sam kept his eyes on his work, ignoring the little cluster of women bonding over their mutual acquaintance with *him*. Oh, the irony. Dane claimed a seat in front of him and ordered a beer, glancing over his shoulder to where Paige drew the girls together, no doubt plotting another act of chaotic fuckery. "No good can come from this."

Grunting in acknowledgment of Paige's uncanny ability to spark mayhem wherever she went, Sam started setting up a row of shots for the crew of frat boys in the corner. Handing them off to one of the waitresses, he stood back and ran his hand over his crown, enjoying the level texture of the stubble beneath his fingers. It was a curiously soothing gesture he performed multiple times a day, and it helped to redirect his thoughts whenever they grew troubled. An annoyingly shrewd bastard in his own right, Dane gave him an astute grin. "Looks like there've been some changes since last time we were in town."

"*One,*" Sam corrected him, fixing his friend with a warning glare. "There's been *one* change."

"And for once, Murphy didn't exaggerate. She's cute as hell." Dane pressed the bottle to his lips, arching an eyebrow. Sam narrowed his eyes, and Dane held up his hands, adding a blameless smile. "Hey, it's a small town. People talk. Frankly, it's refreshing to not have all the gossip directed at whether or not Paige and I are engaged."

Sam gave him a pernicious smirk. "Speaking of, when are you two crazy kids getting hitched?"

"Fuck you, dude." Dane laughed. "You know how she feels about the wedding industrial complex. Besides, the minute I put a ring on it, all the questions about when we're going to 'start a family' begin. I love that girl more than my own life, but have you ever listened to a fucking gender studies professor rant about reproductive autonomy? You'll pray for death."

A peal of riotous female laughter rose from the nearby pool table, and Dane turned to crane his neck in their direction. "What's the story, because someone like her can't be hanging around this place for the ambiance."

"It's convenient," Sam bit out. "She's renting the cabin up the hill."

"Wait, *your* cabin?" Dane coughed, his eyes widening. "I thought you'd torn it down already."

"I still might," he grumbled. "She'll be leaving in a couple weeks."

"Too bad." Dane cast another appreciative glance over his shoulder.

The implication wasn't lost on Sam. Gretchen Clarke was a breath of air so fresh that she made him lightheaded.

Too bad he couldn't trust himself to be around her. "It is what it is."

Dane looked dubious, but was savvy enough to let the topic drop. "Oh, hey...we brought the new bike up. We were thinking about getting a group together and taking a ride down to the Blues Festival this weekend."

"I'd be into that." Sam smiled, grateful for the change of subject. He'd been so busy with the bar that aside from a few sunny days where he'd taken the Harley on runs into town, the bike had been sitting neglected in the storage shed all season. The idea of getting out on the road for a day lifted his spirits.

# CHAPTER
## Five

To think, a few short hours ago, she'd been looking forward to this little outing. Then she came down the steps to meet the rest of the crew in what she *thought* was a sensible ensemble of jeans, boots, and a denim jacket over her favorite Freddie Mercury T-shirt. Sure, she was two-thirds of the way to a Canadian tuxedo, but it seemed like a small sacrifice to make to protect her arms from potential third-degree road rash. Soren took one look at her and made a face that most individuals would reserve for a sunbaked skunk carcass on the side of the highway. "She's not riding in that."

Feeling defensive, she started buttoning the front of her jacket. "What? It's too hot for leather."

"Yeah, Soren," Paige piped up, already perched behind Dane on the back of their cherry red motorcycle. "Cut her some slack. It's hot as balls out here."

"That's easy for you to say," he answered, casting an accusing glance at Paige in her proper riding jacket. "If Dane lays your bike down, you won't end up smeared across the pavement."

"Come on, man," Murphy interjected, shooting Soren a cajoling grin. "Cricket's wearing the same damn thing."

Soren looked to where Cricket sat mounted behind her unassuming paramour, Paolo, and huffed out a growl. He put his hands on his hips, staring down at the ground for a few seconds. His jaw flexed. Gretchen felt her cheeks burn, and not just because it was creeping toward ninety degrees. He was right, and she knew it. "Hey, I can go get my leather jacket, but it's butter soft. It probably wouldn't provide any better protection than what I'm already wearing."

"For fuck's sake," Soren barked loud enough to make her jump. Yanking the zipper down on his lightweight armored jacket, he ripped it off and shoved it at her. She took it without a word and laid it over the tank of Murphy's bike, unbuttoning her denim jacket and replacing it with Soren's.

It was absurdly large on her, hanging down to her mid-thigh once she had it zipped up. She had to fold up the sleeves several times just so she could see the tips of her fingers. Holding out her arms, she gave him a petulant glare. "Satisfied? Or do you think I should belt it?"

He folded his unprotected arms, towering over her for a moment. His jaw ticked again. The moment stretched to an unendurable, near-painful level, and then Murphy's goofy high-pitched laugh sliced through the tension. He reached over and tugged her elbow, handing her the loaner helmet he'd brought along. "All right. Lid up, babe. Let's get our asses on the road."

"You've got to be fucking *kidding* me," Soren rumbled behind her, earning a collective groan from the other riders. "Murph, I love you man, but you *just* got your Class M. I've seen the way you drive."

"What the *shit*, man." Dane laughed. "There aren't a lot

of free seats right now. So, either let her ride with you or shut the fuck up about it."

Soren exhaled a loud, disgruntled snarl and muscular hands clamped over her upper arms, steering her away from Murphy's bike and over to the imposing black and chrome Fat Boy parked under the porch's shade. Throwing a leg over, Soren jammed on his helmet and kick-started the bike, shooting an expectant glare over his shoulder, inviting her to climb on.

---

THIS WAS A GODDAMN CONSPIRACY. All Sam wanted was one day on the road. *One day*, to leave all the stress that'd been weighing him down behind for a few hours. Then he'd stepped out his door and caught sight of Gretchen wearing that pathetically inadequate jacket. She was braiding her hair into pigtails to avoid helmet hair and chatting with Murphy like she'd known him for years. Suddenly, it felt less like a relaxing day out and more like a cosmic bait and switch.

Now she was wearing his jacket with the sleeves cuffed as far as they would go before the armor in the elbow wouldn't allow them to be folded any further, looking so unbearably cute that he didn't think he'd ever be able to put it on again. He'd have to burn it and buy a new one, and that shit wasn't cheap.

He'd gone *way* too long without the touch of a woman. That revelation struck around the time when Gretchen climbed behind him and hitched her thighs around either side of his body. Her hands slid over his ribs and, for one terrible instant, every muscle in his body tensed so fast that he could barely push off the ground. Soon they were winding along the backroads, and he was becoming one of those reckless assholes who drove way too fast just to get the girl to hold on tighter. He'd feel her fingers biting into his sides and rev the engine just to feel her legs grip his hips harder, his rock-hard cock straining against the front of his jeans like a jack-in-the-box that never popped.

They rolled into Plymouth just after two o'clock and stopped for lunch at a brewery with a comfortably shaded deck. Everyone ordered burgers, and the conversation flowed. Gretchen had just produced a full-sized bottle of hot sauce from her backpack and was dressing the top of her "shroom n' blue" burger with a criminally excessive amount of hot sauce when Paige leaned across the table to snag an onion ring off the side of her plate. "So, Gretch, what is it you do for a living? Cricket wouldn't tell me when I asked."

Sitting next to him, Cricket snorted softly, keeping her eyes on her mint-chip milkshake. Sitting on her opposite side, Gretchen propped the top of the bun on her burger and set about sawing the whole thing in half, a covert smile playing over her berry-pink lips. "I'm an electronic design consultant, specializing in sexual wellness products."

Instant, all-consuming silence.

Cricket slurped her milkshake, her sun-kissed cheeks lighting up in a shade of vivid tomato red. The boys gaped. Paige sat motionless for a moment, her elbows on the armrests of her chair, her hands folded over her waist, a funny look on her face.

"So, like..." Sitting forward again, Paige made a grab for another onion ring. "Would I be familiar with any of your work?"

"Depends on what you're into." Gretchen pushed her

plate closer to the center of the table, making it easier to reach. "And before anyone asks, yes. I *do* get free samples."

More silence. Paolo appeared to have discovered something fascinating on the ceiling. Murphy's mouth opened and closed like a goldfish in a bowl, as if he were trying to speak but couldn't quite force the sounds out of his mouth. Sinking back in his seat, Dane slung an arm over the back of Paige's chair and turned his head, speaking to her in a stage whisper. "How do they know to come to you?"

Sam couldn't help it. He laughed. Because beneath the candy floss facade there lurked the mind of a Grade A freak; the type of mad genius who was ostensibly getting paid *crazy* money to meditate on other people's pleasure centers all day long. Of all the possible occupations he could have ascribed to this girl, building a bigger, better *vibrator* would have placed nowhere on that list. Nobody else seemed to get the joke, though, which only made him laugh harder.

"Well, that did it." Dane slid a sideways grin to Paige. "Soren has finally snapped."

"I'm sorry, it's just..." Sam sniffed, the laughter fading to a few light guffaws. Waving his hand in Gretchen's general direction, he brushed a tear from his lashes. "Fuckin' *look* at her! She looks like a—a goddamn fairy princess! Never in a million years would any reasonable human being guess..."

"A fairy princess?" all three women parroted in perfect harmony, setting off a fresh round of laughter from the men at the table.

Gretchen folded her arms and studied her water glass, gnawing her lip in a way that both played at his heartstrings and made his cock roar to life. Christ, nothing slayed him like a bratty little pout, and he was one hundred percent certain that it wasn't an affectation on Gretchen. Dead. He was fucking *dead*.

---

"YUL BRYNNER," Gretchen spoke without taking her eyes off the Zydeco band onstage. The guys had taken off for one last round of beer fifteen minutes ago, and Bechdel Test be damned, Paige had, with a distinct lack of subtlety, steered the conversation to which male celebrity Soren most resembled—a ridiculous question considering the lone shared similarity between any of the men listed was a shaved cranium. She was well aware they were baiting her, trying to tease out some indication of her interest level, but she was only human. Eventually, her need to set them straight outweighed her sense of self-preservation. "But with a longer face and more muscles."

She concealed a smirk as the other two women whipped out their phones and got to searching. The images loaded, and Paige let out an astonished laugh. "Holy shit! That's friggin' *uncanny!*"

Gretchen slid a grin toward them as they stared in rapt amazement at their phones. "It's the eyebrows."

"I wonder how hard it would be to get him to dress up as a pharaoh for Halloween, because..." Cricket turned her head sideways, making a show of admiring a promotional photo from *The Ten Commandments*. She shook it off, blinking at Gretchen as if she'd just remembered where she was. "How'd you even make the connection, though?"

"Mom's a fan of musicals." Both women's eyes lit up at the answer, and they began combing the internet anew, spurred on by the prospect of seeing Soren's doppelgänger sing a jaunty tune. The three women were cackling over a

YouTube video of the waltzing scene from *The King and I* when the menfolk returned.

"What are you ladies clucking at?" Dane queried, settling onto the picnic blanket and pulling Paige between his bent knees.

"Oh, just this..." Paige grinned evilly, holding her phone out to show Soren the now-muted clip. "And now we all know exactly how nasty-hot Soren would look wearing harem pants."

Soren lowered himself onto the adjoining blanket and leaned forward to assess the video, his almost-smile plummeting into a splenetic scowl. Satisfied with the results of her ribbing, Paige turned off her phone and tucked it into her jacket as Cricket traded her phone to Paolo and Murphy for a plastic cup of draft beer.

"Dude, that's bizarre!" Murphy chuckled, passing the phone over to Dane to complete the circle.

"I know!" Cricket chirped, just as Soren started to pass Gretchen the cup he'd brought back for her. "Gretch pointed it out, and now I'll never *not* see it."

"So, this is your doing, huh?" he asked.

"I didn't do it maliciously." Gretchen reached out to accept the beer, only to have it snatched back and overturned onto the grass. The others howled, and Soren took a long, satisfied slug from his cup, his black eyes glittering with an unspoken challenge. Undaunted, Gretchen shrugged and twisted back to the stage. "Well, fuck you, too."

Any laughter was swallowed up in a vacuum of uneasy silence. Gretchen turned to find everyone else's gazes snagged on a couple standing a hundred feet away. The woman balanced on tiptoe, speaking to a fatigued-looking man sporting a baby carrier. The infant strapped to his chest waved her chubby limbs, enjoying the music as her parents shared what looked to be a very intense conversation.

Everyone in their party was sneaking glances at Soren and attempting to hide their discomfiture behind masks of practiced stoicism. Cricket caught her gaze and made an almost imperceptible nod toward Soren, widening her eyes. *Oh.* Gretchen sucked in a breath, casting a glance over her shoulder at the man in question, who was hanging his head and petting his close-shorn scalp as if he was trying to make a wish.

# CHAPTER
## *Six*

Of all the places in the world, his shitheel brother and that flesh-eating demoness Trinity had to come *here* to fuck up the first decent day off he'd had in months. He could feel everyone around him waiting for a reaction, and he was just doing his damndest to avoid making eye contact, so he didn't have to see the looks of pity on their faces.

*Fuck.* They were coming right at him. He could hear Trinity's strident, contentious voice approaching and practically feel hives breaking out all over his body. His face felt hot, there was a ringing in his ears, and his heart was pounding so hard that he could see the front of his shirt move.

Cool hands came to rest on his forearm, and then Gretchen was pushing herself up to kneel in front of him. She leaned in, her cheek brushing his, and he inhaled the scent of sunscreen as she whispered into his ear. "I hate to ask but would you mind leaving early? This music is kinda giving me a headache."

He sat back to look at her for a moment, her kneeling

position putting her right at his eye level. She stared back at him with earnest eyes, and for the first time, he could pick out the stria of copper flecks in the center of her green eye, and the deep forest green of the limbal ring. Struck dumb with gratitude, Sam shoved the rest of his beer at Paolo and grabbed his jacket and their helmets off the blanket, leaping to his feet to follow her. Bringing one hand to the small of her back, he left everything else in their wake and focused on ushering her between the checkerboard of blankets on the grass.

Neither uttered a syllable until they rounded a row of food stalls and started for the parking area. The fog lifted, and he hazarded a glance at the sublime creature walking next to him. She had an indecipherable expression on her face, staring straight ahead with just a tiny hint of a smile. He'd been so relieved to have an exit that he'd jumped on the excuse like a grenade, without considering the convenience of the timing. "Someone told you, didn't they?"

"Nobody had to. It's all in the 'Welcome to Halberd Peak' pamphlet," Gretchen teased, raking him with an acerbic grin. "There's a comprehensive list of all the biggest town scandals spanning the last fifteen years, and a map of the Vermont Beer Trails."

"That so?" *Fuck her for being funny right now.* Sam dropped his hand from her back, not trusting himself to be touching her anymore.

"Oh, yeah." She snickered, and Sam put a little more space between them. "It comes in the gift tote along with a box of maple candy and a bottle of patchouli beard oil."

"I feel so cheated." He chuckled despite himself, watching the ground as he walked. "I never got the tote."

"You have a nice smile." She beamed, her grin impish. "So much better than resting asshole face."

"No one's making you look at it." He wiped the cheer off his face as the bike came into view, preparing himself for the trial of her closeness again. He straddled the bike's saddle and waited as she started gathering her hair into pigtails again, securing them with thin elastics.

"Do you think we could stop for coffee?" she asked, tugging on his jacket. It was so long on her that she had to bend down to start the zipper. "We don't have to stay here, but I could use a little more time to regain feeling in my ass."

"I think that can be arranged."

They'd passed a drive-through on the way into town, the shop standing at the edge of a sunny pasture. It was dark now, and they were able to order their drinks and sit outside on the post and rail fence, watching the stars puncture the darkening sky. It would have been a perfect evening, if he wasn't so hyper-aware of the woman next to him that he kept burning his tongue on his French roast.

---

Communicating with Soren came down to interpreting the nuances of his grunts and the movement of his eyebrows. The man spent most of the time mugging, the muscles in the corner of his jaw working overtime, as if he was chewing all his pithy responses. Gretchen didn't let it bother her. That day at The Paper Frog, when Cricket explained what had gone wrong in Soren's life that had given him all the wholesome sweetness of a swarm of enraged paper wasps, she insisted that Soren didn't *hate* her. He'd simply been hit so hard last time he opened his heart that now whenever someone likable came along, his immediate response was to straight-arm them.

Still, by the time she reached the halfway point on her coffee and Soren's word count remained in the single digits, she'd tired of the companionable silence. Toying with the lid of her coffee cup, she looked to her right and noted the intensity with which he appeared to be observing the grass. "Geez Soren, how about you let someone else get a word in edgewise, huh?"

He chuckled halfheartedly and slid down to lean against the railing, his gaze bouncing up to meet hers. "Sorry. I'm distracted."

"I get that." She paused to look up at the stars for a second. "If it makes you feel any better, they obviously weren't happy. He looked like he was about to beat her to death with the baby if she didn't stop harping on him."

His grin hitched up higher on one side. "Thanks, but I don't need cheering up."

"So, it wouldn't make a difference if I said that you clearly got all the looks in the family?" She dipped her head, catching the subtle deepening of the brackets around his lips and the dimple he had in one cheek. He looked, at least in this light, almost boyish. "I know it doesn't count for much, but I think she made a huge mistake. I can't imagine him being better than you, and not just because you *never* would have..." She pushed an escaped strand of hair behind her ear. "...done what he did."

"I wouldn't, huh?" He looked down, popping another button on the plastic lid of his coffee cup. "You know me so well?"

"I know Cricket. She likes you," she reasoned, scrunching her nose in the way she did whenever she thought of something amusing. "Now that I think about it, I haven't met anyone who had a single bad thing to say about you—if you ignore the fact that nearly everyone always begins their description with, 'He's kind of an asshole, but once you get to know him.'"

"I didn't realize I was such a popular topic of conversation."

"Oh, I start *all* my conversations by pumping everyone I meet for gossip about you." She nudged him with her shoulder, extracting another modest smile from him. Satisfied, she allowed herself another sip of coffee. "I'm teasing. I'm new in town and the only piece of information people have as an opener is that I'm renting your house. There was a solid week there where all anyone spoke to me about was avoiding looking you in the eye before noon, lest I be turned to stone."

He scuffed the toe of his boot in the grass. "It's a miracle you talk to me at all."

"Way to put a positive spin on it." She nodded her approval. "See? I'm having an effect already. Give me a week and I'll have you frolicking in a daffodil patch."

"What do I get if I give you two?" He turned to look at her, the intensity in his gaze almost enough to knock her to the ground. "By the time you roll out of town, I could be turning cartwheels in a tutu."

She laughed at the mental image that conjured. "No one told me you were funny."

———

SOREN DRAINED the last of his coffee on the walk back to the bike. She was right behind him, chatting amiably, and as much as he wanted to tune her out, he couldn't. He liked her. Her good humor was infectious, she spoke her mind without reservation, and most important, she seemed to like him as he was.

He wished he could forget she was leaving in two weeks. Perhaps if he hadn't liked her so much, it might've been easier for him to put their built-in expiration date out of his thoughts and do something about it. Instead, he felt his heart sink as they pulled into the pool hall's parking lot, and she climbed off the back of his bike. Taking off her helmet, she tugged her pigtails loose and shook out her hair. "Thanks for the ride."

"No problem." He put down the kickstand and dismounted, reaching into one of his saddlebags to retrieve the denim jacket he'd confiscated before they left. "It was on my way anyway."

"Oh, yeah?" she asked, unzipping his jacket and exchanging it for her own. "I figured you had to live somewhere around here."

"I do." He pointed over one shoulder to the pool hall. "My room's in the back."

Gretchen blinked a few times in rapid succession. "You live *here*? But why don't you just live in the cabin?"

"I, uh..." He ran his hand over his head again, huffing out a sheepish laugh. "I don't go in there anymore. Not since..."

"Right. The *unpleasantness*." She bobbed her head in comprehension. "Sorry to keep bringing it up. It's just, well, don't take this personally, but the pool hall doesn't exactly seem fit for habitation."

"Whoa! Wanna dial back the judgement, there?" He laughed. "I'm not saying I feel safe walking around barefoot, but it keeps the rain off my head and despite what the assholes downtown think, there aren't any rats or cockroaches."

"And I bet you can't beat the commute." She started backing toward the steps leading up the hill. "Well, I won't waste my breath inviting you up for a nightcap. So, I guess I'll see you around the neighborhood?"

"Yeah, thanks anyway." He nodded, then before he could talk himself out of it, jogged after her to the very edge of the ring of illumination cast by the floodlights. "Did anyone tell you about the party Tuesday night?"

"Hmm?" She spun to look at him, and he wondered if this was how moths felt flitting around a bare lightbulb, desperate to get close, but staying just far enough away to avoid the inevitable burn. "Oh, right. Cricket invited me already. I'm not being lured into a cult, am I? I like to know ahead of time, so I can stuff a protein bar in my sock. Helps stave off the brainwashing."

"It's not a cult." Although he could see how someone might think that. The old artist's colony on the northwestern outskirts of Halberd Peak was originally founded by a troupe of first-wave hippies in the Sixties. It had since faded into a neglected trailer camp for counterculture refugees, and because the end of the season coincided with the Birth of Krishna Festival that the first residents loved so much, they simply rolled the two events together. The resulting party had become an annual tradition that further divided the locals from the gentrifiers. "Just a big bonfire and a lot of drunk townies sitting around."

"Well, I'm not really into big social scenes, but it sounds low key enough." Tucking her hands into the back pockets of her jeans, she cocked her head to one side and gazed up at him for a beat. "If I go, does that make me an honorary townie?"

"No," he murmured, so trapped in the gravity of her gaze that it took him a moment to realize he was standing *over* her now. To her credit, she didn't give an inch, even though she had to crane her neck just to look up at him. "There's a ten-year probationary period."

She laughed softly, the sound sending shockwaves up his spine. "Is there a secret handshake?"

"I can teach you." Sweet *Christ*, just being around this girl was awakening instincts he hadn't felt in years. All he could think about right now was lifting her up in his arms until her toes were dangling in the dust and feeling her body thrash when he slammed his mouth onto hers.

"In ten years?"

He was so close now that the shadow of his shoulder fell across the lower half of her face and all he could see were those strange eyes glittering at him. His face hovered above hers, his fingers itching to tangle themselves in her soft curls and pull until he coaxed a sweet little whimper from her lips. "Yeah, in ten—"

His phone went off, jolting him out of his reverie. He stepped back fast, and she exhaled hard enough that he could see the visible dip of her shoulders. Backing toward the steps at the edge of the hill, she gave him a conciliatory smile. "You know what? It was a long drive and I really have to pee, so I'm gonna head up for the night."

With that, she turned and darted up the stairs. Digging his phone out of his pocket, he checked the notification and swore under his breath. It was Murphy, texting to ask if he'd finally made his move. Squashing the urge to launch the offending device into a ditch, he stalked back to the pool hall before he could chase her up the hill.

# CHAPTER
## Seven

"Here, try this." Cricket set a slice of Bundt cake in front of her and sat down, folding her hands in anticipation. Looking up from her computer screen, Gretchen cast a heedful eye at the plate.

She picked up the fork propped on the rim. "What am I dealing with?"

"Roasted peach-rose poundcake with pistachios." Cricket sat up with pride, excitement rouging the apples of her warm olive cheeks. "I've been noodling with this one for a while. I think I finally got it peachy enough."

"Man, there's gonna be big trouble when the Brits open up the baking show to the colonists." Gretchen laughed, taking a tentative bite. She hadn't said so, but she didn't have high hopes for this latest concoction. Neither peach, rose, nor pistachio was a favorite of hers, yet somehow when she tasted the cake, it worked in the most glorious way. Setting down her fork, she touched her lips in surprise. "That's amazing! I was worried it would taste like perfume."

"Rose water can be tricky." Cricket nodded. "That's why you start with a teaspoon at a time."

"Well, you have a gift. And it's definitely peachy."

"I added peach schnapps," Cricket explained, reaching across the table to break off a corner and chewing thoughtfully. "Yup. I think this one's going in the cookbook."

"Let me be the first to congratulate you for finally giving the world a use for peach schnapps." Gretchen smirked, turning back to her computer. Without looking up, she clapped her hand over Cricket's when she moved to take the plate away. "You can leave that with me."

"I'm sure my Nobel Peace Prize is in the mail." Cricket snorted, getting to her feet as a flock of college-aged girls came into the shop. The girl in the lead, a buoyant redhead with an upturned nose, folded herself over the counter until her flip-flops lifted off the floor.

"Is Murphy around?" she asked, peering toward the door that led upstairs, to the apartment Cricket shared with her younger brother. This obviously wasn't the first time she'd been to chez Bonhomme.

"He's at work," Cricket snapped, casting a warning glare at the girl's arms where they folded against her counter. The girl slid back to plant her feet on the checkered tile, chastened. "You can leave a message, or you can check at Rooster's."

"The Christmas-themed biker bar?" another girl exclaimed, grimacing distastefully. "That place is super sketchy."

"Can I get his number or something?"

Cricket pursed her lips, practically snarling with admonition. "If he wanted you to have his number, he'd have *given* it to you."

"Hey, we're *customers!*" an indeterminate peep rose from the gaggle.

"Not until you *buy* something," Cricket shot back without missing a beat. "And my brother isn't on the menu."

The shop owner watched the girls file out, grinning victoriously. Nothing put her in a good mood quite like messing with the entitled jerks that swarmed Halberd Peak in the warmer months, making it difficult for the year-round residents to find parking. Gretchen shook her head, speaking over her shoulder. "Days like this, I don't know how you keep the doors open on this place."

"They weren't going to order anything anyway." Cricket picked up a broom and started sweeping her workspace. "Oh! Before I forget, I gave Paige your number. She was bummed that you took off before she got to say goodbye, and she wanted to know if you'd be sticking around for Dottie's Wedding."

"Dottie who?" Gretchen peered around the high wall of the booth. "'Splain please."

"Okay, you know the inn's haunted, right?"

"I do remember seeing something to that effect in the welcome pamphlet."

"Right. So there are actually a couple ghosts, but the most famous one is Dottie Moller," Cricket explained. "It was during World War One and she was working as a maid at the Quartz River Inn. Her fiancé was fighting overseas, and then one day she gets a letter saying that he'd married a very nice French girl."

"That rat bastard."

"Oh, you don't know the half of it," Cricket continued, reaching for a dustpan. "The story goes that her fiancé's mother had offered to lend Dottie her wedding dress for the big day, and he asked her to return it to his mother, along with the ring. Instead, she swallowed the ring, put on the dress, and jumped off the roof of the inn."

Gretchen paused, weighing her reactions. "That is some amazingly petty payback."

"We haven't even gotten to the best part." Cricket rolled her eyes. "Dottie's ghost didn't show up until her weaselly fiancé came back to town with his new wife and somehow got elected *mayor*. Suddenly, people started reporting seeing a weeping woman in a wedding dress wandering the halls of the inn late at night."

"My god, this is the most *New England* origin story I've ever heard."

"You want me to explain or not?" Cricket straightened, fixing her with an arch look. Gretchen lifted the corners of her lips in an acquiescent smile. "Good. Shut up. So, this goes on for a while, the ex-fiancé gets voted out, and he and his wife get tired of people treating them like pariahs. They pack up and leave, and someone suggests that maybe if they give Dottie her wedding, she'll quit rattling chains at the inn."

"But the inn's still haunted."

"Yeah. They gave up after the first fake wedding." Cricket shrugged. "Then, thirty years back when the town was on its last legs, they decided to bring it back as an annual event for the publicity. And they pushed it back to Halloween to play up the spooky factor. It's very Satan's Bridal Expo."

"I can honestly think of nothing I would enjoy *less* than a wedding-themed Halloween party celebrating a jilted bride's suicide." Gretchen shook her head. Wasn't it enough that she was attending the "townie" bonfire at the hippie commune tomorrow? Between that and the Blues Festival, she'd need at least a week to recover.

"You sure? Paige and Dane usually throw an afterparty at her parents' place. Everyone gets naked and goes swimming in the pool. It's a lot of fun."

"While that certainly sounds entertaining, I probably won't be here anyway."

"Holy shit." Cricket dropped into the seat opposite hers again, a stunned expression on her lovely face. "You and Soren really are made for each other."

"A risky assertion, if ever I heard one." Gretchen sighed, careful to keep her eyes on her work. The moment she'd stepped into the café that afternoon, Cricket had dive-bombed her, demanding to know where she and Soren had gotten off to the night before. Evidently, the running theory was that they'd gone straight home and banged like bonobos on cantharides. *After all,* Gretchen shook her head at the thought, *nothing puts a man in the mood like getting a snoot full of the two people who shattered his hopes and dreams.*

"No, I mean it," Cricket insisted. "Soren is literally the only other person on the *planet* that I've seen turn down an invitation to a Paige party." She seemed lost in thought for a moment, a slow, evil smile spreading across her lips. "Only now you can play with each other."

Gretchen's hands stilled above her keyboard. She slashed a perturbed glare at her friend, her lips tightening. "I was having a good day."

# CHAPTER

*Eight*

The air was turning chilly in the evenings. A haze of wood smoke wound between the trees, combining with the scent of pot and charred sugar as people circled around the bonfire to toast marshmallows. The firelight illuminated the banks of the river, the water table running a little higher than usual after a day's hard rain. The storm moved on just before sunset, but the people sitting around the fire kept one eye turned upward, watching the starless sky for breaks in the clouds.

Murphy already had a decent buzz on and an arm around a random girl by the time Cricket and Gretchen pitched their camp chairs next to the fire. Paolo was there in an instant, supplying them with pre-sharpened marshmallow sticks, and Cricket rewarded him by plunking down into his lap and pulling his face into her tits for a proper hello.

As for Sam, after spending the last two days dodging invasive questions about his dealings with the new girl from every horny old goat who came into the pool hall, he was doing his level best to keep his head down and nurse his beer without engaging. Still, he couldn't help stealing a look in Gretchen's direction as she threaded a marshmallow onto her stick and laughed at one of Murphy's inane jokes.

She was wearing an oversized turtleneck sweater made of something soft and fuzzy, and the sleeves were folded up to her wrists, putting him in mind of the way she'd worn his jacket. He'd hung it up on a hook when he got home that night, but as much as he wanted to put her out of his thoughts, he'd still lifted it to his nose and inhaled her scent from the lining. Then, he'd gone to bed feeling like an idiot teenager.

Someone started pattering away on a set of bongo drums, and within a few minutes, they were accompanied by several guitars and a jaw harp. Cricket got up to dance and dragged Paolo along with her. Murphy and his date were close behind. Sam watched Gretchen hold her marsh-mallows to the flames for a while, then surrendered and moved down a seat so he could talk to her without broad-casting their conversation to everyone else in the circle. "Can I get one of those?"

She scoffed, side-eying him in the firelight. "Get your own!"

"Wo-ow." Sam drew out the word, taking another swig of beer. "And after all we've meant to each other."

"Oh don't give me that," she snapped, affecting an adenoidal Queens accent. "We used to go out. We used to have *passion*. Now all I ever hear is, 'get in the kitchen and roast me a marshmallow, woman' from the second you get home every night."

"Not this again," Sam grumbled, sliding down in his seat and widening his manspread. "I don't bust my butt all day long just to come home to your nagging and no food on the table."

"My mother was right about you, you bastard." She stifled an overwrought sob against the back of her hand. "She wanted me to marry that nice orthodontist. Now, he's got a summer home on Nantucket, and *you* just spent our vacation money on a jet ski."

Sam chuckled and sat up, leaning on the arm of his chair. "This is fun, but I'm not sure how long I can keep it up."

"Just what every girl *loves* to hear." Gretchen grinned, offering the end of her stick to him. "All right, you can have one. But if I do this, you're replacing the cubic zirconia in my ring with a real diamond. I'm tired of being the only mom in the PTA that can't pass out fruit punch on field days because I'm afraid to turn the stone pink."

"Amazing." He plucked a marshmallow off the end of the stick. "It's almost like being there."

"I know, right?" She stuffed her marshmallow into her mouth, licking the remainders off her fingers. "Kind of like going to a playground when you start having the urge to breed."

"All right." He nudged her arm when he spotted the others coming to reclaim their seats. "Be cool."

"Yes, no one must know Sam Soren isn't an axe-wielding Orc," Gretchen spoke out of the corner of her mouth, spearing another marshmallow. Sam laughed under his breath, his gaze lingering on the side of her face. *Fuck.* Why'd she have to be so damn adorable all the time?

"DID ANYONE ELSE FEEL THAT?" Cricket extracted her tongue from Paolo's ear and looked up, her eyes searching the canopy overhead.

"No, but maybe if we switch seats..." Gretchen snick-ered, earning a middle-fingered salute from her friend and a raised eyebrow from the avian featured owner of the lap on which she perched. A split second later, the clouds opened up and unleashed a deluge. It instantly doused the fire and enveloped the clearing in a cloud of steam. People started packing up and shoveling rapidly saturating mud into the fire pit.

"Come on, Cricket's heading back to town with Paolo. You're riding with me." Soren was at her elbow, hustling her down the path to the parking area. Throwing open the passenger side door of a dark SUV, he jogged around the nose of the car to climb in. "Shit, that came out of nowhere!"

"Yeah, what the hell? It wasn't even supposed to rain tonight." Gretchen giggled through chattering teeth, balling her fists up in the sleeves of her sweater. "I'm going to leave Mother Nature *such* a nasty review."

"Hold on." Soren started the car and turned up the heater all the way. "Put your hands on the vents."

She sat forward and warmed her fingers, casting a curious glance over her shoulder at the detritus of discarded clothing and receipts in the back seat. "This is your car?"

"That's what it says on the registration," he said, steering down the long, winding drive leading out of the commune. "You never noticed it in the parking lot?"

"Yeah, but it's a parking lot. I didn't think too much about it." Sitting back in her seat, she tugged the sodden front of her sweater away from her skin and watched the windshield wipers slapping back and forth. "God, I'm *starving*. Is there delivery in Halberd Peak? All I've had to eat since breakfast was three marshmallows, and I'm pretty sure the only food I have in the house is a bag of stale cheddar popcorn."

"I have food at the bar. What are you in the mood for?" When she didn't answer right away, he slid a sideways glance in her direction. "What?"

"Are you offering to cook me dinner?" She arched an eyebrow.

"Do you want food or not?" He raked her with a snide smirk. "Because I'm perfectly happy to make myself a grilled cheese and spend my night off watching *An American Werewolf in London*."

Her hand clamped over his forearm. "Wait. That's on *tonight*?"

They came through the bar's front door to the snare drum cadence of the rain on the roof. Soren flicked on the interior lights and ducked down the hall, leaving Gretchen alone in the eerily deserted front room. Wrapping her arms around her body, she looked at the chairs propped on the tabletops and the unlit neon signs and called into the back. "What's the word for that creepy feeling you get when you're in an empty place? I know it's a thing, but I can't remember."

"Kenopsia," he answered, strolling down the darkened hallway to offer her a worn black hoodie. "That might be more comfortable than a wet sweater."

Unfurling the hoodie in front of her, she giggled at how comically outsized the garment was. "You sure it'll fit? I'd hate to stretch it out."

One corner of his mouth turned up, the boyish dimple

appearing in his cheek. "I could cut that thing in *half,* and it would still fit you."

"Good answer." She laughed. "Can I change in your room?"

"Uh, yeah." He looked somewhat taken aback by the prospect of a woman seeing his personal space but recovered quickly. "You do that, and I'll see what's good in the kitchen."

"You sure this is okay?" Slinging the sweatshirt over her shoulder, she slipped past him into the hall. "Are you absolutely *sure* you've hidden all your porn?"

"Right. I'll be in the kitchen, spitting in your food." Soren shoved through the swinging doors, leaving her to explore the room that he called home.

She smirked when she caught sight of an old girlie calendar on his bedroom wall, Miss September's teased eighties hair and naked skin faded to the same shade of orangey-white after years hanging in the sun. He couldn't have put it there; the woman in the photo was old enough to be his mother, which was an uncomfortable enough thought on its own. There was a framed photo from a billiards tournament in seventy-seven hanging next to the calendar, so she reasoned that his father must have put them both there and Sam didn't even notice them out of habit.

The room was spartan, with a narrow cot against the wall to the left, the sheets folded into perfect forty-five-degree military corners, and a set of book-lined shelves mounted on the wall above it. A scuffed footlocker stood with its lid open, his wardrobe displayed in a monochromatic spectrum of blacks and grays in neatly folded rows.

She located the minuscule bathroom to the right and pressed the door closed, fighting back a palpitation of claustrophobia. There was little room to turn around without barking her shins on the front of the toilet. She did her utmost to avoid meditating on the implausibility of finding herself topless in the same room where Soren regularly got nude, hanging her wet sweater over the shower door to drip dry. A toothbrush and an old-style straight razor hung in the ceramic holder above the pedestal sink, and she couldn't restrain the compulsion to peer inside the medicine cabinet. She found a shaving mug with a disk of pine tar soap in the bottom, a stick of deodorant, a bottle of extra strength acetaminophen, and a box of nearly expired condoms with only two missing. *Good lord, what a waste.*

Opening the door, she cast a wary eye toward the hallway and crept over to the bed. Placing one knee on the edge of the mattress, she leaned in and scanned the spines of the books, a ribbon of consternation winding through her thoughts. She'd been expecting a collection of pulpy mainstream thrillers, but the titles ranged from *One Hundred Years of Solitude* by Gabriel García Márquez to an anthology of poems by Rumi. Reaching up, she thumbed a copy of Henry Miller's *Tropic of Cancer* off the shelf and nearly hit the ceiling as a heuristic baritone spoke from the doorway. "Looking to borrow something?"

"Nope. Nope. Nope." She replaced the book and scuttled past him, her face flushing with red hot mortification. She heard the soft *click* as he pulled the door closed, the latch mechanism sliding into place.

# CHAPTER
*Nine*

S am took another bite of his sandwich and watched Gretchen feed quarters into the jukebox, wondering exactly how he'd gotten himself into this predicament. The most breathtaking woman he'd ever seen was dancing to Al Green in his favorite sweatshirt, swinging her hips in an artlessly sexy way that made him reach for his drink before he choked on his dinner. She reclaimed her seat, resting her cheek against her upturned fist and settling that disarmingly steady gaze on him.

"I have to say, this is *not* how I pictured my night going." She laughed, tipping her head forward and gathering her storm-dampened curls into a messy bun on the back of her head. "And I can't even remember the last time a man made me dinner."

"You haven't been hanging around with the right men." Sam ripped off another bite of his patty melt, shaking his head in disillusionment. It wasn't quite five-star cuisine, but *shit,* what kind of losers was this girl wasting her time with that they weren't looking after her appetites?

"Ain't that the truth," she said, attacking her food again. "You make a damn good Reuben. I'll give you that."

"I'll take it." He washed his food down with another pull of beer, taking the opportunity to study her while she was preoccupied by her dinner. A few soft curls had escaped her bun and laid against the nape of her neck and around her temples. They snagged the light and softened her profile, like a renaissance beauty. "I've been meaning to ask you what the hell a girl like you is doing in a nowhere place like this."

"Probably the same thing everyone else does when they decide to make a change." She sucked a dribble of Russian dressing off the end of her thumb. "I'd lived my whole life in the same twenty-mile radius, so I decided to find a place that suited me better."

"Must be nice, having that kind of flexibility." Sam chuckled. "If I closed the bar, the regulars would commit seppuku."

"Another ten-dollar word," she observed, narrowing her eyes at him. "You're one of those brainy barkeeps, huh?"

"I guess so." Reaching for a napkin, he wiped his fingers and swept his hand around the room, indicating the smoke-stained walls. "This wasn't exactly my dream, but my path was set the day I was born. My grandfather built this place. Then my dad inherited it, and he retired to run a fishing charter in Mexico. My brother and I were supposed to share it, but *that* didn't happen. And here I am."

"So, what would you do if you didn't have a legacy to uphold?"

Sam had to think for a moment, because he couldn't remember anyone ever asking him that question before today. "I honestly don't know. Maybe write?"

"I could see that." She gave him a knowing roll of her

eyes. "It probably won't help, but I never had a plan either. I kind of tripped and fell backwards into a fulfilling career."

"What, you didn't grow up wanting to design sex toys?" he teased, earning a scoff from the girl next to him. Somewhere in the background, the song ended, replaced by a classic Aretha Franklin number.

"No, I started off designing battleships, if you can believe that." She chewed for a moment, smiling at the surprising turn her journey had taken. "I'd been with the company for a while, and one day I looked around and thought: *Every single one of my coworkers is a soulless ghoul who's been farting into the same desk chair for thirty years. If I don't get out now, I'm going to die here.* So I started looking for something else. Turns out industrial espionage is a big problem in the adult industry, and by then I'd spent a little over a decade working under threat of treason, so it was a natural fit. Everyone in my life, my parents, my friends, my boyfriend at the time, all thought I was *crazy,* but I feel like I'm making the world a happier place, in my own way. Plus, I don't have to spend my days chained to a desk in a high-security building."

"Damn," Sam remarked, looking at her with fresh eyes. "Was it hard switching gears like that?"

"Nah, I can design anything." She shrugged. "Once you know what buttons to push, it's just a question of scale and tolerances."

"And there's no heartbroken guy waiting for you to come back home?" Sam asked, then immediately cursed himself for his imprudence.

"No." She snickered, untroubled by the intimate turn in conversation. "As it happens, the triggering event for my little walkabout was the breakup of a shitty relationship.

Nobody's waiting for me to get back, unless you count my parents, and they have lives of their own."

"How shitty are we talking?" Sam asked, crumpling up his napkin and throwing it onto his plate. Folding his arms on the edge of the bar, he twisted to face her. "Because my scale for bad breakups is a little skewed."

"Like, two straight years of getting mind fucked," she explained, pushing the remnants of her sandwich away and reaching for her soda. "At least once a month, he'd get up in his head and start having 'doubts about the relationship,' and I would talk him off the cliff. We'd broken up and gotten back together a bunch of times, and I was so stressed out that my immune system was *shot*. I was sick all the time, and I didn't like who I was being, so when he started having doubts again, I let him go and channeled my pain into fixing all the things in my life that I was unhappy with. Ultimately, I decided that he probably hated himself and projected all his insecurities onto me, and now I mostly just feel bad for him, because he'll likely never be happy."

"Fuck, what an asshole," Sam breathed, trying to fit his head around the idea that anyone could judge this woman to be worthy of anything less than worship. "How long ago was this?"

She stared up at the ceiling for a few seconds, doing some quick calculations. "Going on about five months or so?"

"And you chose Vermont at random?"

"Chose is a strong word. I was vegging in front of the television, and it hit me that there was nothing keeping me in Connecticut. So, I dragged everything I couldn't pack out to the curb and got in the car, but the old girl crapped out after a whopping six hours on the road. And that pretty much gets you up to speed."

The song ended, and Mavis Staples filled the void. Gretchen trilled out a happy little sound and hopped off her stool, beaming a thousand-watt smile at him over her shoulder. "Whoever loads your jukebox is a *champ*!"

"Well, thank you." Sam mimed buffing his nails on the sleeve of his shirt. "Everyone else thinks I'm trying to keep people sad, so they'll drink more."

"They just don't know what's good." She laughed, throwing her hands over her head and dancing between the tables. "It was very important to my dad that I grow up cool, so I was fed a steady diet of blues and classic soul."

"Sounds like a good guy."

"He's a studio musician. I was really disappointed when I didn't inherit any of his musical ability, but we're not actually genetically related, so—" She bumped into a table and giggled. "Anyway, he's my hero."

"At least his taste in music rubbed off." He spun his seat outward and leaned back, resting his elbows on the lip of the bar to watch her. "What happened to your biological dad?"

"Ah, well..." She danced a little slower. "They got divorced when I was in kindergarten. He didn't stick around after that."

"Jesus, I'm sorry," Sam said, feeling mildly queasy. "My dad's a dick most of the time, but I still can't imagine him noping out on us like that."

"I was young. I'm sure it was much harder on Mom." She gave him a temperate smile. "It all worked out though. She married Elton when I was six, and he officially adopted me. I don't feel like I missed out on much."

She twirled away again, dancing into the center of the floor. Sam watched her for a while longer, a strange tugging feeling rooted on the left side of his ribcage. It was already too late, he realized; she was under his skin.

---

THE SONG on the jukebox ended, and she rocked on her feet, waiting out the silence. Joe Tex's *The Love You Save (May Be Your Own)* started playing, the first few bars building slowly, almost swallowed up by the rain pounding on the roof. She closed her eyes and moved with the music until a hand skated down her shoulder.

Soren was drawing her into his arms, pressing one palm against her ribcage and lifting her right hand in his. Realizing what was happening a moment too late, she uttered a melodramatic protest. "Oh, noooo!"

"You don't want to dance?" He smiled down at her as they started to sway.

"No, it's just..." Bringing her other hand to his bicep, she felt her face heat as the muscles flexed under her fingers. "Everyone knows that the first song you dance to becomes *your song*. Ours is gonna be a homily about not fucking up your love life."

"Hey, you're the DJ," he rumbled, leading her right hand to his shoulder and pulling her closer. "Beats having Aretha tell me I'm no good for the rest of...whenever."

Laughing softly, she let him spin her, turning her back to his front. They stayed like this for a few beats until he spun her again, pulling her into the safe harbor of his arms. Resting her forehead against the firm plane of his chest, she let her hands slide up around his neck, her fingers brushing the skin over his vertebra. She felt him lay his cheek against the top of her head, and for a few precious moments, everything felt wonderful. Maybe this was how it felt to be cherished by a man as secure and solid as the mountain where he lived.

Damn, he smelled good. Like, *crazy* good. Like spicy evergreen trees and warm sandalwood. She wanted to bury her face in the front of his shirt and just breathe him in. Flattening the pads of her fingers against the back of his neck, she slipped them up over the back of his skull, scraping her fingernails over the slightly stubbled texture on his scalp. It felt nice, soothing. She could see why he seemed to do this whenever he got caught up in his thoughts.

"Gretchen." His hands closed around her forearms, tugging them down. Holding her at a distance, he ran his tongue over his lower lip, his uncertainty apparent, and then brought his dark gaze to hers. "You should go."

"Why? I thought—"

"I'm sorry." He looked down again, his face tight. "If things were different, if I'd met you a year or two ago, when I didn't want to feel *anything,* this might've been enough. But—"

"Right. Got it," she bit out, feeling his words like a slap in the face. Yanking her arms out of his grasp, she stalked past him into the hallway, ripping his giant hoodie over her head as she went. She found her sweater where she'd slung it over the shower door and pulled it on. Ignoring his plaintive call, she let herself out the back door and sprinted up the steps in the driving rain.

# CHAPTER
*Ten*

He'd composed a hundred apologies to Gretchen over the last twelve hours, and every time he started again, he was excruciatingly aware of the time ticking down. That was the hang up in all of this. Back when he was treading water, trying to get through each night, everyone looked like a quick fuck to him. It didn't matter how fantastic the girl was; he just didn't have the band-width for anything deeper than that. Once the grieving was over, it was easy to see that keeping things simple only made them about a million times more complicated. He'd hurt people that didn't deserve it, and he had to face the uncomfortable reality that he didn't *want* casual. He wasn't good at it, and it didn't make him happy.

Being able to finally put his arms around Gretchen had cemented the thought in his mind: One week wasn't going to be enough. If things went any further between them and he had to let her go, that'd be it for him. He'd never recover.

That's what he'd been trying to tell her, but he'd fucked that up, too.

Cricket had murder in her eye as he came through the

door of the café that afternoon. She had a shop full of people, but she still hauled him into the back room to interrogate him about why Gretchen was in a sudden sour mood. Once she'd extracted the full story from him, she'd ripped him a new one, whisper screaming up at him and jabbing her pointy finger into his chest.

"You insensitive fuckwit!" she'd snarled, whacking him with an oven mitt. "She just finished telling you about her loser ex, and then you went and did the same damn thing? Exactly how far is that big penis top head shoved up your ass?"

"I know!" He held up his hands, backing up against the walk-in door. "I was right there, but I couldn't put her leaving out of my mind. I just fucked up the wording."

"Might leave, you coward," she'd enunciated sharply. "Might! The only reason she hasn't reupped her lease is because you're charging her out the ass for a house with no internet access, like a rural slumlord. The girl has to work!"

Sam's jaw went slack, and he'd fumbled for words. "Can you just tell her I'm sorry? I don't expect anything to come from it, but I don't feel right about leaving it that way."

"Bitch, I'm not your errand girl." She whacked him with the mitt again. "She lives two hundred feet away from you. Talk to her yourself!" Shoving him to one side, she yanked the door open and snapped at him over her shoulder. "I have a business to run. Go handle your shit."

He spent all day waiting for her to come trotting through the parking lot, checking under the deck every ten minutes to see if her bike had somehow appeared. Then, sometime before midnight he'd gotten busy breaking up a scuffle, and when he looked again, the bike was there. He'd peered up the hill and saw the lights spilling out into the dark, like a beacon on a stormy coastline.

Another missed opportunity. He'd sighed, going back

inside to pour another round of drinks. The night wore on, and soon enough it was time to lock the doors, put up the chairs, and retire to his room at the back of the building— another day done.

Stripping off his shirt and jeans, he tossed them into his hamper and turned to consider his bookshelves, in desperate need of an escape. This was how he unwound at the end of a long night, after hours of sports television and voices warring for attention. Sliding *Tropic of Cancer* off the shelf, he laid back on the bed and smiled despite himself. He wondered if she knew she was going for the horniest one on the shelf or if it was pure chance. Didn't really matter, he decided, cracking open the book.

———

HALBERD PEAK WAS FAR REMOVED from any major cities, just a blip along the uninterrupted highway. In earlier times, the economy revolved around a paper mill, but it shut down in the eighties, taking an entire generation of young people with it. It wasn't the kind of place that screamed hot spot. Then the brewery opened in the old brick mill atop its namesake Milksnake Falls, and a series about haunted hotels featured the Quartz River Inn. Now, a leg of the Vermont Beer Trails ran right through town and every weekend from May to November, the sleepy little hamlet was awash with tipsy ghost-hunting hipsters.

To someone passing through, as Gretchen had been a mere three weeks earlier, it appeared like any other charming, small New England town, with its quaint Main Street boasting a post office on one end and library at the other, and a white colonial church standing watch over the green. Upon closer inspection, though, it was a tad bit *too* perfect;

a homespun false front hung above a sleek, urbane nucleus.

The town hall was situated on an immaculately groomed lawn next to the police station, which rested opposite the fire station, neither of which *ever* went without new fire trucks, ambulances, or shiny black and white Dodge Chargers when the need arose. The plows were always stocked with rock salt in the winter, and the schools never had to choose between new computers for the media center or canceling the music program.

Further indication of the rampant privilege in town— aside from the fleet of BMWs and Teslas lining the streets— was the complete absence of tchotchkes littering the store-fronts. There were no clever T-shirts announcing the town as a vacation destination, no driftwood and fishnet window dressings like the ones found on the coast.

Everything was functional and unadorned; a butcher shop, a bakery, and a small grocery stocked with runny cheeses and artisanal meats in coolers in the back. There was a liquor store with a sommelier on staff, an indepen-dently owned garden center, and a clothing store offering whatever country-club-casual attire was appropriate for the current season. That meant brushed wool pea coats, puffy vests and plaid cashmere scarves in winter and boat neck tee shirts with French navy stripes and hiking capris in summer. If one needed a haircut or a manicure, a well-known New York beauty guru had just opened a spa, choosing to live out his semi-retirement giving soccer mom shags.

There was a hardware store, and a mechanic, and a stately old movie theater with a deco-style marquee. It ran two movies a month: whatever boasted the most buzz for award season and a nice, harmless children's movie. Each weekend, they showed classics after eight p.m. If anyone wanted to see a midnight showing of *The Rocky Horror Picture Show* or a superhero flick, they'd have to make the drive out of town. There was even talk of a big box store a few years ago, but the mayor laughed the developers out of his office.

Cricket assured her that the sleepy season was almost upon them. The residents were looking forward to getting their town back, and should Gretchen decide to stick around, she'd stand a better chance of finding a long-term rental that didn't belong to the man topping her shit list. Soon, it would be just the lifers and the transplants, the privileged newcomers who could afford to live removed from the cities and were fast-outpacing the generational legacies.

Carrying her shopping basket through the aisles at Lundy's Grocery, Gretchen bit her lip and weighed her desire to eat over the knowledge that in five short days, she'd have to gather up any remaining personal property in the cabin and cart it all to Cricket's, where she'd be couch surfing until a new option presented itself. Gravitating toward the prepared foods section, she perused the selection. These were not the typical cold salads and premade sandwiches. The coolers here held duck liver pâté and wrapped sampler plates of unpasteurized cheeses and cured meats arranged in feathery ruffles, wrinkly French olives and squat green chili peppers stuffed with provolone and prosciutto, and fig jam. There was even a roasting machine that emitted the scent of spiced almonds and candied pecans all day long.

Tickled by the idea of eating an extravagant picnic dinner all by herself, she loaded up her basket with crackers, cold cuts, olives, and crudités. She also grabbed a magnum of Champagne and a box of chocolate-covered strawberries on her way to the register. There were no wine glasses in the cabinets back at the cabin, but there was something wonderfully decadent about the thought of sitting on the living room floor and defiling one of Soren's utilitarian coffee mugs with Moët. Maybe after she ate, she'd draw herself a bath in the big jacuzzi tub upstairs and enjoy dessert while sunk neck deep in fragrant lavender suds. Yeah. That'd teach the smug bastard.

Her phone chimed just as she stepped out into the cool September air. She sighed, transferring the canvas totes full of overpriced appetizers to one hand, and reached into her pocket, regretting lingering so long at the cheese counter. If she'd left ten minutes earlier, she'd be further up the mountain, where cell service trickled off to nothing. She wouldn't have gotten the message from *Maybe: Brian Harris* until tomorrow, when Cricket would be around to talk her out of sending a reply. As it was, she felt a familiar fog of helplessness settle around her shoulders, the natural response to Brian's intrusive presence in her life.

*Jenny and I got engaged. Just thought you should know.*

Wow, Jenny worked fast. Gretchen was tempted to ask *why* he felt she needed to be told, but she already knew. Jenny jumped into Brian's bed before he even had time for a post-breakup linen change, and now the poor weak bastard was hoping Gretchen would talk him out of marrying his rebound girl. Setting her jaw, she tapped out an answer. *Congratulations.*

*Can we meet?* Brian's reply was almost instantaneous. She could picture him sprawled on his sofa, one leg propped up, awaiting her answer with bated breath. Then, before she could formulate a snappy way to tell him to kindly fuck off: *Please? I just want to talk.*

She scoffed under her breath, a dull sense of self-condemnation nibbling around the edges of her disdain. Her plan had worked exactly as she intended it to. Even if she'd been gullible enough to believe him again, she was too far away to accept. Still, she could feel his desperation radiating through the phone. She knew what would come next if she didn't answer. The pages-long message pleading for another chance. The hollow promises. Sucking in a steadying breath, she typed her answer and sent it before she lost her nerve. *Don't contact me again.*

The three little dots in his reply window started bouncing, but she'd already blocked this new number before he finished. Stopping to tuck her phone into her pocket and redistribute the weight of her groceries, she blinked with disorientation, turning to look at her surroundings. She'd somehow walked for almost a half mile while trading five lines of text. She'd left her bike parked at the café. Hefting the canvas bags over each shoulder, she sighed with resolve. It would have been a pain in the ass to ride her bike back to the cabin with all these cumbersome bags anyway. She might as well go back for it tomorrow.

---

SHE CAUGHT him by surprise that afternoon, trudging through the parking lot with grocery bags slung over each shoulder and no bicycle in sight. He was on his hands and knees, scrubbing out one of the big trashcans from the kitchen. Pulling his head from its foul depths with a band of grime and soapy water smeared across the front of his shirt, he looked up just as she rounded the end of the building. Sitting back on his heels, he dragged an arm across his forehead and watched her walk by, hair gilded by sunlight, eyes downcast.

She didn't acknowledge him as she passed, and he waited until she was out of range before he got up and overturned the trashcan, letting the soapy water spill out into the dust. Carrying it around the side of the building, he slowed his steps as a flash of dark green caught his eye. Setting down the trashcan, he bent to retrieve a book from the ground, turning it over in his hands. *Jane Eyre*, by Charlotte Brontë.

It had to be hers, of course. No one else was around, and it hadn't been there earlier. She obviously loved it dearly to carry it with her, and if the shabbiness of the curled paperback cover—held closed with a rubber band—was any indication, she had the compulsive habit of rereading it in her idle moments.

Glancing up at the place where she'd disappeared, he sighed. She would want this back, and it wasn't like he could leave it where he found it. Tucking it into his back pocket, he continued inside.

Striding down the hallway, he laid down on his cot and unwound the binding from around the cover, flipping it open. He ran his fingers over the handwriting cascading down the edges of the pages, her thoughts forming delicate vines in the margins. He could track her growth in the way the handwriting had evolved. It began as awkward and loopy, a middle-schooler's first attempts at "grown-up" cursive, with the most recent notations shrunken down and spare, the tight-packed missives written fast and slanted, as if her hand couldn't keep up with her racing thoughts.

Was it a violation to read someone else's comfort book? It wasn't like it was her diary, a record of her private thoughts. Millions of people had read the same exact words, himself included, although it had been a while. Reading them now felt like an unexpected meeting with an old friend; familiar, but a little awkward because so much had changed since last time they'd seen each other. Halfway into the sixth chapter, Sam realized he'd stopped reading the *book*. He'd become more interested in her scribbles.

He ran his hand over his scalp and sighed, staring at the wall for a few beats before he felt his stomach twist with realization. There was an old girlie calendar up there. He didn't know why it never occurred to him to take it down, except that he didn't even *see* it anymore. His father put it up when this was still his office and, Sam surmised, he'd liked the look of Miss September enough to never turn the page. It only occurred to him now that Gretchen had been in here, and he'd told her off when she teased him about hiding his porn. *Fuck,* she didn't think he was in here jerking it to a faded picture of a woman bent over a motor-cycle, did she? Sitting forward, he yanked the calendar off the wall and flipped the page. Miss November grinned up at him, the picture as glossy and vibrant as the day it was printed. Folding the whole thing in half, he aimed and chucked it into the garbage can in the corner.

# CHAPTER
## Eleven

*Something's burning.* Gretchen looked up from her work, the thought finally registering. She'd been warned many times that keeping strange hours would catch up with her eventually, so when she'd first caught a whiff of smoke on the air, she'd assumed she was suffering a mental breakdown, or a possible stroke. It was getting stronger though and beginning to overpower the scent of citronella on the deck.

Lifting her legs off the railing, she set aside her computer and sat forward to peer down into the crevasse below, but it remained dark. It wasn't coming from inside either. She could tell as she passed through the downstairs, sniffing the air, and couldn't detect the slightest hint. Pushing open the laundry room door, she was relieved to see that the dryer had not burst into flames, a dark fear her mother had put into her from childhood.

Moving to the front of the house, she stepped out onto the porch and felt her heart wedge itself into her larynx. It was the billiards hall. Rooster's was on fire. Rooster's was on fire. ROOSTER'S WAS ON *FIRE*. She went dodging to the top of the stairs, her hand clamping to the railing.

*Wait.* Her brain finally caught up, stopping her in her tracks.

"*9-1-1...*" she breathed, rushing back through the living room and out onto the deck to snatch her phone off the table where she'd left it. "9-1-1. 9-1-1."

She'd had nightmares like this, where she was trying to call for help, but her fingers were shaking so much that she couldn't press the buttons. After several failed attempts to unlock, the screen displayed the emergency function, and she swiped her thumb over it, holding the phone to her ear as she dashed out the door.

She managed to convey the nature of the emergency while sprinting down the stairs, skipping complete sections and jumping from landing to landing. By the time she hit the ground, flames engulfed the entire roof of the building. She stuffed the phone into her shirt pocket and ran around the side of the pool hall, ignoring the prickers slashing at her ankles as she waded through the bushes to Sam's bedroom window. *Shit.* There were bars on all the windows on this side of the building, and they were at least six feet off the ground. She could hear alarms blaring inside as she bent and felt around in the dark for something to throw at the window. Coming up with a fallen tree limb, she struggled to lift the heavy branch and swung it over her head.

Glass shattered. A stream of black smoke exploded into the chilly night air, blotting out the stars. The sound of the alarms got louder. Somewhere inside, she heard a series of muffled thumps. Pushing her hair out of her eyes, she screamed up at the window. "Soren! Soren, can you hear me? The fire department is on its way!"

She waited, fingers twisted into the hair at the top of

her head, and then called out again. "Sam! Do not open the door!"

No answer. Breathing hard, she tore through the prickers and stared up at the rear door. There were bright orange flames lapping at the wired glass panel. She heard sirens in the distance and raced around the corner of the building, gasping in relief at the sight of red and white lights flickering through the trees. The air she sucked into her lungs was acrid, and she doubled over hacking as the engines pulled in, the firefighters piling out and rushing around. Someone was grabbing her shoulders, trying to ask her questions, and she dragged her gaze from the burning roof to the man's face.

"Is there anyone else inside?" he was asking, his words somehow out of sync with the movement of his lips.

"Soren." She nodded, her attention snagging on the firefighters as they unfurled the hoses and turned on the water, directing it at the burning roof. "I broke the bedroom window, but there were bars on it..."

The man released his hold so fast that she collapsed into the dirt. A pack of firefighters went barreling around the end of the building as someone else helped her up again. A paramedic led her to the back of an ambulance, rattling off questions. She shook her head, pushing their hands away as they pressed her to sit on the tailgate. Then her eyes fell to the exposed flesh beneath the cuffs of her cropped jeans and the blood beading up through the scratches on her skin. The paramedic lifted her leg and dislodged a thorn from her ankle, still attached to a slender green branch. She hadn't even felt it happen. "Oh. The prickers got me."

"It's no wonder if you're running around out here bare-foot." The paramedic dabbed the scratches with an alcohol pad. "But you did the right thing, not stopping to grab anything."

"Huh?" She blinked at the woman applying bandages to her ankles, her meaning seeping in through the fog of adrenaline. She glanced down at her torn-up feet, realizing for the first time that she wasn't wearing shoes. "No, I wasn't inside. I live up the hill."

"*Shit.*" The paramedic glanced over her shoulder at the burning bar again. "It's a damn good thing you were up."

Someone shouted, and she watched as a pair of firefighters lurched into view with a body slung between their shoulders; dressed only in sweatpants and dangling by the arms, feet scuffing in the dust. Gretchen's superficial injuries were forgotten as the paramedics jostled her to the side and pulled out the stretcher. She watched in horror as they strapped Sam's limp body to the gurney, covered his soot-smeared face with an oxygen mask, and lifted him into the back of the ambulance. His head lolled to the side, and for one hopeful moment, she thought she saw his eyes flutter before the doors slammed shut.

Something inside the bar ignited, sending up a blinding fireball and collapsing the roof in a funnel of sparks. Gretchen was so stunned by the sound of the explosion that she failed to notice the ambulance pulling out of the parking lot and speeding in the direction of the hospital, sirens screeching.

SAM CAME to in the back of the ambulance, remembering very little about how he got there. The paramedics were talking across him, and when he jerked against his bindings, two strong sets of hands flattened against his shoulders, pushing him back down. His eyes burned. A face floated into the watery foreground, Nicky Meyers staring down at him with sedate blue eyes. "Stay calm, Soren. You're safe now."

"Wha—" he croaked, pulling down the oxygen mask as a coughing fit racked his chest. The mask covered his face again, and he laid back, feeling as if he'd been swallowing razor blades.

"There was a fire." Nicky leaned down close, speaking calmly as she undid the straps across his chest and legs. "The new girl called 911."

*The new girl?* he repeated internally, searching the thick fog of his memories for a shred of recollection. His brain dredged up the sense memory of being awakened from a dead sleep when his bedroom window shattered. There was a sudden rush of panic as he realized that the fire alarms were shrieking and he'd somehow managed to sleep through them. He instinctively rolled off the bed and gazed at the door. Seeing the thin band of golden orange light moving beneath it, he snatched his blanket off the bed and stuffed it against the crack.

It did nothing to keep the smoke out. The fire was already in the drop ceiling. A hunk of burning tile fell to the floor, missing the tip of his nose by inches. His eyes were stinging from the smoke, and every breath was agonizing. His thoughts were fading, becoming less ordered. Somewhere in the distance, someone was screaming.

There was nothing beyond that. He must've lost consciousness. Realizing that he'd come close—terrifyingly close—to never waking back up, his stomach roiled. He ripped the mask off again, twisting to the side. Someone barked, "He's gonna boot!"

Nicky's partner jammed a kidney basin under his chin,

and he emptied the contents of his stomach into it. They pressed an ice pack to the back of his neck, and he groaned, spitting the remnants into the basin. The stomach acid was *not* helping his scorched esophagus. "Jesus, *fuck*!"

"*Language,* please," Nicky scolded, and Sam hacked out a pained laugh, falling back onto the gurney. She'd been a tight-ass in high school, too.

He had plenty of time to contemplate the ruination of his life on the drive to the hospital. The doctors wanted to keep him overnight to run a bunch of tests and make sure he didn't die in his sleep, which was fine since everything he had in the world was just reduced to a pile of smoldering ash.

# CHAPTER
*Twelve*

"My god, this is awful." Cricket kicked aside another piece of charred wood, looking stricken. By morning, the entire town knew that the pool hall was gone, and Soren was in the hospital. The church ladies were already cranking out casseroles, though no one was sure where to bring them. His regulars had also taken up a collection, but the money was hardly enough to cover a week at the Sugar Birch Motor Lodge. Now it was just Gretchen and Cricket sifting through the ashes under the watchful gaze of the fire marshal.

"Concentrate on this area over here and be careful not to step on any nails." Gretchen pointed to the corner where Soren's room used to be, picking her way through the rubble and trying to differentiate between fire damage and salvageable items. *Of course, everything the morose motherfucker owned had to be black.*

The building was a total loss, but she was still holding out hope. Toeing aside a hunk of collapsed roofing, she yipped out a gleeful cheer, dragging the remnants of his footlocker from under his twisted bed frame. It was badly burned on one side and the plywood was warped with heat and water saturation. As she pulled it free, the damaged end came away completely, spilling Soren's clothes into the ashes.

"Sweet!" Cricket crowed, shaking out a trash bag and stuffing a stack of black tee shirts inside, followed by a fistful of boxer briefs, giggling as she did. "Better wash these or his junk is gonna smell like jerky."

"The important thing is, he won't have to raid the church donations box." Gretchen bent to retrieve a familiar hooded sweatshirt, still damp. There were seed holes burned into the cuffs, but it was miraculously intact. So were the black Levi's she pulled out from between a set of overhanging floor joists.

"Hey," the fire marshal shouted, stepping away from his pickup truck. "You girls stay away from that part of the structure! It could give at any second!"

"Sorry Bob!" Gretchen waved, stepping back with the jeans in her hands and stuffing them into her bag. Bending down, she pulled a single motorcycle boot out of the wreckage and spent a few minutes looking around for its mate before moving on. Given the good drenching the place had taken, any books that had survived the flames were little more than mush at this point. Taking out her phone, she snapped pictures of the titles she could decipher; once they took care of the immediate concerns, they could dig up fresh copies.

"This is such a nightmare." Cricket straightened, looking overwhelmed by the devastation around her. "Can you imagine? Just losing your whole life like this?"

"He didn't lose his whole life." Gretchen dug what appeared to be the medallion from a Purple Heart out of another pile, stuffing it into her pocket. "He still has whatever's in the storage shed, his car, the house I'm moving out of, and people who care about him enough to pull his shorts out of the rubble. By my estimation, Soren's a lot better off than most people."

"You know, I *was* thinking about baking his favorite raspberry white chocolate cheesecake to make him feel better." Cricket cocked her head to one side, a slow smile spreading across her lips. "But when you put it that way, fuck 'em."

Gretchen grinned, slinging her bag over her shoulder. "He did almost die. That's gotta rate at least a cake, right?"

---

MURPHY WHOOPED out a shrill laugh when he caught sight of the orderly rolling Sam out of the hospital. Shoving away from the side of his truck, he opened the passenger side door and bowed with all the pomp of a regency era footman. Sam growled and launched himself out of his wheelchair, vaulting into the truck. After two days shut up in a hospital room having blood drawn, chest X-rays, and even getting a camera scope shoved down his throat to assess the damage to his lungs, he was ready to be anywhere else —even if it meant putting up with Murphy's insufferable good mood.

"I hope you're hungry." Murphy grinned, hopping into the driver's seat and throwing the truck into gear. "Because there's about a year's worth of casseroles waiting for you back at the house."

"The house?"

"Yeah, man." Murphy laughed, looking at him as if he had suffered actual brain damage. "The *other* building you own? The one that's still standing?"

"But what about Gretchen?" Sam demanded. By his count, she still had five more days on her lease. Unless... *fuck*, had he lost more time than he thought?

"Oh, she already found another place, which is awesome since Cricket was ready to let her stay with us. I'd have died of fluid loss in a matter of hours," Murphy explained, miming vigorous masturbation, silver thumb ring flashing. "So, now you have a place to sleep that isn't a Red Cross trailer, and Cricket made you a cheesecake."

"Great." Sam sighed, tamping down the bolt of disquietude that coursed through him.

"Look, dude, I know it's not ideal, but things could be a lot worse, right?" Murphy sounded chastened, and for a brief moment, a crack appeared in his perpetually upbeat facade. "We're all really glad that you're okay, but you're gonna have to suck it up. Besides, it's only—"

"Temporary. I know." Sam swept his palm over his scalp. He was getting sick and fucking *tired* of that word.

It was dark when they finally made it back to town and Murphy dropped him at the base of the stairs. He was grateful for the dark as he made the long climb up to the cabin. It was impossible to look down at the blackened shell of the bar. Someone had left the lights on, and as he stood outside the door trying to work up the fortitude to use the hidden key, a flicker of movement on the other side of the glass drew his eye. Looking up, her ethereal gaze suddenly captured him.

Resting his hands on either side of the casement, he waited as she crossed to the door and opened it. She stood staring up at him for the space of a few breaths, then without warning, she catapulted herself into his arms with enough force to make him stagger backwards. She wrapped her legs around his waist and buried her face against his shoulder, and he forgot how long the last couple days felt and how badly he'd slept in the hospital, surrounded by all its strangeness. Her voice cracked "Oh my god, that was so scary!"

"Yeah, it was," he murmured into the tart, fruit-scented nebula of her hair and closed his arms around her. Damn, this felt good. "I'm sorry for being an asshole and ruining a good time the other night."

"That's okay." She sniffled, her tears soaking into the shoulder of his hospital-issued scrubs. "I felt a lot better after I lit your bar on fire."

He chuckled, sliding his hand up the back of her neck and tightening his hold. "I've been wondering who I should thank for that."

Gretchen gave a weepy little laugh and climbed down, swiping the back of her hand over her eyes. "Okay, I'm done now."

"That's good, because I'm so tired I was about to tip over."

"I should be going anyway." She nodded, edging past him. "I wasn't supposed to be here, but I realized that I forgot to swap a load into the dryer, and I didn't want everything to turn sour."

"No machine at the new place?" He grinned in confusion.

"No, Cricket and I went down and saved some of your stuff and I wanted to wash the smoke out of the clothes, just in case," she explained, sweeping her hair over her ear. There was an odd tempo to her voice, as if she was trying to get everything out in one breath. Sam was distressed to see fresh tears gathering in her eyes. "Actually, it was kinda funny. Your car keys were still hanging right on the wall like nothing ever happened."

"Hey." He gathered her tight against him, pressing his cheek to the top of her head. "Come on, Trouble. You're *killing* me with the tears."

"I'm sorry," she mumbled into his chest, pushing away to wipe the tears from under her eyes. Reaching into her pocket, she handed him his grandfather's singed Purple Heart. "Anyway, I found that, and you need rest, so I'll go."

"Thanks." He turned it over in his hand, feeling an unexpected pang of nostalgia. This medal hung above the bar since his grandfather built the place. "It's probably better that you're here. It's a nice distraction from having to come back to this house."

"Geez, that's bleak, Soren." She gave him a watery smile, dabbing her eyes with the sleeve of her shirt. "You sure you're gonna be okay? I could hang out."

"You want to stay for dinner?" he asked, skimming the side of his hand down her arm. "I bet Mrs. Fingerhut sent over a funeral potato casserole. I'm pretty sure she adds crack."

"Sure." Her smile was resplendent. "I've been looking for an excuse to spend some time with that cheesecake."

# CHAPTER
## Thirteen

"Okay." Sam sat back against the corner of the sofa, considering for a moment. "My first vehicle was a Vespa, I once attended a weekend-long rap festival, and my first time was with my best friend's mom."

"I can't decide if you're really good or really terrible at this game." Sitting cross-legged next to the coffee table, Gretchen took another bite of casserole and narrowed her eyes at him for a moment. "It's the mom thing, right?"

"Actually, my first vehicle was a hand-me-down Ford Contour." Sam chuckled, tucking his hands behind his head in triumph.

"Wait, you slept with your best friend's mom?" She gasped sharply, her hand flying to her mouth. "Wait, you went to a *rap festival?*"

"What can I say? I was twenty-one and the girl I was dating was a fan. I would've done just about *anything* to get some." He shrugged, unaffected by the shock written across her face. "As for the other thing, it was Halloween, and she ran out of candy. She had to give me *something.*"

Gretchen slapped her palm on the top of the coffee

table, her laughter echoing around them. "How old were you? Didn't that make things weird with your friend?"

"Sixteen, and I never told him."

The giggle died on her lips. "I don't even know how to respond to that."

"Yeah. Looking back, it was really fucked up." He gave her a rueful smirk, propping his hands on top of his head. "But in the moment, it was *awesome*."

She arched an eyebrow. "How was it for her?"

"I was sixteen. I didn't *ask*."

"Typical man." She snickered, looking away. There was another question on her mind, one that had been weighing on her thoughts for a while, but she wasn't sure now was the right time.

"Hey." He hailed her attention. "Whatever it is, just spit it out."

Gretchen bit her lip, staring at him for a beat. "Did she ever tell you why she did it? Not your friend's mom, because there's really only one reason for a grown woman to sit on a sixteen-year-old's dick...but your ex?"

"Ah." His grin tinged with melancholy. "Put it this way: She didn't want to be stuck in Halberd Peak for the rest of her life, and I had a business to run; she wanted to have a baby, and I didn't; or she thought I took everything way too damn seriously."

"Shit." She exhaled a deep, slow breath. "The serious one?"

"Nope." He looked down, picking at a piece of fuzz on his scrubs. "All true. She was always complaining that I had zero sense of humor."

"Why get engaged in the first place?"

"Things weren't that fucked up in the beginning." He shrugged, lifting his eyes to hers. "We were good for a long time. Then one day I woke up and she didn't like me anymore."

"Probably a hot take, but I think your brother did you a favor." Gretchen sat forward, resting her elbows on the coffee table. "It doesn't sound like you guys would've been happy together anyway."

"You're more right than you know." He yawned. "God-damn, I'm tired..."

"You want me to go?"

"Nah, it's late, and I'm not gonna sleep upstairs anyway. You can take the bed." He crossed his arms, nestling deeper into the couch cushions.

"Ummm..." Gretchen's gaze flicked from Sam to the stairs and back again. "Okay. Cricket bought you a multi-pack of toothbrushes. Can I steal one?"

"Sure." He nodded, his eyes already closed. "Bring me one, too?"

"You're really not going to go upstairs at all?" She stood for a moment, observing the passive look on his face. "You want a shower? I won't run the water if you do."

His eyes flew open, and he grinned up at her. "Was that an invitation?"

Gretchen pinched her lips into a flat line before she could manifest a smile and encourage his bad behavior. "You know, I don't know what the hell your ex was talking about. You have a *fantastic* sense of humor."

---

CRACKING HIS EYES OPEN, Sam peered into the kitchen, where Gretchen Clarke was wearing his favorite hoodie and flip-ping pancakes. Was he dreaming? Was this heaven? He wasn't sure, but it seemed possible when she turned away and reached for something on a high shelf, the bottom of the sweatshirt riding up enough to reveal the perfect crescents of her ass. *Fuck.* He sat up, clapping his hands over the pup tent in his scrubs bottoms.

"Hey, you're up!" She smiled, saluting him with her spatula. "How do you like your eggs?"

"However you want to make 'em." He smacked his lips against the funky taste of morning breath. "I think I'll grab a quick shower."

"Go ahead." She waved him off. "But I never use the downstairs bathroom, so I don't think there are any towels in there."

He paused at that, then huffed out a sharp sigh of resolve; might as well suck it up and get it over with. He'd been bracing himself for this moment, but as he climbed the stairs and walked into the bedroom, he was surprised by how unaffected he felt. This place didn't feel the same anymore. The house smelled like her now, and last night when they microwaved dinner, she had to remind him where the silverware was.

He liked the place better now that it wasn't his anymore.

It was surprisingly luxurious, not having to wash one side of his body at a time. Standing in the steamy shower enclosure, he popped the cap on a forgotten bottle of green apple shampoo, giving it an exploratory sniff before returning it to the ledge, satisfied that he'd sussed out the source of her delectable scent.

It didn't even occur to him that he'd forgotten his fresh clothes in the dryer until he was climbing out of the shower. Wrapping a towel around his waist, he was approaching the top of the stairs when he heard Gretchen talking to someone, a hard edge creasing her voice. "... because I do not *know* you."

He heard the drone of an unsettlingly familiar voice, though he couldn't make out what was being said. Stopping at the top of the landing, he could see the lower half of her body, her bare feet squarely planted. "Oh, I'm sorry. Let me rephrase: I don't *want* to know you."

A craggy rumble of laughter ricocheted around them, and he felt his spine stiffen. He could've picked that sound out of a lineup while blindfolded. Gretchen was unmoved. "Wait. Here."

The door slammed, and as she stepped away, he took stock of the two pairs of legs on the other side of the glass, both clad in denim. One in heavy black boots; the other in white tennis shoes. Yup. It was official: This day was ruined before it even started. Gretchen was crossing the room, those two-tone eyes snagging on him as she mounted the stairs. "You want the good news, or the bad news?"

"What the hell." He sighed, feeling a small kernel of gratification at the way her gaze lingered on his body. "Gimme the good news, since I've already got an idea what the bad is."

"Looks like the insurance investigator found your fire safe and left it on the porch with a note." She shot him two halfhearted thumbs-up. "Assuming your social security card and birth certificate are in there, that should make it a lot easier to replace your license. So, ya-ayyy."

She stretched the word out, doing a thoroughly unconvincing job of remaining upbeat. It was sweet to watch, and Sam couldn't help but smile. Putting one hand on his hip, he skated the other over the crown of his head and gazed over the railing. "And the bad news?"

"Right, uh..." She let her hands fall to her sides. "Apparently you never updated your emergency contact info, and the hospital contacted your brother."

"Shot in the dark," he said, his smirk sardonic. "But he called my father to back him up?"

"Yup." She nodded, pressing her fingertips together in the international sign for evil doings. "Now, I've already taken the liberty of treating him like garbage, but if you want, I can go down there and cut up his face while you put on some clothes."

"I don't think that'll be necessary." He chuckled, securing the waist of his towel with one hand as he ambled down the stairs. It might've been nice to be wearing pants when confronting the piece of shit who'd dealt him the greatest betrayal of his life, but fuck it.

"Can do, boss." She moved to the side as he passed, then fell into step behind him. "But I know how to hit a guy and make it look like he tripped. So, if you need me to punch him in the nards, just tug your earlobe."

Sam stopped short and heard her surprised squeak as she collided with his back. Turning to look down at her, he smiled in bewilderment. "What kind of dickless, myopic asshole let you get away?"

"Probably on par with the same brainless, disloyal, down-trading simpleton that cheated on you." She lifted her chin, her eyes smoldering with amusement.

"Man..." He folded his arms to stop himself from yanking up the sweatshirt and nailing her to the wall. "If I didn't have to deal with the terrorists outside, I'd be doing some *real* nasty shit to you."

"Aww..." She giggled, giving his shoulder a playful punch. "Right back 'atcha, sweet talker."

# CHAPTER
## Fourteen

Lyle Soren looked just like a wiry, kiln-dried version of his son, but with a pirate's hoop earring and a horseshoe mustache. This was Gretchen's first thought when the man stuck out his hand to introduce himself, his gold incisor glinting in the morning sunlight. He was nowhere near as bulky as Sam, but he had the same intense dark gaze and full lower lip; his eyes had acquired more crinkles at the corners, and the brackets running from the flare of his nostrils to the corners of his mouth were more pronounced with age.

He stood back and observed as she faced down Sam's brother in the doorway, covering a laugh by coughing against the back of his hand when she got in one last good jibe. Then, as she stepped back and dug her heel into the toe of Justin's shoe to stop him wedging it into the door, the old man shot her an approving wink.

"Nice girl you've got here," Lyle pronounced when he shook Sam's hand a few minutes later. He stepped back and angled his chin in her direction, hooking his thumbs under his belt. "This one seems to have the sense God gave her."

"Jesus *Christ,* Dad," Sam's brother barked at the not-so-subtle barb, his face reddening.

"Can I get you some coffee, Mr. Soren?" Gretchen piped, beaming. Sam sliced a warning look at her over his shoulder. It was obvious he had no intention of letting the two of them at each other. Whether he was worried she'd charm his father into taking her side or she'd fall under the old buccaneer's thrall remained to be seen.

"They're not staying." Sam took a step to the left, blocking her line of sight and affording her a perfect view of the screeching Dürer griffin, wings pointed skyward, occupying the entire left hemisphere of his back.

"Yeah, thanks *hermosa.*" Lyle leaned to one side, giving her another fourteen-carat smile. "But we were just hoping to have a family huddle. We didn't realize Sam had a lady friend over."

"That was entirely by design, Dad." Sam shifted his feet, his hackles already up. "As for the huddle, I'd much rather spend my day at the DMV."

"Yikes, kitty likes to *scratch,*" Gretchen murmured, slinking away to get dressed and gather her things. Sam snorted, shooting her a parting grin.

Sam was shoving the door closed when she returned a few minutes later, his good mood from earlier well-squashed. Seeing the rankled expression on his face, Gretchen hitched her bag over her shoulder and started gnawing her lip. "So, what'd they want? Aside from making sure that you're not dead."

Sam groaned and flopped onto the sofa, running his hands over his head as if he was trying to start a fire on his scalp. "Probably to talk about what happens now that the bar's gone."

She took another step in his direction, trying to ignore

the tantalizing way the towel gapped open when he spread his knees. The only thing stopping her from getting an eyeful was the way he slung his hands over his thighs, letting them dangle between his legs. She cocked her head to the side, attempting to capture his gaze. "And you don't want to?"

"I don't know," he muttered, scrubbing his hands down his face. "I thought I'd at least have some time while I waited for the insurance to get settled."

"All right, Mountain King..." Skirting the edge of the coffee table, she perched on the arm of the sofa, setting her feet on the cushions. "What do you need to get done today?"

"*Mountain King*? Are you calling me a troll?"

"Just *humor me,* Sam." She swatted at him. "What do you need to get done?"

"I like when you call me Sam." He let his head fall against the back of the sofa, gazing up at her.

"Your preference has been noted." She laughed, nudging him with the toe of her shoe. "Come on, now. Focus!"

He huffed, then started rattling off tasks, looking more dejected as the list went on. "I have to get a new license, replace my cellphone, buy new boots..."

"Okay. Just for today, do those things," she suggested. "Those other problems don't even exist until you take them on as your own. Right now, handle *your* business. Who knows? Maybe getting some stuff done without worrying about other people's expectations will help you make up your mind."

"Jesus." He smiled up at her, blinking as if such a thought had never even occurred to him. "How do you make everything sound so simple?"

"Meh. You're just too close to the project." She got up again, checking the clock on the wall. Slipping around the back of the sofa, she crouched down, folding her arms against the cushions. "I know it feels overwhelming, but you're going to be okay."

―――――――

THE HOSTESS LED him through the dining area of The Axe & Bow Pub and directed him to a table in the corner, where his father was already entertaining several waitresses with tales of his Mexican fishing exploits. Steeling himself for the inevitable revulsion that came with watching a pack of breathless women vie for the attention of Blackbeard the Pervert, Sam slid into the opposite side of the booth. The waitresses scattered like seagulls off the back of a trash barge, hovering nearby with one ear turned to the conversation so they knew the best time to swoop back in.

"Don't worry. Dipshit isn't here yet," his father grunted, sucking the meat off a chicken wing. "So, what's the story with that hot little number you've got answering your door?"

"Gretchen's a friend." No way was the old man getting more than that. Not when Sam himself had yet to figure out what the hell was going on. His father snorted, shooting him an astute arch of his brow.

"I've had friends like her." He reached for his beer, chugged back a mouthful, and then rattled out a burp. "Not for nothing, though; that's not the kind of girl you keep around for a casual piece of ass."

"And what the fuck would you know about it?" Sam sat back as the waitress delivered his beer, then contemplated the menu. Stupid gastropubs. What if all he wanted was a damn steak? Did it *have* to come rubbed with coffee and drizzled with whiskey glaze? "I've never seen you keep a woman around for longer than a few months, and that includes Mom."

"Watch it, ya little bastard." His father chuckled, waggling a finger in his direction. "For your information, your ma was a keeper. I was the one who wasn't worth shit. And look what happened. She went off and met someone who treated her right."

The old man chortled, oblivious to the deep undercurrent of self-hatred he was swimming in. "Shit for brains' mother, on the other hand—"

"Don't," Sam bit out, slicing a glare in his father's direction. It was the worst kept secret in Halberd Peak that Sam and Justin had two different mothers, and good money had it that there was more spawn out there. Somehow, by the time they reached high school, both boys wound up in the care of their shameless Lothario of a father. Sam, because his mother moved to Plattsburgh with the new husband, and he wanted to stay with his friends. Justin, because his mom went off her meds sometime after he started fifth grade and the state awarded full custody to Lyle. Gulping his beer, Sam let the bitterness wash over his tongue and grimaced. "And lay off Justin. I'm not saying I've forgiven him for what he did, but that's between him and me."

"Is that so?" His father's eyes glittered. "If I didn't know any better, I'd say that little firecracker's been a good influence on you."

"Fuck off," Sam snapped, resenting the look of triumph in the old bastard's eyes. He'd been verbally abusing Justin for years, just waiting for Sam to stick up for him. "Gretchen has too much going for her to waste her time trying to fix me. Or anyone else."

His father stilled, a shrewd smile spreading across his lips. "You're already off your nut, aren't you?"

"You're drunk."

"No, I'm serious." The old man chuckled, shaking his head at his son's supposed lack of self-awareness. "I never liked Trinity. It was plain as day that she was wrong for you, but you had those iron-clad love goggles on, and we all knew if we said anything you'd double-down and elope."

"Come to a point before I step into traffic."

"The point *is*..." His father grinned, sinking his teeth into another wing. "You've always been the type to go all in, even when the girl wasn't worth it. If I'm honest, I admired that stubborn streak in you, because I figured, hey...at least all those years around me didn't fuck you up that bad. You saw the good in everyone, even the cheap goods."

Discarding the bones on the edge of his plate, he licked his fingers and chewed for a beat. "I think this is the first girl I've ever seen you with that was actually worth a damn."

"Sorry, Trinity's up my ass because I had to go out of town and the baby's got a temperature." Justin appeared before Sam could decide how the hell he was supposed to respond to his father's unexpected outpouring of approbation. Clamping his mouth shut, he hunched over his beer as Justin dropped in opposite him, looking chastened by the shuttered expression on his brother's face. "Never mind. Let's just get this over with."

"Good idea." Their father continued to glare in reproach for a moment, then flicked his gaze to Sam. "Heard back from the insurance company yet?"

"Not yet. They're not going to cut a check until the investigators clear it." Sam sighed, smoothing his palm over his skull. "The fire marshal says it was a freak electrical issue; it's just a question of submitting the written report, which could take a couple weeks."

"I have a contractor buddy who can help with the rebuild," Justin spoke up. "Better to keep prices down."

His father was already nodding at the wisdom of the sentiment, but all Sam heard was a dull rushing sound in his head, like he was holding a seashell over each ear. Something in him snapped, and he slapped his hand down onto the table. "So that's it? No discussion?"

Justin looked to their father. "Rooster's is an institution, right? People are counting on us."

"But I'm the only one actually doing the *work*," Sam ground out. "Dad's in Mexico and you're—I don't even give a fuck what you're doing. Are *you* going to pull your weight for a change?"

"Hold up." His father sat forward, eyes flashing dangerously. "My father built that place. I spent a lifetime keeping it afloat."

"Well, maybe I don't want to sacrifice the rest of *my* life to it." Sam threw up his hands. "It's never going to be the same again, so maybe it's time to accept that it's gone and cut our losses."

"This is our legacy." Justin looked equal parts offended and hurt. "I know that things haven't been good between us, but—"

"You want it?" Sam flagged down the waitress and asked to borrow her pen. He flipped over his paper placemat and scrawled out a quick missive. "Here you go. I'm signing over my share of the bar, and the land. Hell, you can even have the house. Ever since you and Trin dicked me over, it's been ruined for me anyway. When the insurance company sends the check to *me,* since the policy's been in *my* name since Dad retired, if you two want to split Dad's share of the money and rebuild the bar, that's your business."

He shoved the placemat across the table to his brother, and Justin slammed his hand down to stop it from sailing onto the floor. "Trinity won't go for this. You know she doesn't want—"

"Oh, I know, because I had that exact same fight so many times, I can recite it in my *sleep*." Sam scooted out of the booth and grabbed his new jacket. Standing over the table, he felt a fresh sense of liberation thrumming in his bones. "Now she can either move back to town and help you uphold *your* legacy, or she can divorce your ass."

"Great. Fucking *great*." Justin pushed the placemat aside, and his father snatched it up, gaping at the words on the paper. "And what are *you* gonna do?"

Sam paused, because for the first time *ever*, he didn't have an answer. It wasn't as if he'd planned for this. He'd never *needed* to. He waited for the panic to set in, but none came. Instead, there was only an odd sense of exhilaration. Shoving his arms into his jacket, he grinned as a lifetime of tension uncoiled between his shoulders, unexpected tranquility expanding throughout his body and sending tingles racing over his scalp. A laugh bubbled up. "I have no idea."

# CHAPTER
*Fifteen*

The streetlights were just coming on as Gretchen hopped off her bike in front of her one-bedroom rental cottage. Catching sight of a familiar motorcycle parked at the curb and Sam's dark shape sitting against the thick trunk of a nearby sugar maple, she put the kickstand down and plucked out her earbuds, sauntering across the yard.

"Hey!" She tucked her hands into the rear pockets of her jeans as she approached, fixing him with an inquisitive smile. "What's up?"

"It's a nice night," he began, flipping his book shut and looking up at her in the dying light. "I thought you might want to go for one more ride before it gets too late in the season."

"Okay, sure." She nodded, pleasantly surprised. "You want to come in while I change?"

He followed her up onto the porch and through the screen door. Leading him into the kitchen, she directed him to sit down at the ugly white farmhouse table and set a glass of iced tea in front of him. "Hang out here. I'll be right back."

"Take your time." Sliding down in his seat, he stretched out his long legs and crossed them at the ankles, looking surprisingly relaxed in a space that she herself had yet to settle into. She paused, looking him over again. There was something in the air around him, a sudden lightness of spirit that hadn't been there before.

The weirdness continued when she emerged from her bedroom a few minutes later. Getting to his feet, he cast a disapproving eye at her fashionable but inadequate outer-wear, but rather than giving her a hypercritical sneer, he reached for the heavy leather jacket he'd been carrying when he arrived. Unfolding it, he took out a smaller one. "Try this."

"You brought me a loaner jacket?"

"Sure. Let's go with that." He waited patiently as she started to put it on and encountered an obstacle in the left sleeve. Pulling out a crumpled brown paper bag, she gave him a curious smile and unfolded the top, feeling her heart skip a beat.

"*Jane Eyre*. You brought me *Jane Eyre*."

"I found your old copy in the bar's parking lot." He dipped his chin, his expression turning apprehensive. "I meant to give it back to you, but you were still pissed at me. Then the fire happened and…"

He put his hands on his hips. "I know it doesn't have all the notes in the margins, but—"

He bit off the end of his sentence as she took two big steps and, splaying her hands across his chest, hopped up on the toes of her boots, intending to press her lips to his cheek. Unfortunately, he stooped to give her access. Too late to correct her trajectory, she ended up catching him on the ear. Stepping back, she shook her head at their lack of coordination and zipped the book into her bag. "Thank you."

He was right. It was a perfect night for a ride, just cold enough to stop her sweating into the lining of the coat. He'd brought matching gloves too, and a matte black helmet to keep off the wind. Sam aimed the bike north, the darkness adding to the rollercoaster sensation of chasing along the backroads. Holding on tight, she lifted her head to stare up at the strip of stars flowing above the gap in the treetops, like light glinting off the scales of a great black snake.

The moon was high by the time they pulled into a parking space alongside a seafood restaurant, the low-lying structure framed by silvery pine-thatched mountains in the near distance. It was dazzling—if isolated—and as they dismounted and pried off their helmets, Gretchen took a deep breath and folded her arms above her head, turning to observe their surroundings. "Wow, doesn't it smell amazing here?"

"I could eat roadkill right now," Sam rumbled impatiently, starting for the door.

"I was talking about the fresh air, but you're right. The food smells good, too." They were just settling into a booth against the window when her phone rang. Reaching into her jacket pocket to silence it, she frowned when she saw Cricket's name light up the screen. This had to be serious, knowing her friend's distaste for calling versus text. "Uh, I'm sorry. I really need to get this."

She got up and walked to the door, letting herself out into the cool night air. "Hey, what's up?"

"Holy shit, girl! You will not believe what's been going on here!" her friend exclaimed breathlessly. "Soren's gone totally AWOL. Tracy Post went over to the cabin to get her casserole dish back and found his *brother* there."

"Really?" Gretchen turned, watching him study the menu from her place outside the window.

"Yup!" Cricket confirmed, her voice laced with anxiety. "Murphy let him park his SUV in the garage out back this afternoon, but no one has seen him since then. Rumor has it that he just signed over ownership of everything to Justin and took off!"

"He didn't say where he was going?" Gretchen closed her eyes, further amplifying her sense of internal conflict. She'd be damned if she'd be the one to contribute to the rumor mill. He obviously needed to get away, and if he really signed over everything to his brother, he may not be planning on going back. "Do you have his new cellphone number?"

"I didn't even know he *got* a new phone," Cricket hissed. "I called Paige, because I thought maybe he might've reached out to them. He doesn't trust that many people, you know? But now I'm getting scared because he *hates* his brother, and for good reason!"

Leaning back against the split shingle siding, she stared at the clouds drifting across the face of the moon. "I'm sure Sam's fine. He probably just needed to step away and get his head screwed on right. I'll send you his new number as soon as we hang up."

"Sam?" There was a long, pregnant pause from the other end of the line. Cricket giggled maniacally. "Gretchen Clarke, I should have guessed."

Deciding it was best to let her get it all out of her system, Gretchen exhaled a slow breath between her teeth. Cricket was relentless. "So? Details! Were you guys hooking up before, or is this a recent development?"

"Wow." Gretchen pinched the bridge of her nose, smiling through the mortification. "For starters, Soren and I are *not* sleeping together."

"Nuh-uh." Cricket's melodious laughter rippled between them. "Don't give me that. He's a leather harness and studded helmet away from driving point in a post-apocalyptic horde. And sweetie, you're...how do I put this... you know those videos of baby animals in cute costumes? You're like the human embodiment of a baby goat dressed up like a marshmallow chick. It's so weird it almost makes sense."

"Cricket, my love, is it fun in the shōjo manga fever dream where you live?"

"Laugh all you want," Cricket shot back. "It's only a matter of time before you two bone down. I can only hope and pray that you're still able to walk upright when it's all over."

"And now that you've branded that incredibly disturbing visual onto my brain..." Gretchen sighed, eager to put an end to the conversation. "I'm about to sit down to dinner right now, but as soon as we hang up, I'll send you Soren's new number so you can confirm his safety. All I ask is that you please refrain from saying *any of that* to him."

"You're the worst kind of killjoy, you know that?"

"Uh-huh. Love you." Gretchen ended the call. Walking into the restaurant again, she shot him a look of pure vexation. "Head's up. Cricket is about to start blowing up your phone, and she doesn't know I'm with you."

---

SAM SWIRLED the whiskey in the bottom of his glass and watched Gretchen twirling another forkful of seafood

Alfredo. There was no putting off the conversation anymore, not after that frantic call from Cricket. "There are some things we need to talk about."

"Okay. Shoot," she chirped happily. It was nice, sitting in a restaurant and having a meal with a woman again— even if this particular woman swallowed oysters at such a clip, she'd have to stay away from the beach for fear of reprisals.

Sam cleared his throat, resting his folded arms against the tabletop. "When Cricket called you, did she mention I signed over everything to my brother?"

"That does ring a bell."

"Why didn't you say anything when you came back?"

"I figured you'd tell me when it became pertinent." She chewed for an instant. "So. What happened?"

"I'm not really sure; I lost it." He gazed down at the tablecloth, shaking his head in gloomy recollection. "Rooster's wasn't only mine. When my grandfather died, he left equal shares to all three of us: my dad, Justin, and me. Any major decisions relating to the business or the land had to be agreed upon. We were supposed to sit down and decide what we wanted to do, but they'd already decided that everything would go back to the way it was before."

"And you weren't a strong supporter of that plan?" She pushed away her bowl and mirrored his posture, resting her elbows on the table.

"I don't know why I was surprised," he mused, scratching the side of his nose. "I'd already assumed that was going to happen. Then I was sitting at the table, and they were talking about getting started as soon as the check from the insurance company cleared. But the policy has been in my name for the last five years, ever since Dad moved to Mexico. Even before Justin took off, he never contributed to the payments, and once he was past the age where Dad could force him to bus tables as punishment, he never worked there."

Sam sat back and folded his hands behind his head. "I'm sitting there listening to them spending my money without giving me any say in the matter, and before I knew what I was doing, I'd signed everything over to Justin. Dad's listed as an additional beneficiary on the policy, so I told them that if he wants to spend his half of the payout on bankrolling the rebuild, that's up to him. But I'm not giving everything I have left to stay trapped in thankless drudgery for the rest of my miserable life."

"Then why not sign the property over to your dad?" she asked, cocking her head. "Why involve your brother, especially when he's done nothing to deserve such a big share?"

"Dad retired because he couldn't handle the job anymore. All that time on your feet, the heavy lifting, it takes a toll," Sam explained. "They left me holding the bag last time. I wasn't about to stick around and let Justin skip out again."

"I see." Gretchen's eyes shone. "And the fact that your brother will have to move his family home to the place they thought they'd escaped for good? That's just gravy?"

"Pretty much." Sam chuckled. "The kicker is, if they decided to sell the land, he'd make a nice chunk of change —at least as much as I'll walk away with once the insurance company pays up. But he never will, because that would mean sacrificing the moral high ground."

"Damn, Mountain King." Gretchen reached for her iced tea, her eyebrows jumping. "I'm impressed. Sun Tzu *himself* would be impressed."

"I'm choosing to take that as a compliment, rather than a commentary on how petty I am." Sam grinned, running his hand over his arm. Once again, it struck him how effort-less it felt connecting and feeling understood when he was talking to Gretchen. It was as if they spoke the same language, and every other woman he'd ever been with had spoken ancient Phoenician.

"What are you going to do now?"

"I don't know. I was set on a path before I even knew there was a choice. Now I've stepped off that path, and I can't seem to make myself worry about it." He sat forward and brushed his palm over the tablecloth, searching for the words to articulate the inexplicable sense of calm he'd gained. "Right now, I'm letting the high of uncertainty carry me through."

"Fair enough." The ease with which she accepted this reasoning surprised him, seeing as it made little sense to him. "Personally, I found that my life got a hell of a lot easier when I stopped holding on so tight."

"What would you do? If you were me?"

She swallowed, contemplating the question. "First, I'd figure out where I was going to live, since I'd effectively rendered myself homeless. Then, I guess I'd ask myself what I love to do and try to find a way to make a living doing it."

*Sure, and as soon as I can find a job reading all day, I'll have it made.* Sam smiled at the thought, tracing a finger through the condensation on the side of his glass.

# CHAPTER
## Sixteen

I t was well past midnight when they made it back to town. Dismounting at the curb, Gretchen took off the helmet and jacket, moving to give them back. He threw her a modest smile, waving it off. "Nah, you keep 'em. They won't fit anyone else anyway."

"Oh." She dropped her hands. She didn't know how much a motorcycle helmet cost, but she knew they weren't *cheap*, nor were top grain leather jackets with armored elbow patches. She watched him disengage the kickstand, preparing to speed off to places unknown, and made an involuntary reach for his handlebar. "Hey, where are you staying tonight?"

"I'm at the motor lodge." He took off his helmet and slung his forearm over the top, holding it against one thigh. Gretchen gave an involuntary shudder at the thought of the sleazy road motel, and his responding chuckle held a hint of gloom. "I know it's not ideal, but it's only a few days. I'm gonna be working over at Scarver's Garage, so they offered me reduced rent on one of the places behind the shop. I just have to wait a week for the old tenants to clear out."

"Just try to avoid brushing against the walls." She chased her laughter with a yawn. "God, I'm so tired, I could cry."

"Me too." He matched her yawn with one of his own, taking his helmet off his knee. "It feels like a hundred years have passed since I woke up this morning."

"Technically, that was yesterday morning." She noticed his eyes straying to the place where she leaned on his handlebar and snatched her hand away, backing up onto the curb. "I'm sorry. You're trying to leave, and I'm holding you hostage."

"Don't worry about it." He gave her a sleepy but reassuring smile. "I'm not looking forward to going back to the motel. I'm probably going to catch syphilis from the bedspread."

She laughed at the thought. "You could crash here tonight. I'm reasonably certain you won't catch a venereal disease sleeping on the couch."

Sam paused, holding his helmet suspended in the air in front of his face. Lowering it again, he squinted at her for a moment, as if he was weighing the suggestion in his mind. Then he laughed, swinging his leg off the motorcycle's saddle. "Fuck it. You're on, Trouble. I'm too tired to fight."

Leading him inside, she fetched him a quilt and a stack of pillows, then excused herself to brush her teeth and wash her face. The thought of finally closing the book on the day filled her with a welcome buzz of anticipation. Dressing fast, she walked into the tiny sitting room just as he was shaking the quilt out over the length of the couch. He paused to smile in puzzlement at her oversized "Sorry Girls, I'm Gay" novelty T-shirt. "Trying to tell me something?"

"What?" She looked down at the bright rainbow-printed lettering on the front of the shirt and giggled. "Oh. No message, I just hadn't anticipated having a guest, and this is all I have in the way of pajamas." She pushed a strand of hair behind her ear and felt her cheeks flush. "Last year at the Providence Pride Parade, some drunk guy threw up all over me, so I bought the first shirt I could."

"I used to have an 'I heart Oklahoma' T-shirt with a similar backstory." He nodded as she presented him with a fresh toothbrush, still in its box.

"When did you go to Oklahoma?"

"I didn't." He chuckled, walking past her to take his turn in the bathroom. "I was standing a few doors down from a Goodwill when I got puked on."

Gretchen watched him go and resolved to keep the living room wall between them, just in case. It was a peculiar quirk of the old cottage that the bathroom opened directly off the kitchen, and she'd already discovered the door hung an eighth of an inch too low, preventing the latch bolt from engaging. The only thing the lock did was give the person inside a false sense of security.

Putting her hands on her hips, Gretchen turned in a half circle, surveying the room. Like many homes in Halberd Peak, this place was originally built as company housing for the old paper mill. It was never meant to accommodate more than one person, or perhaps two, as long as they were already sharing a bed. As a result, the bedroom laid beyond a set of French doors at the end of the living room, the glass panels affording anyone sitting on the sofa a perfect view to her bed. She hadn't considered that when she extended the invitation.

She was already arranging a horseshoe of pillows

against the headboard when he strode out of the bathroom a few minutes later. She bent to connect her phone charger while he pulled his shirt over his head and unbuttoned his jeans, leaving them in a pool on the floor. He sat down on the couch, sliding off his watch and setting it on the side table next to his new phone and wallet. He spoke without turning his head to look at her, his voice easily heard through the closed French doors. "You don't snore, do you?"

"I don't think so," she returned, shimmying down under the covers and pulling her sleep mask over her forehead. "Did you hear me snoring last night?"

"No." He gestured between them and lifted the quilt, extending his legs along the length of the cushions. "But you were a lot further away then."

"We'll just have to see," she mused, swishing her feet around under the blankets to create a pocket of warmth. "How about you?"

"I used to." He laughed, elbowing all but one pillow onto the floor and punching the remaining one into shape. Lying on his stomach, his feet extended over the arm of the sofa. "You'll have to let me know if I still do, because I'll have some choice words for the surgeon that fixed my deviated septum."

"Noted." She reached over to kill the lights. "Hey, can I have your extra pillows?"

"Huh?" He looked at her. "Why do you need so many? You only have one head."

"I like to make a nest."

"Of course, you do." He groaned, reaching down to rescue the discarded pillows as she climbed to the end of the bed and unlatched the doors, pushing them open. He tossed them to her, and she added them to the cumulus of fortifications on either side of her shoulders. Nestling into the softness, she hummed with contentment. Finally, she reached up and tugged her mask over her eyes, sealing out any remaining light in the room. A minute ticked by, then he spoke again, his voice gravelly with impending slumber. "When do you have to wake up?"

"Whenever." She sighed into the darkness afforded by the mask. "I'm so excited to be in a house with a proper internet connection. It was like the Dark Ages at your place."

There was another pause. "Hey, Trouble?"

"Yeah?"

"What do you usually wear to bed?"

"*Just* the mask." She beamed into the void. A sound of rough lamentation issued from the sitting room.

"Fuh-king hellll." He groaned into his pillow.

---

SAM STARED up at the ceiling, listening to the ominous warbling of the wind coming through the fireplace, and ran his hand over his aching cock. This was sick. He couldn't stroke himself off with her lying ten feet away. Snarling under his breath, he damned himself for not hauling his ass back to the motel when he had the chance. He didn't even know what had possessed him to stay. They'd come to the end of a perfectly pleasant evening, and she was standing there, her hair shining like a halo under the yellow glow of the streetlamp. He felt like he was being hypnotized—by the refreshing night air and by that damned inviting smile. He couldn't say no.

Lifting his head, he gazed into the bedroom and watched her spooned up against the protective barrier of her nest, snoozing behind her satin sleep mask. She couldn't fathom the beast she was cozying up to. One look at the fabric covering her eyes sent his thoughts to an unholy place. That stupid mask. To any normal person, she might've looked like a woman trying to avoid being disturbed, but all he could think about were the sounds she'd make if he bound those slender wrists. Told her to spread her legs, slapped her thighs red, then soothed the burn with a chunk of ice, running his tongue over every inch of her unprotected flesh until she was twisting against her bindings and mewling like a needy kitten. He wanted her to beg, and she seemed intent to go on torturing him right back—not that she was at all aware of the torment she was putting him through.

Getting to know her had done nothing to dull the lustful infatuation that seemed to dog his every step. She was open and kind, inviting him into her world and creating a safe place without judgment or pressure. She dangled love and acceptance within his reach, and in the next breath reminded him it would disappear the moment she decided she'd had enough of Halberd Peak and everyone in it.

She terrified him with her impermanence, but what could he do? He had no hold on the girl. They weren't together. He'd never even kissed her, and it was probably too late by now. As of tomorrow morning, they would have spent two nights sleeping in the same house like brother and sister.

Pushing himself up to sit against the corner of the sofa, he ran his hand over his scalp. He should go; just get up and leave. There was no way he could survive another morning waking up to that sweet face. Not without doing or saying something that he couldn't take back and breaking his own heart in the process. Kicking off the quilt, he reached for his jeans and shook them out, preparing to put them on.

"Sam?" her dusky voice rose from his right, and she propped herself up on one hand, pushing her mask onto her forehead. "Something wrong?"

"No, I'm fine." He surrendered, dropping his jeans on the ground again.

# CHAPTER
## Seventeen

Gretchen Clarke had a filthy mouth. He'd barely opened his eyes and the girl was already swearing up a blue streak. He rolled over as she paced into the room wearing a pair of washed-out jeans and long-sleeve T-shirt, whacking one foot against the coffee table hard enough to make him wince. She spat out a string of muted curses. "Shit-motherfucker-fuck! Balls! Balls-balls-balls!"

"Everything okay?" He smiled sleepily, eliciting a startled yelp from the girl hopping around in front of him.

"Oh, you're awake." She limped to the end of the room and fell back into the floral upholstered chair in the corner, massaging her biffed toe. "I lost a fucking contact." She shoved herself to her feet and walked into her bedroom, moving somewhat better than she had a few seconds earlier. "I lost a contact, and I don't have any more."

"I didn't know you wore contacts," he mused, clutching the quilt across his front as he bent to grab his jeans off the ground. There was no way he was walking around in his boxers right now—not when he had an erection that could drive railroad spikes.

"What?" she called, opening and slamming drawers as she went in search of something.

"I said..." He stood up, sauntering toward the open French doors. "I didn't know you wore conta—"

She came rocketing out of the bedroom and almost face-planted into his chest. Jumping back, she pushed a pair of oversized tortoise shell glasses up her nose with a discombobulated frown and stepped around him. *Fuck, that's cute.* "They're the kind you leave in. Most of the time, I forget they're there."

Sam spun to track her movements. Just when he thought she couldn't possibly get more disarming, she brought out the big nerdy glasses. "You should wear those more often."

"I know." She threw up her hands. "They're friggin' adorable! Until they fog up, or I'm doing literally anything where I have to worry about them falling off, or I can't find them."

She stood in a visible pique for a moment, hands on hips, and scanned the room. Locating her computer on the skinny writing desk against the wall, she stalked over and snatched it under her arm, carrying it into the kitchen.

"You sure your foot's okay?" Sam watched her settle cross-legged on a chair at the table. "You need any ice?"

"I'm good," she murmured, her tone absent, nibbling her lip as she drummed out a few quick sentences on her electronic notepad. "I just want to jot down a couple thoughts before they go out of my head."

"Suit yourself." He picked up a bag of coffee from the counter and unfolded the top. "Do you mind if I make coffee?"

"Knock yourself out."

He spooned Cricket's special "Stronger Than The Devil"

blend into a filter and filled the reservoir with water, starting the machine. "Can I ask you a question?"

"Might kill some time," she returned in the same preoccupied tone, engrossed in her work. The machine hissed to life, and Sam started opening cabinets until he located the mugs.

"What exactly is this big deal project you're working on?"

"Well..." She twisted to lay an arm across the back of her chair, the light catching on the lenses of those damned adorable glasses. "We're working to close the orgasm gap."

---

THE DRIP STARTED, and the scent of freshly brewed coffee filled the air. Sam leaned against the counter and bobbed his head, the corners of his lips quirking up. "Noble stuff. Closing that damn orgasm gap."

"I know it's not something a lot of men think about, since it's merely a question of hydraulics for you." She started pushing back her cuticles. "But eighty percent of women can't orgasm from penetration alone. Most require additional sustained stimulation, but that's often neglected during intercourse, because they don't want to make their partner feel inadequate or they simply don't know what they need."

"Jesus, that many?"

"Sounds pretty fucked up when you hear it out loud, right?" She laughed knowingly. "Basically, the whole point of this is to take the female orgasm out of the foreplay stage, when it's often rushed or simply ignored, and make it possible for any woman to achieve climax during intercourse. There are a lot of companies working on it, but they mostly focus on the physical aspects of orgasm. The issue with that approach is that the female orgasm is largely *mental*, and when you factor in the huge variances in anatomy, it's impossible to build a single device that works for everybody."

"Okay, I'm with you." He folded his arms over his chest, watching her with curious fascination. "How do you engineer a solution to all that?"

"How technical do you want me to make this?"

"I'll take the broad strokes."

"Right. Okay..." She bit her lip again, thinking of the years of hard work that led them to this point. "First, we had to determine how to quantify what worked for each individual, both physically *and* mentally; help them to redirect intrusive thoughts and stay in the moment; and teach them how to communicate those needs to partners. Ultimately, we settled on a combination data gathering approach that allows us to make personalized recommendations for positions and mental techniques that help women reach orgasm with greater frequency."

"Hold on." He held up one hand, a wolfish grin lighting his angular features. "Are you saying that there's some kind of electronic sex therapist out there that knows how to hack your body?"

"Well, I did participate in the beta trials." She pointed at her computer over her shoulder. "So, yeah."

"Can I see it?" He tilted his head, gazing at the device in question.

"That's not what my file is for." Although the look of disappointment on his face was unexpectedly gratifying. "It's about taking ownership of your own pleasure, not handing everyone you meet a report on how to get you off. Where's the fun in that?"

"Why the fuck not?" He laughed, turning to pour himself a cup of fresh brew. "It's not great for guys either, always wondering if they're getting it right. If this thing really works, it'll make an enormous difference for a lot of people."

"Yes, I'm sure when I get up to the pearly gates and they have me waiting behind the woman that spent her life inoculating orphans in sub-Saharan Africa, it'll all feel worth it."

"You won't have to wait in line." He chuckled, sipping his coffee. "Mary Wollstonecraft'll be waving you through the side door."

She looked back at her work. He knew what he was doing, standing there shirtless and name-dropping feminist icons. "You're a dirty fighter."

"I'm a dirty lot of things," he retorted, his voice devoid of any irony. Pressing her knees together, she ignored the pointed look he shot her over the rim of his cup. "Think I could use your shower before I go? The one at the motel could double as a mushroom farm."

She hucked out a pained laugh at the thought of the motor lodge bathrooms and the way the white caulk around the shower enclosure had a permanent black mildew stain. "Yeah, of course."

Hearing the soft roar of the water turning on, she put the ineffectual nature of the door's hardware out of her thoughts, reasoning that someone would have to push against the door for it to open. Then, of course, fate intervened.

A stiff mountain breeze swept down the chimney,

creating a wind tunnel effect and popping the trick door. She hopped out of her seat and reached for the handle, freezing in her tracks at the sight of a very wet, very nude male body a few short feet away.

He leaned into the spray, pressing both hands to the tiled wall as if he was waiting to be frisked. The steam on the clear, plastic shower curtain did precious little to stop her eyes from roaming over the sinuous knotwork of his back. Dropping his head under the nozzle, he let the water run over the back of his neck for a second or two, then straightened, the rounded musculature of his ass flexing as he pivoted, turning his back to the water. He cupped his semi-hard cock as he did, giving it a single stroke and letting it drop between the powerful heft of his thighs. He performed the gesture with such ease; it looked like an afterthought. His movements remained unguarded until he stilled, both of his hands tensed at his sides.

Realizing she'd been caught, she slid her eyes up the front of his body, over the laddered muscles of his abdomen and marble-hewn pecs, and met his gaze. A nervous giggle rose in her throat, and she half turned, her line of sight dropping to his crotch before she could stop herself. He was now fully hard and pointing straight at her like a divining rod. *You could swing a wrecking ball off that thing.* Clearing her throat, she forced her gaze back to his face. "I'm really sorry. The wind took the door."

Sam shifted his stance, wiping the water from his eyes with his thumb and forefinger, and the tiniest ghost of a smile touched his lips. They stared at each other for a beat, neither speaking, until she finally unrooted her feet and backed out of the room. The door felt like a load of bricks in her hand as she eased it closed, making a mental note to hang a rubber band on the knob from now on. Wedged between the bolt and the strike plate, it should create enough tension to keep the door from flying open at embarrassing moments in the future.

# CHAPTER
## Eighteen

Sitting on a bar stool and nursing a beer at The Axe & Bow, Sam looked up as a heavy hand descended on his shoulder and Justin claimed the seat next to his. Despite being almost five years younger, his brother looked *ancient*, with gaunt cheeks and bags under his eyes. If he was not mistaken, he even detected a slight thinning of the hair at his crown, the very beginnings of a monk's cap forming. He didn't know why Justin bothered growing his hair out in the first place. History had shown that Soren men didn't look good with hair.

"Thanks for coming man." Justin heaved out a sigh, signaling to the bartender. "I wasn't sure you would."

"I won't lie." Sam slashed a glare in the other man's direction. "It took me a minute to decide."

"Then why'd you come?"

Sam shook his head, taking another long pull from his beer. Short answer? He'd been climbing the walls at the motor lodge, thinking about the moment when he felt a tongue of cold air lash his bare back and turned to find Gretchen standing in the bathroom doorway, staring at him. Or more to the point, staring at his dick. He'd frozen like a lawn sculpture, unsure of what to expect, and then she'd *apologized*, killing any horny shower sex fantasies stone dead. He glowered at Justin. "What do you want? Because I'm not taking that shit back. It's on you now."

"Yeah, man." Justin's answer was characteristically passive. "I'm not gonna try and talk you into it, anyway. You've been doing more than your share for—"

"Fuck off with that." Sam released a dark chuckle. "You might've buffaloed the neighbors in whatever town you two ran off to with this selfless martyr act, but don't think for a second that it's going to work on me. Or anyone else in Halberd Peak, for that matter. The people around here have *long* memories."

"I don't know how many times I can say this, but I didn't want to see you hurt." His brother laid the blade of his hand against the bar top, a hard edge creeping into his ordinarily mild tone. "It just happened."

"And not a day goes by when I'm not grateful," Sam groused, reaching out to give Justin's shoulder a firm squeeze. "I have no illusions about what kind of hell I'd be living in if I'd married Trinity. We would have made each other fucking miserable."

He waited until he felt his brother relax, then slammed Justin's face onto the bar. Just once, so he could feel like he got his licks in. He pointed a finger at him, suppressing the urge to laugh, the way they used to when they would sock each other and scream *dead arm!* for fun. "But that doesn't make it okay."

"*Jesus,* dude." Justin dabbed at his nose with his fingers, checking to make sure he wasn't bleeding. "I said I was fucking *sorry*."

"And I believed you." Sam let a chuckle slip, feeling the tense gazes of the other patrons on his back. They were waiting for the brothers to trade blows, but when it became clear that a fight wasn't about to break out, activity resumed around them. "You wanted her; you got her. There isn't a goddamn thing I could do to you that'd be worse than that."

Justin didn't respond. The bartender set his brother's beer in front of him, adding a cautioning glower in Sam's direction. Sam waved him off, unimpressed. There was a football game playing on the flatscreen above the bar, and for twenty minutes, they sat shoulder to shoulder, pretending to pay attention to the television. It started feeling almost comfortable, and then Justin spoke again. "You're right, you know. About all of it. Things were good at the beginning, but now..." Justin raked his fingers through his hair, hunching over his beer. "Things have been fucked up for a while."

"What do you mean, 'fucked up'?"

"She's in a terrible mood. All the time," Justin explained, one hand opening palm up against the bar, telegraphing helpless confusion. "Sometimes, I feel like she got what she wanted from me, then immediately took all the energy she used to put into us and started putting it into Ellie."

"Ah, shit!" Sam groaned. "She actually convinced you to name the kid Elliot?"

"It was a family name!"

"No it *wasn't,* dude. It's the name of the guy she dated in college!" Sam snapped. He wasn't surprised. Trinity was like that, willing to snow whoever she had to to get her way. Sam huffed out a sharp breath, sitting forward again. "Don't tell me you didn't put that together."

"She could've told me that. It wouldn't have made a difference to me where it came from."

"Since when did Trin need a reason to lie?"

"Fuck my *life*." Justin's jaw slackened, and he ran his hand over the length of his face, as if it was *just now* occurring to him he didn't know the woman he'd married. "You know, when I called to tell her we'd have to move back, she told me not to bother coming home. So, I guess if you still need a place to stay—"

"Don't get it twisted. Just because I haven't curb stomped you into oblivion doesn't mean we're friends." Sam shook his head, the look of deepening despondency on his brother's face dousing whatever sense of schadenfreude he may have felt before. Of course, this would happen to Justin. He'd spent the first twelve years of his life managing his mother's instability. He'd learned to normalize the nonstop mind games so well that he didn't see the blinking emergency EXIT sign above the door. Lifting his beer, he hesitated, speaking from the corner of his lips. "I'm sorry things aren't working out."

"No, you're not."

Sam set his jaw, reminding himself that he couldn't fix *everything*. Maybe even a little surprised to feel the old instincts coming back. He told himself that his brother made his decisions, and that he didn't owe him a damn thing. He fought it for a solid thirty-seconds before he finally gave in.

"*Fuck,*" he snarled under his breath. "What the hell are you doing hanging around here? You need to find a lawyer, or a marriage counselor, or whatever."

"I've put out a couple feelers—"

Sam clamped his hand over the scruff of his brother's neck, pulling him in close. "This isn't about you anymore,

Jus. It's not even about Trin. You have a daughter, and that baby deserves to grow up better than you did. Find a lawyer *yesterday*, dumbass."

Justin blanched as Sam released his hold. Pushing his empty bottle across the bar, his brother slid off his stool, mumbling his appreciation for the advice. Giving Sam one final, mournful half-smile, he slunk out the door. Sam folded both elbows on the bar and rested his hands on top of his crown, blowing out a tight breath. The bartender approached to ask if he was ready to close out his tab, but where the hell else did he have to be? He reached for a dinner menu.

---

"Hey, Soren!" Murphy crowed as they walked through the door of The Axe & Bow, peeling away from the rest of the crew and jogging over to the bar, where Sam was tucking into a plate of brisket and mashed potatoes. Standing at the back of the crowd, Gretchen was swept along in their wake, feeling somewhat undone by his surprise appearance. Soon, they were all picking off shared appetizer platters as if this had been the plan all along, and she was doing her level best to remain unbothered by the glum looks Sam kept flicking in her direction.

She distracted herself by chatting with Cricket about driving into the city to pick up her new car. With the cold weather coming, she needed something more roadworthy than a ten speed, and she was finally feeling strong enough after the untimely death of her last ride. Paolo and Murphy were speaking across Sam, who was being even more laconic than usual, an irksome island unto himself in the center of their otherwise merry company. The others got up to start a game of darts, and she surrendered to the quantum pull of his dismal mood, moving down to sit next to him. "Okay. Is this about this morning? Because you've been sitting here looking like someone shot your dog since we—"

"No, it's not about this morning."

"Cool." She'd wasted enough time chasing emotionally unavailable men to know she had zero desire to do it ever again. Pushing back her chair, she got up to join everyone else at the dartboards.

A scant minute later, he slid up next to her at one of the high-top tables behind the oche, leaning on his folded elbows and speaking close enough that their shoulders touched. "So, are we talking about it or not? Because I'm confused."

"Okay, firstly? *Shoosh,* please," she hissed at him, tossing her mane over the side of her face, grateful for the protection it provided from the rest of the bar. "And secondly, it was an *accident*. I apologized. Can we just leave it at that?"

His eyes moved over her face, and that dimple appeared in his cheek. "You're blushing."

"I do that sometimes." She snapped her eyes forward, watching Murphy step up to the toe line and take his next shot. "Was that it? Or is there something else on your mind?"

"I had a beer with my brother. It looks like his marriage is in trouble."

"And now you're beating yourself up, because you were wishing all kinds of terrible things on them when you thought they were happy?"

"It's bullshit magical thinking, but yeah. Something like that," he murmured, a guilty smile bending those compelling lips. "Also, this is going to sound awful, but there's another part of me that keeps wondering how I didn't see the signs when she and I were together. Trinity was..." He paused, pondering—Gretchen presumed—how best to describe the woman who'd handed him his own raw, dripping heart a few short years ago. "Not good for me."

Gretchen turned her head, noting the tension at the corner of his jaw. "Refreshing to meet a man who doesn't fall back on calling his ex 'crazy.'"

"Too easy."

"I get it," she admitted. "Mine texted me a while ago to let me know he got engaged to one of my former friends. I might've felt passed over, if I didn't know he was only reaching out hoping that I'd offer myself up as an alternative. Or if I actually gave a fuck about marriage."

"And you don't?"

"I think there's more to life than getting my ring popped," she answered, giving him a sanguine smile. "We both know you didn't destroy your brother's marriage any more than I made that douchebag reach out when his new relationship got too serious."

"Yeah, but Justin has a little kid. And he'll probably be raising her on his own."

"He also has a brother who just handed him the keys to a house to do it in, the rights to a property to support her with, and the inexplicable munificence to actually care when his life is falling apart, despite how dirty he did him," she reasoned, cocking her head to one side. "You want to work on a real problem?"

"World hunger?"

"Vertical farms. Next?"

"Hey!" Murphy appeared at the table, offering a

nosegay of darts to the man next to her, arm outstretched. "Want a game?"

"We can play teams," Cricket called, pulling a fistful of darts out of the other board. "Paolo and me, versus you and Murph."

"You're not playing?" Sam looked at Gretchen, a challenging smirk ticking at the corner of his mouth.

"I don't compete," she answered, earning a sparkle of amusement from those dark eyes.

"In art as in life." He smirked, pushing away from the table.

They played one quick game before Murphy got distracted by a gaggle of girls near the bar. The waitress came to deliver a fresh pitcher of beer, and Cricket and Paolo refilled their glasses, alternating between taking shots at the board and playing grab-ass on the oche. Sam returned to her side, pouring himself a pint from the communal pitcher.

"How do you do that?" he asked quietly, setting his gaze on her again. "Just cut through all the bullshit. Make things easy."

"An unassailable sense of optimism, coupled with a career spent in the STEM world." She lifted one shoulder in a casual shrug. "Date a few engineers and you learn that they only speak logic, and they have a spreadsheet for everything."

He chuckled. "You'd be wasted on a man with the compulsive need to quantify everything."

"Where was this guy a month ago?" She surprised herself with the query. "I might not have dismissed you as a human root canal if I'd gotten a glimpse at him before."

"He was always there." Sam swept a watchful eye toward the inattentive couple nearby, his close-lipped smile accentuating the dimple in his cheek. "I've been keeping him buried pretty deep."

"Is he gonna disappear when the high of uncertainty wears off?" she teased, nudging him with her shoulder.

Sam laced his fingers together around his glass and tilted his head, those dark eyes drilling into her. "Will you?"

This was dangerous. Having him this close to her, smelling spicy-warm and rumbling at her in that deep voice, was screwing with her natural defenses. She cleared her throat, facing forward again. "I'm happy for now."

His brows knitted together. "Are you always so noncommittal?"

"I didn't used to be." She laughed, her tone self-deprecating. "But then I decided I need to start taking up more space in my own life, which means not tailoring my world around the demands of others."

Another deep, secretive chuckle caressed her ear. "You really know how to kick a guy right in the balls and make him apologize for standing within range."

"What the hell does that even—"

"I like you, Gretchen." He leaned closer, dropping his voice to a gruff murmur. "I like you, and I'd like to get to know you better."

He took another drink, his stare not leaving her as he did. "The thing that has stopped me until now is that I don't want to get involved with someone who won't be around in a few months. I don't enjoy casual relationships. When I was young, I might've worried that admitting something like that made me less of a man, but frankly, I'm at a point in my life where I'm over playing games. The things I want to do to you require a level of trust that comes with strings attached."

"I—" She jumped at the sound of a dropped glass, and a wave of sarcastic applause rippled through the bar.

"I'm throwing a lot at you," Sam conceded, his gaze unwavering. "I'm going to give you some time to consider whether or not you're willing to make space for someone else in your plans. Sound good?"

Stepping away from the table, Sam picked up the empty beer pitcher and carried it back to the bar. Murphy trotted over to meet him, trailing a line of girls in his wake. Cricket recognized a handful of school friends and waved Gretchen over to make introductions. Slapping a smile over her stunned expression, she did her best to look unruffled by the sudden revelation he'd dropped in her lap.

# CHAPTER
## *Nineteen*

"Tourist girls, man." Murphy leaned back against the bar, nodding toward a nearby table, where a cluster of tipsy bachelorettes enjoyed another beer flight. His young friend shot him a sly sideways smile as one girl executed a flawless hair flip and come-hither smile. Murphy nudged him. "Dude. That's all you."

"Pretty sure she's looking at you." Sam sighed, waiting for the bartender to finish cashing him out so he could get out of there. Unlike his young friend, he had no desire to make time with a woman who wouldn't remember his name by morning. Murphy snorted, looking supremely disappointed in him.

"Her name's Rachel. She just broke up with someone." Murphy leaned in, giving his shoulder an encouraging slap. "Come on, dude, the pickings don't get easier than this! She's been staring at you for the last five minutes!"

"Tell you what," Sam began, fixing his friend with a perturbed smile. "I'm going to pay my tab and leave, and you can stay here and be the meat in a sorority sandwich."

The bartender returned with his change, and Sam gave his friend a parting cuff on the arm, heading for the rear exit of the pub. He'd parked in the lot behind Main Street, and as he jogged down the stairs, he caught sight of someone sitting on the bottom step, a familiar corona of brown curls rustling in the chilly autumn breeze. "Hey, you okay?"

"Hmm?" She hopped to her feet, smoothing the front of her sweater dress over her legs. She sounded wrung out, her voice hoarse with overuse. "I just needed some time to recharge." Pushing her hair out of her eyes, she gave him a feeble smile. "Socializing with so many people all at once…"

"One of the hazards of hanging around Cricket." Sam felt a pang of sympathy. He knew that sensation well; he'd dragged himself across the finish line on more nights than he could count, feeling like all the people he'd come in contact with at the bar had siphoned every ounce of equanimity straight through his asshole.

"Strap in and hang on for the ride." Gretchen laughed, bundling her hands up in the sleeves of her coat, avoiding his gaze.

"Listen, Gretchen." He took a step toward her, holding out one hand. "I didn't mean to make you uncomfortable. If you want to forget—"

He stopped talking as she reached out and gathered two fistfuls of the front of his shirt, pulling him under the overhanging landing at the back of the building. Stepping back until her shoulders pressed against the masonry foundation, she lifted her chin. "I want you to kiss me, Sam."

"Kiss you?" he repeated, his voice dropping to a low rumble.

She nodded slowly; her gaze going to his lips. "The thing where you put your mouth on another mouth."

"Sounds familiar." He hesitated for a moment, then notched his left hand under her jaw, laying the opposite forearm against the wall above her head. Bending close enough to feel her trembling breath against his face, he forced her chin back with the pad of his thumb, enjoying her pliability. "Say it again."

Eyes glazed with subdued reverence, she exhaled another quavering breath, the muscles of her throat flexing under his hand. "I want you to kiss me."

"And who am I?" he coaxed, adjusting his stance and caging her in against the length of his body. He'd never craved the sound of his name on a woman's lips before, but damn if hearing it pass hers didn't get him hard as a rock every time.

"Sam." She gasped as he forced her chin higher with the immovable abutment of his thumb. Rising up on the balls of her feet, she pressed her fingertips to the wall at her sides.

*Again.* Sam released a low, sinister laugh from deep in his belly, his jaw ticking with crude gratification. He felt her shiver, those sweet lips parting as he hovered above her, close enough that their breath blended. A devilish grin spread across his face. "Pull up your skirt. I want to watch you touch yourself."

She exhaled a soft laugh, a spark of pure obstinacy lighting up her eyes. "How far are you willing to take this, Sam?"

"As far as you'll let me." He lifted his arm from the wall, stepping back to run his hand over the bulge in his jeans. "Now, spread your legs and fucking *show me.*"

He waited, staring her down as she worried at her bottom lip, the gears in her head turning. Then, in an act of true mercy, she tugged the hem of her dress up to her waist.

Looping her thumbs under the waistband of her lacy black panties, she peeled them down her legs, bending to pull them over her boots. Opening her legs wide, she afforded him a glorious view as she started stroking her index and middle finger over her clit.

Breath hitching, she beckoned him closer, looping one leg around his thigh and angling her hips away from the wall, opening herself further to his gaze. Releasing a ragged breath, he reached for the buttons on the front of his jeans.

---

Sam stood over her, devouring her with his eyes. She massaged her clit in slow, feathery circles, shutting her eyes and riding the sensation. Sam clasped her throat with one large hand, speaking against her ear. "Look at me."

She did as she was told, prying her lids open, before looking down to watch as he pulled himself free of his jeans. She felt her core clench at the sight of his hand stroking over the thick club of his erection, working his fingers over the head of his cock and down, before he forced her chin back up, those dark eyes searing into her. His nostrils flared, his words coming out in a rough whisper, as if he'd been gargling iron filings. "Are you close?"

She ran her tongue over her lower lip and nodded, feeling the pulsing in her core intensify at the sound of his voice. "Yes or no, Gretchen?"

"Yes!" She gasped, rocking back and forth, pushing her fingers inside of herself. Her eyes started to drift shut, and he immediately corrected her, his fingers tightening around her throat.

"*Look* at me, Gretchen."

Dragging her stare to his again, she felt an insistent

ache in her core. There were storm clouds in those eyes, his brows forming a fierce frown. His teeth flashed with the intensity of his command. "Make yourself come. And don't you *dare* close your eyes again."

*Oh god, yesss...* Hitching her knee higher up on his thigh, she tensed her core and rocked against her fingers until a wave of scorching heat spread through her limbs. She moaned, electric shocks spiderwebbing along the backs of her arms and legs, and her hips bucked, her leg clenching over his until the other foot lifted off the ground. She fell forward, breathing hard against the tightly bundled muscles of his shoulder.

"Jesus *fucking* Christ," she heard him snarl. He pressed closer, until she could feel his knuckles brush her skin, pumping fast and hard until he came with a loud grunt, his come splashing against her belly and thighs and dripping into the dirt beneath their feet.

He panted for a few seconds, releasing her neck and pressing his hand to the wall, then he leaned back to admire his work. Looking down at the pearly fluid splattered across her skin, she started to tug her dress back down. "Can I get something to clean up wi—"

She squeaked as he seized her hands, yanking her arms above her head. He smeared his palm over her front and spun her around, one giant hand on her shoulder, stapling her to the wall, forcing her cheek to the cold bricks. Bringing his sticky palm down on her ass cheek with a sharp, wet *thwack*, he teased a yelp of surprised laughter out of her throat before he spun her again, leaning down to growl in her ear. "No, you fucking well *can't*. You're going to let it *dry* that way."

She nodded, feeling a fresh rush of arousal pooling between her legs as he turned and stepped out from the cover of the stairs, walking fast toward the car. She felt her face heat, realizing too late that he really intended to leave her there with his spooge marking her thighs. Tugging her dress down over her hips, her grin malevolent, she muttered under her breath, "*Motherfucker.*"

# CHAPTER
*Twenty*

"Cute town." Gretchen slid her glasses down her nose as a gaggle of girls in near-identical puffy vests, turtleneck sweaters, and knee-high riding boots wandered past the window of the restaurant. "Not sure I'd call it a city, though."

"Closest thing we've got around here." Cricket tore a handful of fresh basil into her pho, adding a squeeze of lime for good measure. "Burlington used to be the pinnacle of culture to me. That was before I'd seen New York and Paris."

"And you never wanted to get out? Try someplace else?" Gretchen asked, slurping back a mouthful of spicy noodles. "With your skills, you could be a pastry chef anywhere you wanted."

"Where do you think I *got* my skills?" Cricket gave her a bittersweet smile. "Four years at Le Cordon Bleu. Made my bones at a place in Miami." She stirred the broth in her bowl, exhaling a long sigh. "Vermont's in my blood, though. I moved back and set up shop. No regrets."

"I get that." Gretchen nodded, bristling at Cricket's

incredulous snort. "What? I mean it! I can see how a person could miss it here."

"You never miss Hartford?" Cricket asked, watching her from across the table. Gretchen paused, waiting to feel something. Sure, there were upsides to living in any city: the wide variety of restaurants, ready availability of public transportation, and entertainment on tap. But there were downsides, as well: traffic, lack of personal space, the constant feeling of being lost in the shuffle and *crime*.

She shook her head. "Things weren't happening for me there."

"What about now?" A shrewd smile bent her friend's lips. "Your month is over. You're still here."

"My project's ramping up." Gretchen plucked a piece of beef tendon from her bowl, avoiding her friend's prying. "I'll be chained to my computer for a few months. Can't be on the road."

"That makes sense." Cricket nodded, staring into her bowl. "Did I mention the guys are helping Soren move into his new place today?"

Gretchen stopped chewing and lost herself for a moment in the remembered sensation of Sam's fingers against her throat, firm enough to show dominance, but without causing pain. She felt a telling ache between her legs as she recalled the menacing rumble of his voice in her ear, promising all sorts of discipline she most definitely intended to deserve. Shoving those thoughts aside, she swallowed hard, reaching for her water glass. "Yup."

"And you two were okay last night?" Cricket asked around a mouthful of noodles. "I wouldn't ask, except I noticed him saying something to you and you had this *look* on your face."

"A '*look*?'"

"Yeah, kind of like a kid lost in the grocery store." Cricket shrugged, her expression taking on a pensive undertone. "Nervous. A little nauseated."

"We kept it civil."

"Good." Cricket exhaled a sigh of relief. "I mean, it's not like he's a predator or anything. I know you two aren't exactly on good terms."

"Your concern is appreciated, but unnecessary. Soren was a perfect gentleman." Dipping her head, she hid her smile behind her napkin. Christ, she couldn't even get through the lie without laughing.

"Good." Cricket nodded, preparing to lift her bowl to her lips. "Not that I would have expected anything less. Soren can be a prick, but he's an equal opportunity prick. I honestly think he respects women more than any man I've ever met."

"That's a bold claim."

A penitential smile painted Cricket's expression. "I'm selling this too hard, aren't I?"

"Lil' bit." Gretchen laughed, feeling certain that her friend could see right through her mask of false cheer. Why'd he have to say those things? They'd finally moved past the awkwardness of the morning, and then he said all those wonderful, perfect things, leaving his proposition to hang over her head like the Sword of Damocles.

***

"Ah, fuck." Frank Scarver stepped out of his office, narrowing his eyes at the red electric car stopped behind Cricket's Beetle at the light on Main Street. The grizzled old mechanic hocked a mouthful of phlegm onto the ground, looking every bit like a scale model of his bearish husband with his full beard and white hair, but with skin of such a rich, dark umber that the creases in his face appeared to be carved from a solid hunk of obsidian. "Man can't make a living in this town with all these holier-than-thou hippies."

Sam leaned around the hood of the car he was servicing and wiped his greasy hands on a red rag. He didn't know why being a mechanic never occurred to him before; he'd been doing his own engine work since he was fifteen, and this new arrangement worked out great. He needed to bring in a little cash while he waited for the insurance money, and he didn't hate what he was doing.

The light turned green, and the new car veered off, pulling into the lot. Frank sucked his teeth and grimaced as it rolled to a stop, and Sam sauntered out to meet it, calling to the old man over his shoulder. "Relax! There will always be purists in the world."

The window rolled down, and Gretchen's sweet face slid into view. He bent down, resting his hand on the roof of the car. "Nice ride."

"I know, right?" She grinned, casting an assessing glance at Frank, standing in the open bay of the garage and glaring daggers at the nose of her car. "I'm not taking you away from anything, am I?"

"I've got a minute." Sam shook his head, his heart rate doubling as their eyes connected again. This was a mistake. There was no going back from what they—what *he*—had done. He'd never again be able to look at her without seeing the way her eyes went wide and flooded with stars a split second before she came. He swallowed, his voice rough. "So, what's up?"

She held a paper gift bag toward him. "Picked up a housewarming present in Burlington."

"What is it?" He eyed the proffered bag with caution.

"See, the way this works..." She smiled, dangling the gift in front of his face. "Is you open it and then make an appropriate noise of appreciation."

"Right." Sam took the bag and glanced inside. "A can opener and a shower curtain."

Gretchen sat back in her seat, resting one hand on the top of the steering wheel. "Two things no one ever thinks about until they need them."

"Thank you." Sam nodded, impressed by her forethought. He had indeed forgotten to buy a shower curtain.

"Very good, Sam!" She clapped her hands. "Given a little more practice, I could see you getting really good at that."

"So, uh..." He leaned one hip against the car door, sweeping a gaze toward the giant plywood pumpkin cutout on the town green. The Lions Club put it up every year, flanked by hay bales and bundles of calico corn. In another month, it would come down and they would drape the trees with twinkle lights, another turn of the seasons in Halberd Peak. "You want to come for dinner tonight?"

"Dinner?" She quirked an eyebrow.

"If you're interested." He looked down, kicking at the dust. Goddamn, he was an idiot. He knew he should've left the minute she took hold of his shirt and pulled him into the shadow of the stairs. She knew how to play him just right, looking at him with dreamy eyes, asking him to kiss her. His higher brain went offline, leaving his lizard brain to prowl. "I'll cook."

"I could be convinced." There was that teasing little smile again; the same one that broke him when she asked him how far he was willing to go. He'd wanted to see her pleasure herself, but then she got bratty, and his whole damn body was in on the game. He wanted to push her, to mark her, so there'd be no doubt who she was playing with.

"So come," he said in a low octave. It'd really happened, right? He hadn't imagined it. He thought about the limpid look in her eyes when he put his hand on her throat and the startled amusement she'd manifested when he told her to pull up her skirt. He'd relished the way her breath shook when she capitulated to him at last, and *sweet fuck,* the image of her leaning against the wall and stroking herself... that would live in his memory for the rest of his days.

Later that night at the motel, he stood in the shower with the tepid water running down his body, grinning like an idiot at his own good fortune. Trin treated his darker impulses like an unfortunate foible, shooting down every attempt to find mutuality until he stopped trying altogether. Gretchen Clarke gave her submission like a *gift*, with complete and unreserved trust. Even when he was pinning her against the wall and painting his come across her body, the only detectable emotion in those motley eyes was pure, enthusiastic lust. No fear. No shame. No judgement. That blew his fucking mind.

"Okay." She laughed, flipping her hair. "Should I bring anything?"

Sam looked at her again, grateful that his mechanic's overalls were baggy enough to hide a semi. "Just yourself."

Charlie and Frank Scarver didn't look like real estate moguls, but they owned a nice chunk of Halberd Peak, including the little bungalow she was renting on Garnet Lane and the white Italianate Victorian housing Sam's new apartment. While the rest of the town was pulling up stakes and making for the cities, the Scarvers were buying up rental properties all over town, quietly amassing a nice little empire for themselves as they went about the business of keeping Halberd Peak on the road.

The irony of it all made her laugh, sitting on the floor at Sam's place, eating a surprisingly refined meal of white wine braised lamb shank and goat cheese polenta. Only in a delightfully backward place like Halberd Peak could Charlie Scarver and his husband be magnates, and she'd be eating dinner with a man who'd come on her thighs but refused to kiss her. Everything about this evening felt surreal, from the wonderful food to the hideous burgundy and green south-western patterned sofa against the wall.

"This may be the nicest meal I've ever eaten while using a box as a table," she mused, handing him her bowl when they were finished. "I never realized you knew how to *cook-cook*."

"It's my mother's recipe," he explained, carrying their empty dishes to the tiny kitchen in the corner. "That was really important to her. If I was going to be spending every summer with my father, learning to flip burgers and dip fries, I was going to damn well know how to make something classy, too."

She smiled, watching him filling the sink with warm water. He'd met her at the threshold that evening wearing his typical uniform of black shirt and jeans, the grease scrubbed from under his nails, and explained that a friend had just gotten married and given him everything from his old bachelor pad. Another person had stepped up for a man universally regarded to be the asshole of the county. "You want help with that?"

"I'll just leave everything to soak for now," he answered, piling dishes into the sink.

"Are you two close? You and your mother?"

"Sometimes I wonder if we used to be, or I'm just remembering things better than they were." He drew a deep breath, keeping his eyes on what he was doing. "She married my stepdad when I was eleven, and he moved us to upstate New York right before my little brother was born. The baby took up a lot of their attention and I was missing home, so I moved to my dad's."

"You still see each other?"

"Around the holidays, mostly." He turned to face her, folding his arms. "It's probably better for her this way. My brother's a lawyer now. Her husband just retired. They travel a lot. She got the life she wanted."

"That's it?" She canted her head. "What does that make you? The ugly little secret?"

"Something like that." He shrugged, settling onto the unsightly sofa next to her, running his hands over his knees a few times. "What do you want me to say? I wasn't an easy kid to be around, always fucking up at school and acting like an obnoxious little shit."

"So, you took yourself out of the picture. At what? Twelve?"

"Thirteen."

"Oh. Well, in *that* case..." She turned sideways, tucking one foot under her. "I guess it never occurred to you that if you felt unwanted, it was a failure on *their* part. Not yours."

He chuckled, but there was a sad undertone to it. Sliding down in his seat, he stared up at the ceiling. "I'm sure when you have your own kids, you'll do it different."

"That's not going to happen," she snapped, earning a puzzled look from the man sitting next to her. She shook her head, an apologetic sigh slipping past her lips. "Sorry, that wasn't about you. You'd just be surprised how many times I've heard that, and it never stops pissing me off."

He lifted his head, frowning. "You don't want kids?"

"Ah. This conversation." She smirked, her eyes downcast. "No, I always figured if my biological clock finally started ticking and I felt the sudden need to be a mother, I'd adopt. No reason to add to the surplus."

Sam's expression transformed, blending pleasant surprise with amusement. "I like that."

"Glad you approve." She paused, her smile fading. "I bet your mom's proud of you."

"Eh..." Sam looked down, a subdued smile lifting one side of his lips. "I was just a first draft."

SAM DIDN'T WANT to be talking about this. He hadn't gone to all the trouble of getting her here and cooking dinner just to sit around talking about where his parents dropped the ball. And he hated the way she was looking at him right now. His life hadn't been that rough. His parents never hit him, even if his father threatened him with an ass-whooping at least once a week. He always had a roof over his head and food to eat. Maybe his parents hadn't been forthcoming with their affection, but he wasn't murdering people and making collages with their entrails to make up for it. He was a functional adult, if one set aside his catnip-like attraction to unsuitable women.

He clapped a hand over her knee, giving it an amiable jostle. "Let's change the subject."

"Hey, it's your party." She shifted, sitting back and propping her feet on the box in front of the sofa. "So what's for dessert?"

Now *that* was a subject he was looking forward to. Getting up and crossing to the kitchen, he opened the freezer and took out a box of fruit ice pops. "Cherry, straw-berry, or lime?"

She raised a quizzical eyebrow, but answered with certainty, "Cherry. *Always* cherry."

He took out a single pop and stashed the rest, tearing open the paper wrapper. "I've been thinking about this all day."

"Sure, because who doesn't enjoy a fruit pop on a balmy forty-degree day?" she quipped. "Is this another game?"

"Only if you want it to be." He settled onto the far corner of the sofa and offered the dessert to her. A slow smile touched her face, and she slid closer, reaching out. He snatched it away and ran his fingers through the hair at the nape of her neck, swiping the pop across her lips. Her tongue darted out, and he chuckled. "There you go. Get a taste."

He brought the stick down against the top of his leg, watching her. "You want to stop?"

A defiant light glittered in her eyes, and for a split second he wondered if she'd balk. Maybe she drew the line at deep-throating a frozen novelty treat. Then he saw that bratty little smile bend her lips, and she climbed down to kneel between his feet, resting a hand on each of his legs.

"This is what we're doing?" she asked, teasing him. "You want to watch me fellate an ice pop?"

"That's right, I want to watch you." His voice dropped to a husky rumble, and he tightened his fingers in her curls. "Go ahead. Lick it."

*Oh, fuck me.* Sam clamped down on the instinct to unzip as she locked her gaze on his and, starting from the bottom, ran her tongue up the pop in one long, languid caress. She hummed, wrapping her fingers over his, and closed her lips over the top, working the thing with her mouth until it started melting. Sitting up with her lips stained bright red, she wiped her chin. "Satisfied?"

He threw a pointed look at the pop in his hand. "It's not gone yet."

"I've had enough sweet," she purred, scoring her nails over the tops of his thighs. Catching one of her hands, he sat forward, close enough that he could see the oscillation of her pupils dilating. She froze, her voice barely above a whisper. "Please kiss me, Sam."

He searched her face, then leaned back and tossed the rest of the ice pop overhand, sending it sailing into the sink with a splash of soapy water. Settling against the back of the sofa, he sucked a drip of molten cherry syrup from the crook of his thumb. "Not yet."

She knelt rail straight, all the sultry sweetness gone out of her tone. Her eyes flashed. "Not *yet*?"

Jumping to her feet, she looked prepared to storm out in a fit of indignation. With an exultant bark of laughter, Sam clapped his hands around the backs of her knees and hauled her into his lap. She flattened both forearms against his front, digging her pointy little elbows into his chest as she struggled to get free, but he held her fast, snaking both arms around her waist and forcing her to settle, her knees sinking into the cushions on either side of his legs.

"O-ooh!" He chuckled, watching the sparks of fury snapping in her eyes. "I like you angry, Trouble."

He flipped her onto her back under him, and she responded by driving a knee into his ribs, coming danger-ously close to throwing him off. She shoved at his shoul-ders, her cheeks flushing prettily. "This is just a giant power trip for you, isn't it?"

"Hold on. Just wait." Pinning her hands over her head, he fixed his eyes on hers, deadly serious. "This isn't a game for me, Gretchen. Kissing you is all I fucking *think* about. I'm just not there yet."

They stared at each other for a beat, her breath feath-ering against his face in tiny gasps. He was throbbing so hard that the zipper on his fly was biting into him, but he was already lost in the feeling of her thighs pressed against his sides. Seized by the instinct to move, he ground against her, rolling his hips in a slow, tortuous circle. A shiver ran through her body, and she whimpered, flattening both hands against his ribs. He let out a ragged groan, speaking through clenched teeth. "Trouble, when I kiss you, it'll mean something."

She was moving with him now, wrapping her legs around his waist and digging her nails into his arms, while he was hinging on the limits of his self-control. *I need to stop.* If he didn't, he'd start ripping her clothes off. Tearing himself away from her, he sat back on his heels, staring down at the tiny, dazed creature under him. *Fuck*, the things he was going to do to this girl.

# CHAPTER
## Twenty~Two

Gretchen woke in a funk, burdened by unsatisfied lust and a heavy dose of guilt. She'd actually threatened to storm out. Over a stupid *kiss*. Draping an arm across her eyes, she groaned under her breath, thinking about every time he waited for her consent, even when he looked like he was a heartbeat away from holding her down and taking all his rage and frustration out on her. *Shit. I really fucked that up.*

Jamming a pillow over her face, she screamed until her voice broke, feeling the phantom pinch of his iron grip on her wrists and the sinewy weight of his body between her thighs. She thought about the moment he heaved himself off of her, the fabric of his shirt stretching taut across the muscles of his chest and abdomen as he fought to catch his breath. His eyes bored into her as he smoothed one big hand over her hip, giving her a restrained smile. *"You should go, Trouble."*

At least she'd gone without complaint, rather than beating her fists against his chest and demanding that he fuck her right there. He'd walked her to the door, and she'd just stood there for a second, unsure of what to do. What was the protocol for this? Continental kiss and compliment the dinner? Pretend she hadn't thrown a tantrum like an entitled asshat? Finally, she settled on shaking his hand, thanking him for the dry hump, and walking away as his laughter rang through the hallway.

Putting the events of last night out of her mind, she shoved back the covers and reached for something to wear. She hated to be late on the mornings Cricket was testing a new recipe. There was a chill in the air as she stepped outside, and it surprised her to see the first puff of white leave her lips. Had she really been there long enough to see her breath in the morning? Stranger still, she was able to find her way through town without an upward glance, walking with her head down, her hands shoved deep into the pockets of her coat. Without realizing it, Halberd Peak had started feeling like home to her.

"There you are!" Cricket greeted her as she entered the shop, the sing-song tenor of her voice matching the chiming of the bells above the door. "Don't worry, I saved you one."

"One what?" Gretchen asked, taking a mug and approaching the row of coffee carafes on the wall. She chose her brew, added milk, and slid into her regular booth.

"Dark chocolate-strawberry croissant." Cricket set a plate on the table and took the seat opposite her, looking pleased with herself.

"O-oh, talk dirty to me." Gretchen hummed, sinking her teeth into the pastry.

"Nice to find a girl who knows what she likes." She felt her heart skip a beat as a deep, familiar voice echoed from the stairwell, followed by a yip of Murphy's trademark kookaburra's cackle. Gretchen sipped her coffee, working to rein in her thundering pulse before she addressed the men coming from the upstairs apartment.

"Murphy, honey, you're cute, but that laugh could interfere with a person's pacemaker."

"Aww..." Murphy sat down and pulled her against his side. "You're cute too."

Sam's boots scuffed the tile as he claimed the empty seat next to Cricket, slinging one arm over the back of the bench. He took a slow sip of his coffee. "Murph, man... you're outclassed. Just let her eat her breakfast."

"I don't need help telling anyone to fuck off, thanks." Gretchen unwound the young man's arm from around her waist, ignoring the pointed smirk Cricket slanted in her direction.

"Suit yourself," Sam murmured, tossing back the last of his coffee and pushing his empty cup into the center of the table. "I have a brake job in fifteen."

He got up, tightening the knotted sleeves of his overalls around his waist, and nodded to Cricket. "Thanks again."

Her friend looked a little surprised to be included but recovered fast. "No problem."

His eyes snapped to Gretchen's for a fraction of a second, then he turned to leave, the bells over the door emitting a happy jingle on his retreat.

Cricket snickered. "I think the new job agrees with him."

"Sure." Gretchen took another bite of croissant. "He was practically skipping."

Cricket waited as her brother got up from the table, then leaned in, plying Gretchen with a cajoling smile. "You know, in his own misguided way, Soren was *trying* to be nice."

"I said thanks, didn't I?"

"He *likes* you." Cricket pressed her hands together. "Cut him a little slack, okay? He *knows* he fucked up."

"What was he thanking you for, anyway?" Gretchen asked, eager to change the subject. It wasn't as if they'd sat down and discussed keeping things quiet, but she'd been in town long enough to understand the perpetual motion machine that was the Halberd Peak rumor mill. A person could get maimed in the teeth of those infernal gears if they weren't careful.

"You know, it was the *weirdest* thing?" Cricket laughed, looking mildly bewildered. "He stopped in yesterday, wanting to borrow my Dutch oven. I was like, 'That is *Le Creuset*, Soren. If I had a child and my house was on fire, I'd have to think real hard about which one I'd save, you know what I'm saying? If you borrow this thing and it doesn't come back in *pristine* shape, there will be no safe place for you. I will chop. You. *Down*.'"

"Did he say what he wanted it for?" Gretchen laughed, already knowing the answer. She'd seen him lift their lamb shanks out of the pretty pink enameled pot last night.

"I didn't ask." Cricket shrugged. "The only thing I care about is that he brought it back in the same condition that he borrowed it in."

———

Both bosses were out when the silver Mercedes came to pick up her car. She laid her elbows on the counter as they waited for her credit card to go through, her pneumatic tits nearly spilling from the neck of her low-cut sweater. "Do you take detailing work?"

"They keep me plenty busy here." Sam turned away, busying himself with some paperwork on the desk behind him. He'd met a lot of women like her while working at the bar. Rich, married, and bored, they liked to sleep with men they considered beneath them because it gave them an excuse to let their hair down and play the dirty little fuck toy they never got to be while running between social engagements. Back when he was still recovering from his stint as love's crash test dummy, a woman like her would've looked like just what he needed. Thankfully, he was feeling more discriminating these days. The machine spat out the receipt and he pressed it to the counter between them, turning to locate her keys. "Just sign that, and we'll be able to get you out of here."

"Uh huh." She scratched her name onto the signature line. "Well, if you change your mind and decide you're interested in making a little something on the side, you've got my number."

Sam slid her keys across the counter. "You should be all set."

The client toddled out, and he returned to the garage to finish the job he'd been wrapping up when she arrived. It was an unseasonably frosty day. The garage doors were closed, and there was a space heater running, the hot air stinging the top of his head as he laid on the rolling cart, his mind once again snagging on the events of the previous night. How was he supposed to get anything done when he was still living in the ferocious light of Gretchen's eyes, hearing her gasp when he threw her down and pinned her under him?

His hold had been slipping ever since that little slice of sunshine rolled into town with her carefree smiles and steadfast humor, but it was seeing her get angry that severed his last thread of control. Until that moment, she'd presented an unflappable mask of geniality, but there was fire there, a passion to balance his own. She pushed back like a wild thing, teeth on edge, ready to strike. He wanted more of that.

"Hey, quittin' time!" Charlie called into the garage, the statement wafting in on a thick smog of noxious cigar smoke. "You can go ahead and take off."

Sam hauled himself out from under the last car of the day and scrubbed his hands. He trudged down the unpaved drive to his apartment building, his mind swirling with thoughts of Gretchen. That morning at the café, she'd barely looked at him before he was ready to overturn the table between them and tackle her to the floor.

Lost in his memories, he was cresting the stairs before he noticed the woman standing at his door. For an instant, he imagined Gretchen was there to finish what they'd started, but then he saw the fringe of strawberry blond hair beneath the crocheted cap and the chubby baby on her arm. He felt a cudgel of blistering dread hit him right in the solar plexus and set his jaw, shouldering her to one side as he took his keys from his pocket. "What do you want?"

"I need to talk to you." Trinity pulled a strand of hair free from the viscous gloss varnishing her lips, peering up at him with the same coy gaze she used to employ when she wanted something. "Can we come in?"

Sam folded his arms and glared. Like *fuck* was he letting Satan's helpmate spread her pestilence to another of his living spaces. "Just fucking out with it, Trin."

"Well, I—" She turned, gazing down the hallway to check for anyone who might be listening. "I just wanted to say that if this is your way of teaching me a lesson, you've stepped way over the line."

"What are you even talking about?" Sam scoffed, rocking back on his heels. From zero to all about her in five-seconds flat; that was an impressive level of narcissism, even for her. "What? Giving Justin my share of the land? He doesn't have to keep it. He can do whatever the hell he wants with it. You hate this place so much, tell him to sell it."

"I *tried.*" Her voice reached a high, reedy hiss. "He keeps bitching about your *legacy*, like you're the royal family or something. Not a bunch of—"

"Bartenders?" Sam smirked, a blade of frigid vindication sweeping down his spine. His keys jangled as he turned his back on her, unlocking the door. "This has nothing to do with me anymore. It's between you and Justin."

"If he's so hellbent on staying, that's fine." She grabbed his wrist, wedging herself in front of the door. "But I'm happy where I am. I've built a life for myself."

"So *go* there."

"Oh, come on, Sam." Her touch softened, and she lifted her chin, giving him a coquettish smile. "It's kind of perfect, huh? All those years I was dying to leave, and you wouldn't. Now you can go anywhere you want, and Justin is ready to drag me back, kicking and screaming."

"Funny how that shook out," Sam deadpanned, trying to move her to one side without outright shoving her.

"Do you ever think about me?" She stood her ground.

"Sometimes." He gave her a scornful sneer. "When I get a splinter."

"Isn't this what we always wanted?" She stepped closer, holding the baby to one side as she brushed her tits against his arm. "Neither of us wanted to get stuck in this town. Now, we don't have to be."

"Except that you're married to my brother." Sam took hold of her shoulders, moving her away from him again.

*Jesus,* had this tactic *ever* worked on him? He suddenly wanted to go back in time and punch his younger self in the nuts. "And you have a kid."

"I could take her with me." She shrugged, looking unconcerned by the small human clinging to her side. "Justin's great with her, though. I bet he'd be willing to slip me a nice hunk of cash—if I didn't challenge custody."

The bottom of his stomach dropped out. *Holy shit, she's a sociopath.* How the fuck had he missed the fact that he'd shared his bed, been prepared to share his whole *life,* with a monster? Clenching his jaw against the nauseous lump in his throat, he directed his gaze at the wall for a few seconds. "If you want to leave, leave. The baby will be better off here."

"What, you gonna stay in town? Help Justin?" Trinity tittered with derision, raking her eyes down his body. "You'd rather waste yourself helping people who don't give a shit about you. Aren't you tired of getting pissed on?"

"Whatever you have to tell yourself, Trin." Sam opened the door and stepped inside, slamming it before she could slither after him. The baby started crying, and he stood listening to the melancholy wailing traveling down the hallway into the stairwell, weighing his next move. True, he didn't owe his brother a damn thing, but could he, in good conscience, let her skip town with the baby? No one deserved that fate, especially not that poor kid. He sighed in resignation and dug his phone out of his pocket. No doubt, this was exactly what that crazy bitch had in mind when she decided to drop in.

# CHAPTER
## Twenty~Three

Gretchen sat back and stretched, checking the clock on the kitchen wall. She'd worked all day without stopping for lunch; it was pouring outside, and the wind was singing down the chimney like a jug band had taken up residence in her living room. Her brain was fried. She needed to be done for today. Her phone buzzed, and she reached for it, reading the message on the screen. *I need to see you.*

She paused, glancing at the clock again. Okay, so it wasn't past nine p.m., but the message was unmistakable. *Give the Rolodex another spin, Sam. I don't do booty calls.*

*That's not what this is.* She started composing her reply, then jumped when someone knocked on the front door. Leaning to the side, she peered out the window. He was out there, looking more than a little bedraggled. Getting up to answer the door, she gazed past him to the wall of rain sheeting the lawn. "I hope you dragged your rowboat far enough up the stairs. It'd be a shame if it washed away."

"I'm sorry, I just..." He followed her inside and stood

dripping on the hallway rug for a beat, wearing an oddly dazed expression on his face. "I had to see you."

"Well, here I am." She held her arms out at her sides, eyeing the wet patches on the front of his shirt. "You didn't walk all the way here, did you?"

"No, I drove." He rotated to look at the door where he'd come in. "Shit, what the fuck am I doing? My plan ended at getting here."

"Then your plan appears to have worked flawlessly." Another gust of wind swept down the chimney, and she wrapped the front of her slouchy, cable knit cardigan closer around her body. "You want some tea or cocoa? I'm drinking a lot of hot beverages these days."

"You have a flashlight?" he asked, sliding his jacket off and hanging it on the coat rack next to the door. She located the plastic utility light under the sink and handed it to him as he lifted the fire screen and crouched, gazing up into the chimney. Twisting to the side, he reached up and rattled the flue closure, then rolled back on his heels. "It *looks* closed."

"I called the Scarvers, but they haven't gotten back to me." She shrugged as he handed her the flashlight and replaced the screen. "I'm about to stuff a pillow up there."

"I'll talk to Frank tomorrow." Sam stood up, dusting off his hands. "I can pick up a flue plug at the hardware store and bring it by."

"I don't need you to do that."

"Whatever you say," he returned, unruffled by her stubbornness. "Hold onto the receipt and tell them you're taking it out of the rent."

"Oh, is that how it works?" She widened her eyes at him, an irascible edge to her voice. "Please. Tell me more."

She tried *desperately* to look anywhere but at the solid

band of muscles over his abdomen as he lifted the hem of his shirt and wiped the soot from his hands, a slow smile spreading across his lips. "I get it, Trouble. You don't need anybody's help."

———

THIS GIRL. This *fucking* girl. Standing there with that defiant glint in her eye, ready to go down scratching and biting before she'd accept help from anyone. She was so goddamn cute, he could barely restrain himself, but she didn't need him to explain how rent worked. Nor did she need him to warn Murphy off, though that was less about his friend acting like a twelve-year-old and more about his own stupid avarice. He dropped his head, letting out a long, frustrated sigh. "I'm sorry, I explained unnecessarily. But—"

"Oh! So close!" She threw both fists into the air, affecting the pose of a thwarted supervillain. "You were so *close*, then you went and stepped on a perfectly good apology."

"Jesus, there's no *winning* with you!" he barked in exasperation. "Has it ever occurred to you that someone might try to help you because they care about you?"

"Has it ever occurred to *you* that if I need help, I'll ask for it?" she returned without missing a beat, her eyes narrowing.

"This is how it's gonna be?" he ground out. "You brat around, and I wait to be called off the bench?"

"Look at that: He *can* be taught." She smirked icily.

He put his hands on his hips, every muscle in his body on high alert. "Have you ever been tied up?"

"Have I—" She snapped her mouth shut, giving him an appraising look. "Why?"

He took a step toward her, his voice rough. "Use your imagination, Gretchen."

She leveled that unwavering gaze on his. "Once or twice."

*Sweet Christ.* His gaze dropped to her lips, and he felt a frisson of raw exhilaration dash down his spine, rooting in his groin. "You enjoyed it?" She nodded, and without thinking, he reached out to rest one hand on the curve of her neck. "I'd like to tie you up."

"Okay," she breathed her acquiescence. Then, almost as an afterthought, "But no sex."

"No sex," he acknowledged, lifting her chin with the crook of his finger. "Anything else?"

"No water sports or scat play. Nothing that breaks the skin, and never call me names," she answered without hesitation, her gaze unswerving. "Other than that, I trust you."

He tilted his head and stared at her mouth, running his thumb over the pulse point at the corner of her jaw. "You've really thought about this."

"You asked." She took his hand, leading him through the open bedroom doors the same way she had a thousand times in his fantasies. He sat on the foot of the bed as she opened the top drawer of her bureau and selected two folded cotton bandanas, handing them to him. "Clothes on or off?"

"Take off everything but your underwear," he ordered, shaking out each of the bandanas and folding them into slender bands on the diagonal. He watched her strip off her cardigan and shirt and felt his cock go ramrod straight at the sight of her nipples puckering in the drafty room.

Unlacing the front of her pajama bottoms, she pushed them down her legs and kicked them away, waiting patiently.

Christ, she really was something. There weren't words enough to describe the thoughts that went through his head when she released her hair from its low bun and shook it out. Looking at her, his mind wandered. Cruel fantasies took hold, and for a few blissful seconds, he wondered what it might feel like to walk into a room with a woman like her on his arm. Standing up, he nodded to the bed. "Lie down."

"Facedown or faceup?"

Sam paused, observing her direct gaze and the straight set of her shoulders. "Face down."

She allowed him to bind each wrist to the spindle headboard, her hands above her head. When he was done, he stood to one side of the bed and admired the way the divine rise of her ass ebbed to her hips, and the neat taper of her waist rose to the delicate piano keys of her spine.

"You're beautiful." He sat down next to her, drawing his fingertips up the back of one long, lean leg. "You're so goddamn beautiful."

"Thank you." She turned her head, studying him with placid acceptance. "Now what?"

"Now..." He traced the edge of her blue cotton panties with the tip of his finger before covering the curve of her ass, feeling a shiver go through her. He waited, kneading her flesh until the nervous tension left her body and she pushed into his touch. Then he lifted his hand and brought it down with a crisp *smack*, relishing her startled *yip* and the satisfying sting that spread through his palm. She gasped, her back arching as she peered over her shoulder at him, her eyes stretched wide. He smoothed his hand over her skin. "You okay?"

She nodded, her voice thin and shaky. "*Yes.*"

"Good." He smiled, bringing up his hand to deliver another blow. He heard her suck in a breath just before it connected, and she whimpered, scooting away. He clicked his tongue. "Where you going, Trouble? All you have to do is tell me to stop."

"No!" She stilled. "Not yet."

He chuckled in quiet delight, unlacing his boots and kicking them off onto the floor. Climbing onto the bed, he straddled her legs at the knees and sat back, feeling especially blessed. "Christ, you're perfect, Gretchen."

She clasped her fingers around the headboard slats and dug her elbows into the mattress, her shoulders rounding as she braced for the next blow. He started slow, delivering a stinging slap to one cheek and then the other, building a rhythm and working her hard enough to put a shimmer of sweat on her skin and bounce her body from side to side. It hurt him too, the pain reverberating up his wrist, but he had no intention of letting up until she signaled her surrender.

"Stop!" Her guttural shout finally split the air, and Sam roared in pure, animalistic satisfaction. Bracing both hands on his knees, he watched her body go slack under him as her hands fell away from the headboard. She exhaled a ragged gasp, her entire body trembling.

His hand hurt like hell as he smoothed her hair to one side, bending to press his lips to the velvet skin on the back of her neck. Moving to her shoulder, he kissed that too, peeling her panties down her thighs. "This okay?"

She moaned, grinding back against his hard-on. "Yes. Please."

ANY THOUGHT for her sore backside vanished as Sam slipped his hand under her body, his fingers finding the aching place between her legs. He grazed his teeth over the curve of her neck, his laughter rumbling through his chest and creating a pleasant buzzing in her shoulder blades. "You're so wet, Gretchen."

She hummed, sinking her teeth into her lower lip to stop herself from crying out. He was torturing her, circling his fingers around her clit without touching it directly. Even the feeling of his jeans brushing against the sensitized flesh of her ass sent fiery shivers down her legs, the pain jumbling with the percussion of arousal.

"Where's your vibrator?" he asked, stroking his long fingers through her folds.

"In the side table." His weight shifted as he leaned over, and she heard him chuckle again as he surveyed the selection in the drawer. A moment later, he was wrapping one hand under her chin and pulling her against his chest, the other maneuvering a mini vibe down the front of her body. She yelped when it finally made contact with her clit. "Please don't stop."

His hand came away from her throat, and she felt him reach between their bodies to unfasten his fly. Sliding his length against the cleft of her ass, his breath was hot against her ear. "Don't worry. No sex."

She moved with him, riding the toy in his hand until the first ripple of climax blazed through her body. "Right there. Oh god... *Sam!*"

She buried her face against the mattress as the physical release brought with it a stunning emotional one, her orgasm wringing a powerful sob from her throat, a cloudburst of scalding tears spilling down her cheeks. He stiffened, barking out a sharp growl and spilling his load over the length of her spine. It pooled at the small of her back, trickling over the side of her ribs as she laid under his crushing bulk, utterly spent.

"Trouble," he murmured. He pressed his face against the curve of her neck, dusting her shoulder with kisses, and turned her face to meet his, sweeping his thumb through the wetness of her tears. "Baby."

# CHAPTER
## Twenty-Four

"I read somewhere that it's unhealthy to keep a television in your bedroom." Sam reclined on the bed next to her, holding a bundle of ice to her left butt cheek. He looked more content in this moment than she'd ever seen him, his head propped against his upturned hand, secure in the knowledge he was providing proper aftercare. After releasing her wrists, he'd made her tea, cleaned the come off her back with a warm, damp washcloth, and buttoned her into her favorite flannel lounge top so she wouldn't freeze while he iced her bruised backside.

"It's not *in* my bedroom," Gretchen murmured without turning her gaze from the cartoons on-screen. She waved her hand at the open French doors. "This place is the size of a saltine."

The kitchen buzzer went off, and Sam picked up the ice, carrying it into the next room. She listened to him rattling pots and pans for a few minutes. The air filled with the scent of something garlicky and piquant, and he came striding through the living room carrying two bowls. Handing her one dish, he sat back down and passed her a fork. Gretchen took a bite, humming when the bright flavor of spicy tomato and lemon burst across her tongue.

"You like it?" Sam watched her, stirring his own pasta. "Calabrian chili pasta with lemon."

"I had the stuff to make this?" She paused, staring into her bowl. She had a vague memory of coming home from the grocery store and finding an orphaned jar of red chilis in her bag. She'd stashed it in the cabinet, reasoning that she'd find something to do with it eventually.

"Believe me, I was just as shocked as you were."

She took another bite and chewed for a few seconds, reflecting on the improbability of eating a delicious home-made dinner in bed after a scary-handsome man iced her ass. "Maybe you should come over tomorrow, shove bamboo splinters under my nails, and make me fried calamari."

He snorted, leaning back against the headboard. "Calamari's a lot of work. How about I remove one of your kidneys without anesthesia and roast a chicken?"

"If you're planning to take a vital organ," she spoke through clenched teeth as another icy draft whipped down the chimney. "There'd better be mashed potatoes."

---

HE'D TAKEN her too deep. There was slush pelting the windows, the house felt like a goddamn meat locker, and goosebumps covered every inch of her legs—yet she barely reacted. He was tempted to tell her to get her ass under the covers before she lost a toe to frostbite, but she'd already taken his head off once that evening. So be it. Climbing off the bed, he unzipped, ignoring her bewildered expression as his pants hit the floor. Lifting the comforter, he climbed in, offering her a smile. "What? It's cold in here."

"Make yourself at home."

"Thanks, I will," he answered, smoothing his hand over the downy top border of the buffalo checked flannel sheets. "These are great. Did you buy them, or did they come with the house?"

"They're mine." She gave him an impassive look for a moment, then crawled over the bed. Shoving her legs under the blankets, she dug her pointy elbow into his side. "Make some room, you gargantuan freak."

"Ouch!" He chuckled. "That hurts me. You've hurt my feelings."

"No, I didn't." She rolled her eyes, scooting down and curling against his side, directing her gaze at the television. "You love being the tallest person in every room. You get to look down on all of us. Literally."

"You don't understand my pain." He draped his arm over her shoulders, speaking against the top of her head. "Your feet hang off the end of every bed. Extra-long pants are a pain to find. And then there are the constant queries of 'how's the weather up there?'"

She craned her neck to look up at him, her gaze resolute. "I will pay you a thousand dollars to spit on them and tell them it's raining."

"Is that a flat fee, or a thousand dollars per?" *Fuck*, this was dangerous. She was sitting there, arms around him, looking as pacific as an angel in a stained-glass window, and he was hearing warning bells.

He'd learned from experience that he couldn't afford the intimacy of a kiss when he needed to keep a clear head. Kissing the wrong woman felt too much like forcing an emotional connection. Kissing the right woman? He wasn't sure how that should feel anymore. He'd wasted so many on the wrong ones that he felt like his heart was punched full of holes.

Still, she kept slow-blinking at him, lips slightly parted. If he kissed her right now, that'd be it. He was already in her bed. There'd be no stopping him from taking things too far. Flailing for a change of subject, his brain pulled the ripcord, dredging up the stupidest, most unromantic topic it could. "Trinity came to see me today."

"Your ex?" She inched away from him. He felt a pang of withdrawal as her hand fell from his chest. "What about?"

"I'm not really sure what she was hoping to accomplish —aside from fucking up my night." He swept his hand over his face, tracing the outer corners of his mouth with his index finger and thumb. *Fuck*, he was an asshole. "First, she sounded like she wanted me to talk Justin out of moving back. Then when I told her to pound sand, she offered to sell my brother his own baby for seed money to get away without him."

"*Yikes*." Gretchen hucked out an uncomfortable scoff. "What did you do?"

"What do you *think* I did?" He shook his head. "I called my brother and told him to stop dragging his feet on finding a lawyer."

"Good idea." He sliced a perturbed glance in her direction, and she gifted him with a dispassionate one-shouldered shrug. "You want spin? It goes against my grain to tear another woman down, but your ex sounds like a terrible person. You dodged a bullet. That's all I've got."

Why was he telling her this now? Never had a man thrown her such bizarre, paradoxical signals. Lifting his arm from around her, she settled back against the headboard, resting her hands in her lap. "You should probably head home soon. It's getting late and I have a lot of work to get done tomorrow."

He shook his head slowly. "I don't feel right leaving you."

"You want to freeze together?" She reached up to gather her hair into a high ponytail with the elastic around her wrist. "You can go, Sam. I can bundle up."

"You can come to my place for the night," he suggested, pushing back the blankets. He reached down and grabbed his jeans, tossing a roguish smile over his shoulder as he pulled them on. "Don't worry. You'll be safe with me."

"I never thought I wasn't," she spoke evenly, watching him slip his feet into his boots. Wasn't that obvious? Hadn't she just let him tie her down and spank her until her body was so saturated with endorphins it felt like her head was about to float free of her shoulders? She'd never had an experience like that before: the raw emotional detonation that seemed to come from a tightly locked part of herself springing open, releasing a fulmination of fear and anxiety into the ether. "It's not that I don't appreciate the offer, but I think I could use some time to myself tonight."

He turned to lean over her, bracing one hand on the mattress. He captured one of the curls framing her face, toying with it.

"Sometimes I think you might be the woman I've been waiting for my whole life," he rumbled, his eyebrows gathering. "Other times, I think you might be the biggest mistake I'm ever going to make."

His gaze tumbled to her mouth again, and she heard the

soft, ragged edge of his exhale. She dropped her eyes. "I don't think I can handle being kissed right now, Sam."

"No. I know." He pulled back, getting to his feet. "I'm going because you asked me to. But I'm going to call to check in on you later." He turned and bent close, dropping a kiss on the top of her head. "If you change your mind about coming to my place, I'll let you take the bed."

He walked into the front hall and shrugged on his coat. Pausing in the doorway between the living room and the kitchen, he cast one last look at her, then let himself out into the rain. The door slammed, the sound echoing in the eerie, storm-rattled quiet.

# CHAPTER
## Twenty~Five

There were icicles adorning the telephone wires and tree branches by the morning. They hung off the eaves of the garage like the teeth of an angry wolf, threatening to draw blood on the first person to pass through its doors. A few days ago, they'd been walking around in shirtsleeves. Now, it felt like they'd skipped Halloween and Thanksgiving and jumped headfirst into Jack Frost's wintery butthole.

Sam was standing in the garage, watching the town volunteers knocking together stalls and decorating the green for the kooky autumn wedding festival when Dane's sleek luxury sedan slunk into the parking lot. Paige sprung from the passenger-side door, dashing straight for him and latching onto him in one of her signature full-body hugs. "We've been so worried about you!"

"Nice to see you too, Peanut." Sam grinned, giving her a tight squeeze before setting her down. Dane was right behind her, reaching out to shake his hand.

"How you been?" Dane slung his arm around Paige's

shoulder, a frown creasing his brow. "We heard you were working here now."

"It's a job." Sam shrugged, gazing across the green again. "Aren't you guys a little early for the festival?"

"My parents are out of town." Paige beamed, leaning into her partner's side. "We thought we'd take advantage of the empty house."

"It'll be nice having you two around."

"We thought so," Dane agreed. "Maybe we should have some people over for a game night and throw some steaks on the grill."

"Sure. Let me know." Sam watched them climb into their car and huffed, returning to the garage. His groove had been off all day, ever since Gretchen failed to put in her regular morning appearance at the café. They'd spoken last night, after he'd gotten back to his place. Lying back in bed, he'd dialed his phone and felt his heart hammering as he waited for her to answer.

Her voice sounded drowsy when she did. *"Mmm, hullo Mountain King."*

*"I told you I'd check up on you."* He ran his hand over his stomach, staring up at the shadows as they shifted across the ceiling. Her laughter ruffled against the receiver, and they wasted a few minutes talking about nothing. It was the sweetest kind of torture, listening to the voluptuous purr of her voice in his ear, feeling that thread in his chest drawing taut enough to be plucked like a harp string and wanting her *there* where he could feel the length of her body against his.

He'd lain smiling into the dark for a long time after they hung up, and that stupid grin was still in place when he rolled out of bed the next morning. He was looking forward to seeing her at the café, to savoring the tension that hung in the air when they weren't free to talk. He could've spent *hours* baiting her and watching those kaleidoscopic eyes flashing, but she never showed. Now, he was hungry for the sight of her.

When the clock finally struck five and the day's work was over, he trudged home and lifted weights. He made dinner and tried to read, and when that didn't work, he turned on the television. Reaching for his phone, he opened her chat window and typed out a message, striking the send button.

———

Sam's text came through during her last meeting of the day, the quiet chime of the alert nearly lost to a cacophony of distant sirens. Geez, was the whole town burning down? Her supervisor, Cherie, perhaps sensing her distraction, repeated her query. "Gretchen? Are you still with us?"

"Yes, sorry." She straightened, setting her phone face-down on the tabletop. This was silly. Tokyo was the brass ring, and it was within her grasp. This was the opportunity of a *lifetime*, and she was juggling messages from a man who hadn't even kissed her yet. She sucked in a steadying breath, refocusing her smile on the screen. "Can I have some time to think about it?"

"Of course." Cherie nodded benevolently, and the sentiment was echoed by the other three floating heads on the videoconference. "We understand that it's a big change. We can give you a couple weeks to consider it, but that'll be it. We need to get the new team lead installed in Japan before the new year."

"Right." Gretchen looked away, the little voice in her head reminding her that *it wouldn't be forever*. It was just a year in one of the most exciting cities in the world. This was the dream! "I'd like a little time to talk to my family. Make some arrangements."

"That sounds reasonable." Cherie smiled with the confidence of a woman accustomed to giving orders and seeing them carried out. She glanced at another window on her computer screen, checking her agenda, and addressed the rest of the assembly. "Does anyone have anything else?" The silence stretched for a few seconds, and then Cherie nodded. "All right, everyone. See you next Friday."

The screen blanked, and Gretchen jumped to her feet, unsure of what to do with this sudden surplus of energy. Every nerve in her body was buzzing with unrestrained excitement. She hopped up and down a few times, then shook out her hands and settled cross-legged into her chair, her gaze falling on her phone. *Shit. Shit-shit-motherfucker-fuck-shit.*

How could it be possible that her first instinct was to call the same person this news would hurt the most? She felt torn between elation and gut-wrenching forfeiture. Getting up to pour herself a glass of cold water from the fridge, she leaned against the counter and took a long sip, staring down the phone from across the room. Then she huffed and marched over to it, dialing fast.

Sam's deep resonance greeted her, wasting no time on formalities. "Can I see you tonight?"

"Wish I could," she began, a boulder of guilt sinking in her belly. It wasn't right to tell him this over the phone, but she didn't think she could stand to say it to his *face,* either. "I've been in meetings all day. I have a lot of work to catch up on."

"That's too bad." His chuckle sent a shiver down her

spine, and she felt the knot in her stomach lessen by a degree.

She closed her eyes, tipping her face up to the ceiling. "And what makes you say that?"

"Because I've been thinking about you all day." He dropped his voice to a deep, relaxed rumble, sounding so close that she could almost imagine him standing next to her. Brushing her hair to one side. Stroking his fingers along the column of her throat.

"Is that so?"

"Absolutely," he rasped against her ear. "I've been thinking about the way you looked last night, how you moved under me, and the sounds you made..." His voice tapered off into a low, needy growl. "You come so goddamn nice."

"You're trying to tempt me."

"No." She could hear the smile in his voice. "You can hang up. Or you can give me something to get me through the night, since I can't have you here."

She closed her eyes, concentrating on the sound of his breathing. Somewhere in the back of her mind, a hopeful voice piped up, suggesting that maybe there was a way. Maybe they could make this work, just for a year, if they tried. "Like what?"

His laughter took on a provocative timbre. "Like you can make yourself come and let me hear you."

"I can do that." Moving into the living room, she laid on the sofa and unbuttoned the fly of her jeans, slipping her free hand under the waist of her panties. She found the swollen bud between her legs and closed her eyes, massaging with practiced fingers.

"Tell me what you're thinking about," he ordered, his

breathing sounding ragged, the way it did when he was getting himself off.

"You." She arched her neck, invoking the sensation of his cock grinding against her backside. "Putting your fingers inside me. The way you'd feel between my legs." She bit her lip, rolling her head to one side. "I want you to fuck me like a naughty girl."

"*Fuck!*" he barked from the other end, his breathing growing rapid. "You're gonna finish me, baby."

"Don't you dare." She rolled onto her belly and ground her hips, feeling her orgasm building just out of reach. "Wait for me, Sam."

"Say it again," he demanded. "Say my fucking name again, Trouble."

Her body stiffened, her knees clenching around her arm. "*Sam!*"

"That's my good girl."

A strangled gasp tore from her throat as the orgasm careened through her, scrabbling outward to the very tips of her toes, and for a few seconds, her field of vision was consumed by a brilliant flash of white. Floating back to shore, she hummed happily. "Come for me, Sam. Make it count."

"Oh, *fuck*..." The words grated against her ear, and he exhaled a loud grunt. He panted into the receiver, sounding as if he was standing in a windstorm, then he laughed, his voice somewhat lighter than before. "*Christ*, Gretchen. What are you doing to me?"

"Not a damn thing." She grinned at the ceiling, still buzzing with release. "That was all you, kitten."

He cleared his throat. "Kitten, huh?"

"You keep calling me 'baby.'"

"Fair enough," he conceded, growing serious. "Is it weird to say I miss you?"

She sat up, alarmed to feel her heart flutter against her ribcage. This was bad; she should have told him already. "Not to me."

"Well, I do," Sam murmured. She could picture him running his hand over his scalp, a subdued smile on his lips. "I think I missed you before I met you."

"I—" she began, any remaining endorphins thoroughly dampened by a vicious twinge of guilt. She knew they were on borrowed time now, but she wasn't ready to let reality get in the way quite yet. She was relieved to hear a beep signaling an incoming call. Taking the phone away from her ear, she frowned at the screen. "What the hell? Cricket's calling me. It's like she *knows*."

"That's weird," came his disconcerting rely. "Paige is calling *me*."

She lifted her head, recognizing the rhythmic drubbing of a helicopter rotor slashing through the air. "Okay, something's up. Talk later?"

"Yeah."

The line went dead, and she gathered her composure before she accepted the call, a portentous feeling burbling in her gut. Someone released a weary sigh from the other end, and for several agonizing seconds, no words came. Pushing herself to a seated position, Gretchen felt a torrent of icy dread sluice down her spine. "Cricket? Honey, what's wrong? Please talk to me."

Cricket's voice sounded hoarse and robotic, as if she'd been crying so hard that she'd simply run out of tears. "There's been an accident. You should probably get to the hospital."

# CHAPTER
## Twenty-Six

S am shifted in his seat, careful not to disturb Gretchen where she snoozed against his left arm. They'd been there for hours, a small crowd of somber bodies huddled in one corner of the surgical department's waiting room. Cricket was balled up against Paolo's side with puffy red eyes, directing her empty gaze at the floor. Sitting to Sam's right, Paige reached over and took his hand, while keeping the fingers of her other hand plaited between Dane's. Those two had been holding onto each other since they arrived, as if they were afraid to let go and lose their moorings.

Gretchen twitched suddenly and lifted her head, giving him a bleary half-smile. Seeing the fatigue swimming in her eyes, Sam felt a welling of ill-timed anger. Murphy got to sleep through all of this. He'd probably wake up and start making jokes, with no idea the hell he'd put them through.

Sweeping a strand of hair away from her eyes, he pressed his lips together in a wan display of a reassurance and lifted his arm over her shoulders so she could lay her head on his knee. No one acknowledged the intimacy of the gesture, and if anyone noticed that he and Gretchen had arrived together, the observation was overshadowed by the current drama.

The night slogged by. They slept in shifts, taking turns pacing when the act of staying in one place got to be too much, but no one spoke. No one had to. Sam dozed fitfully, knowing he'd regret the awkward position when his neck felt ready to telescope in on itself in the morning.

He'd known something was wrong as soon as he heard the sirens. Sitting in his living room, he strained his ears, trying to determine where they were headed. Ambulances most often went in the direction of the Deer Leap Retirement Home, but today they turned, moving up the mountain, and he felt a heavy sense of foreboding settle over his shoulders. He'd shoved that thought away when Gretchen returned his call, wanting to give her his undivided attention. It wasn't until afterwards, when he was slumped on his couch catching his breath, that he heard the telltale sound of an approaching helicopter. *Lifestar. Someone's having a bad day.*

The pit in his stomach dug itself deeper as the calls came in, interrupting their interlude at exactly the wrong moment. Any feelings of softness or joy vanished as he let her go and picked up for Paige. His heart was pounding, flooding his veins with adrenaline, but his brain managed to suss out a few important words: Murphy. 4-wheeler. Hospital.

Messaging Gretchen to tell her he was on his way to pick her up, he sprinted out the door and clamored down the stairs so fast, he almost put his shoulder through the drywall. He didn't even feel the cold until twenty minutes later, when they were barreling down the highway and he realized he'd dashed out of his apartment without his jacket.

"What time is it?" Cricket asked, the words abrupt enough to make several of them visibly flinch. Dane checked his watch.

"Just after two a.m."

"Oh," she murmured.

"People have to be hungry." Sam gave Gretchen's shoulder a parting squeeze before carefully pushing himself to his feet. Looking around at the others, he caught a few guilty nods. "I'll see what I can find."

"I'll come with you." Dane released Paige's hand for the first time, getting up to follow him. Locating the elevator, they waited for it to alight on their floor, Dane's incisive gaze drifting in his direction. "You and Gretchen, huh?"

Sam stiffened, pivoting to blink at his friend. "Where the fuck did *that* come from?"

"You two looked pretty comfortable back there." Dane shrugged as the doors slid open, trailing after him into the car. He bent to punch the button for the ground floor. "But whatever, man. If I'm wrong, set me straight."

Sam glowered at the dented stainless elevator doors for a beat. "I'm sure this is difficult for everyone else to understand, but I'm not made of stone."

"Is that a yes?"

"That's a mind your fucking business."

"Dude." Dane held up his hands. "It's just a question. Nothing meant by it."

"Good." Sam rolled his shoulders, tight after sitting in those uncomfortable chairs, then slid a sideways look at his friend. "You won't say anything to Paige?"

"Nah, man." Dane loosened, an apologetic smile creasing his lips. "But she's a hell of a lot smarter than me. I doubt I'd have to."

SAM AND DANE returned carrying two cafeteria trays piled with gluey white bread sandwich wedges and mini chip bags. Everyone gathered around the table in the corner, sitting elbow to elbow and picking at their food in melancholy silence. Opening the lid on a paper cup of soda, Gretchen stared at its contents. "Are any of these caffeine free?"

"Take mine." Sam switched it for something clear and fizzy without missing a beat. That shouldn't have made her want to cry, but it did. Maybe it was the woeful look on everyone's faces or the comedown after the adrenaline-pumping trip to the hospital, but she could feel her heart break a little more with each passing moment. Her eyes started misting over, and she peered at Sam, seeking something to steady her. His gaze swung in her direction and his brows lifted with worry. He laid one hand on the back of her chair, his thumb brushing the space between her shoulder blades. His lips moved, mouthing the words, *You okay?*

She nodded, leaning into the solidity of his body as a sudden, grief-mad notion went through her mind.

She could take Sam *with* her.

Everyone held their collective breath as a doctor breached the doorway, going directly to the couple on the other side of the room. Unsettled by the seesaw of emotion, Gretchen's stomach heaved. She shoved back her chair, sprinting into the bathroom across the hall and flinging herself onto her knees in front of the toilet.

Paige was behind her, holding back her hair. "Oh, sweetie..."

Bracing one forearm on the seat, Gretchen waited to

retch, then sat back when nothing came up and swept the back of her wrist over her damp forehead. Paige laid a hand against her spine, rubbing in soothing circles. Gretchen shook her off, closing her eyes against the tears burning at their corners. "I'm fine. I just need a minute."

"Okay, I'll be right outside if you need anything."

"Right." Gretchen sat forward, resting her face in the crook of her arm. This melodramatic bullshit wasn't helping the situation, and to cap it off, she was probably going to catch some horrible disease from sitting on the floor. She gulped back another wave of nausea, quietly berating herself. "Get the *fuck up*, Gretchen. Now is not the time."

"Stay down," a deep voice instructed from the doorway. Sam crouched behind her. There was a brittle clinking sound as he fished an ice cube from the cup in his hand, and he held it to the back of her neck, offering her the soda. "Here. Take a sip."

She gulped down a mouthful of cola, no longer caring if the caffeine would keep her up. The way this night was going, she'd probably be grateful for the bump. There were voices outside the door, Paige's concerned feminine lilt playing off Dane's languid, reassuring timbre. Dane presumably won out, the voices fading as he steered her back to the waiting room. Gretchen released a mordant laugh. "Now they're gonna think—"

"I don't care." Sam passed her a stick of gum, the mint flavor helping to detangle the bilious knots clenching in her stomach. "Do you?"

"No, but I was hoping we could get things sorted before the rest of the town got involved." She sighed as he sat back against the tiled wall and pulled her into the space between his outstretched legs.

"Dane and Paige won't say anything." He stroked his fingers through her hair. "She just wants to make sure I'm not in here making things worse."

"I really don't see how you *could* make this night worse."

He rested his cheek on the top of her head. "I could give you a swirly."

She hiccupped out a single *ha* and then clapped her hand over her mouth, physically smothering her laughter. She was sitting on the floor of a hospital bathroom, waiting to find out if her friend had survived the surgery to repair his lacerated organs after driving a four-wheeler off a cliff. Now was not the time to be laughing. Sucking a breath through her nose, she felt her chin wobbling. "Please don't be funny right now."

He swept her hair over her shoulder, bringing his warm hand against the back of her neck. She let out a tremulous breath, clinging to the anchor of his dark gaze. That little voice was back. She could ask him to come with her to Japan. It was crazy, and if he were any other man, she'd be afraid that he'd dismiss her as clingy or desperate, but this was *Sam*. He was different. She swept the heel of her hand under her nose, dropping her eyes. "My—"

Someone rapped on the door, cracking it open by an inch. Dane's voice echoed through the room. "Hey guys, we're coming in."

Sam loosened his hold as Dane and Paige slunk inside. It was a small space, and Sam's legs occupied much of the limited floorspace, so they stood in front of the sink. Dane leaned back against the counter, his pale brows crinkling together. "Murphy's out of surgery. He's down a spleen, and they've got him in a medically induced coma until the swelling on his brain comes down, but he's stable."

Sam folded around her like a puzzle box, wrapping her in those tree trunk arms and dropping his head against the back of her neck. She felt his chest swell against her back as he drew a deep breath and blew it out, shuddering on the exhale. His voice thickened, emerging as a strangled whisper. "Thank *fuck*."

---

"I DON'T THINK Cricket ever told me what happened to their parents." Gretchen's voice wound through the darkened interior of the SUV. It surprised Sam that she was awake. She'd been so quiet for the last hour, he'd assumed she'd drifted off.

"Their mom was diagnosed with breast cancer when she was pregnant with Murphy. She refused chemo." Sam sighed, maneuvering the car along the deserted mountain road. "Norm Bonhomme keeled over in a lane at Lucky Bowl six or seven years ago. Brain aneurysm. Never felt a thing."

"That's awful." She propped her feet up on the dashboard, nibbling a thumbnail.

"The world's fucked that way." A second or two ticked by, and Sam blew out a quavering breath. "When that cocky little shit wakes up, I'm gonna beat his ass."

"Great idea," she replied, her voice dripping with sarcasm. "That'll fix everything."

"Well *shit*, Gretchen," he snapped, at a loss for what else to say. "One of my best friends in the world is fighting for his life, possibly brain damaged and paralyzed. I feel entitled to be a little fucked up about it."

"So, try shedding a fucking tear." She threw up her

hands, sounding perturbed. "I'm scared too, but you don't see me threatening violence."

"Scared," he repeated, feeling a grudging sense of affirmation. The car rolled to the stoplight at the southwestern end of Main Street, and he took his hands off the wheel, scrubbing them down his face. "Jesus Christ. He's just a fucking kid."

She reached out, resting her hand on his shoulder. "I know."

"What was he thinking, taking that pass after all that rain?" He turned his head to look at her, waiting for her to say something clever and forthright. He wanted her to make it all feel manageable again, but he could see from the heartsickness in her eyes that there would be no easy answers this time.

"You said it, Sam." She looked down, brushing a tear off her cheek. "He's a kid. He did a dumb kid thing."

Sam looked out at the darkened street ahead of them and hesitated. The sun would be up in a couple hours, and there was a cool, low-lying mist hanging in the air, forming a halo of refracted light around the blinking red traffic signal. His building loomed to the right, a boxy white form beyond the dark structure of the garage. The road to the left led to her bungalow. He peered at her again. "I have an extra toothbrush at my place."

She nodded. "Okay. Your place, then."

# CHAPTER
## Twenty-Seven

The drive behind Sam's building might've been paved at one time, but decades of freeze and thaw had gotten into the cracks, and the summer grasses had taken root. Now it was just a deep set of wheel ruts running alongside the old Victorian, and the six-car lot in the back was muddy enough to suck a person's shoes off their feet.

Sam got out first and drudged through the swampy parking area, lifting her over the ankle-deep puddle under the car. He held her hand as they climbed the stairs to the second floor, surprising her by slipping his arm around her waist and pinning her to the door of his apartment. His fingers traced the underside of her jaw, coming to rest against the back of her neck. He nuzzled into her, trailing his lips over her temple, the apple of her cheek, and finally, his mouth met hers, tasting of the sugary cola he'd been sucking down all night. A sob escaped her lips, the intensity of the contact mingling with the desperation of the last twelve hours.

"Hey." He pulled back, searching her face. "You okay?"

"Yeah." She nodded, brushing a fresh tear off her lashes. "Yeah, I'm good. Don't stop."

He gave her a sad smile, the sentiment clear, before he lowered his head to try again. They failed to sync up for a moment, their mouths colliding awkwardly as hunger overrode technique and all the raw emotion of the night spilled into it. Then he put his arms around her, one hand closing around the back of her head, and crushed his lips to hers. A shiver ran through her limbs, and she twined her fingers around the nape of his neck. His tongue pushed into her mouth, tangling with hers until she caught his full lower lip with her teeth and bit down *hard,* wanting to see the evidence later. A snarl ripped from his throat, the iron bar of his arousal pressing to her belly as he fumbled to turn the key in the lock. His hands were under her coat, peeling it off her shoulders as he pulled her inside, kicking the door shut without losing his hold on her. He shoved his hand under her sweater, yanking down the thin lace front of her bra to close his lips over a nipple, bending her backwards until her feet came off the ground.

"Jesus, I needed this." He straightened, picking her up and holding her legs tight against his sides as he strode into the next room, where his mattress laid on the floor.

She squeaked as he bent to lower her onto his bed, and himself on top of her. He pulled his shirt over his head, his muscles flexing in the pale light streaming through the windows. Taking hold of the bottom hem of her sweater, he stripped it off her so fast that she felt nothing but the cool rush of air against her skin. The rest of her clothes went the same way, tossed haphazardly behind him. Then, he was hopping backwards and towering over the bed, his eyes never leaving hers as he unfastened his fly and shoved his jeans and underwear off his hips, stepping out of them. He was hard already, his erection hanging heavy between his legs. Pointing with his chin, he ran his hand over his cock. "Get the condoms."

She followed his gaze, to where an unopened sleeve of condoms rested atop the upended milk crate serving as his side table. "Wow. You thought of everything."

"I like to be prepared," he said, kneeling on the end of the mattress as she army-crawled across the bed to retrieve them. He seized her ankles, dragging her under him the moment she closed her fingers around the package. She tensed as he plucked them from her hand and flipped her over, her knees snapping tight against his sides.

"Relax, Trouble," he murmured, pressing his teeth to the curve of her neck, hard enough to leave two stinging half-moons branded into her flesh. "I'm not going to hurt you."

"I know, but..." She trailed off as he moved lower, grazing his lips along the valley of her breasts and down her belly. "Sam?"

"Yes?" He lifted his eyes to hers, the stubble on his chin scraping the flesh just above her pubic mound.

"Oral really doesn't do it for me. I'll give all day long, but receiving..."

"So, tell me what you want." He gave her a studious smile, stroking his fingers along the seam of her sex. "Like this?"

She hissed as he notched his fingertip under the hood of her clit, making her hips jolt upward. "There. Faster."

For a man who seemed to get off on being in charge, he took direction well. Dipping his fingers inside, he worked her in slow, patient strokes until her thighs were slick and she was fighting for breath. Then, just as her knees started to quake and that delicious swell of pleasure began to build in her center, his lips brushed the shell of her ear, his breath hot against her skin. "Tell me what you want, Gretchen. You want to finish this way, or on my cock?"

There was a pulse of need deep inside, her body clutching at nothing, and she bit her lip. *We've come this far. Just say it.* She met his gaze. "I want you inside me."

He took his hand away, and she mewled in distress. "You can't stop!"

"Relax, Trouble. You want me inside you, this is a two-handed job." He grinned, ripping a condom open with his teeth and rolling it on. Her breath hitched at the sight of him moving over her with his erection in his fist. *This is it. We're doing this.* He grew serious, seeming to sense her jitters. "I won't do *anything* you don't ask me for. You understand?"

"Yes." She nodded, the conviction in his eyes bringing her back to the moment and soothing her nerves. She didn't have the words right now to explain that she wasn't *scared*, just nervous. This part always made her nervous, but in the best way. The word was barely out of her mouth before he was twisting his fingers in her hair and crushing her into the bed under him, kissing her hard enough to bruise.

---

ELEVEN HOURS SPENT WAITING for news of Murphy. Another hour on the road, battling his own burning fatigue. He should be ready to pass out, but the taste of surrender on her lips had a strangely energizing effect. All he wanted to do now was let all the stress roll off his shoulders and focus on being in the moment with Gretchen while losing himself in the liquid oblivion of climax.

Disbelief washed over him as he lifted her arms and

pinned them over her head, transfixed by the trust in her eyes. He'd been numb for so long that the notion of finding connection with another person started to feel like a pipe dream, but now... *This*, he thought, guiding himself into her body. She was perfect, so snug and warm, and *hungry*, squeezing every inch of his cock like she was made for him. *This is how it's supposed to feel.* He took his weight on one elbow, dropping his head. "I wanted this so much."

"Me too." She bit down on his shoulder as he started to move in her, and he closed his eyes, concentrating on the feeling of her nipples brushing his chest, and the flat of her belly kissing his in time with each stroke.

"Sam." She wriggled, locking her heels around the underside of his ass. "Sam, I need to be on top."

He gasped out a laugh, his first of the night. "Really?"

"Either that or flip me over. But I need a hand free."

"Works for me." He rolled without pulling out, taking her with him. She laughed in surprise, then flattened her palms to his sternum and stirred her hips, drawing a deep groan from him. "*Fuck*, Trouble!"

"Here. Sit up." She reached for him; her hand cupped at the back of his neck. He did as she asked, covering the narrow butterfly of her ribs with his hands and pulling her to him, needing her mouth on his again.

"*Goddamn*," he ground out, wetting the pad of his thumb and reaching down to stroke her, savoring her breathy little moan. "You're so fucking perfect."

She gasped in response, looping her arms around his neck and rocking into his touch. He sat up tall, pressing his lips to her throat and letting her take what she needed from him, until her body started to shake and grow slippery in his hands.

"Just like that. Just...like..." she murmured breathlessly. "I want you to come with me, Sam."

He gulped back a moan and nodded, mesmerized by the unbridled lust veiling her eyes. "I'm close."

"No, I mean—" He knew the moment before she came, the first flutter of her muscles around him like a warning shot before the full-scale clench-and-roll of her orgasm. She released a feral cry and tipped back, the nails of one hand gouging into his shoulder, the other braced on his knee, giving him a gorgeous view of his cock sliding in and out of her as she rode him, greedily extracting every last ounce of her pleasure.

He waited until her movements slowed and she exhaled a deep, satiated purr before he flipped her under him and laid one hand above her head, finishing himself off in five hard thrusts. His ragged bark rang against the walls, and he was lobbed head-first into a blinding spiral, electricity arcing along his nerve endings and setting off cascading showers of sparks through his entire body. His abdominals clenched, wringing him out until he had nothing left to give, and he tumbled sideways, still inside her, holding her clutched against his chest. He buried his face against the curve of her damp shoulder, breathing hard. "Jesus *fuck,* Trouble. You don't play around."

She sighed, resting her cheek over his thundering heartbeat. "Sweaty. Need shower."

———

"Hey Sam?" Gretchen laid her chin against the beefy ridge of Sam's shoulder, her legs encircling his waist in the depths of the clawfoot bathtub. He reclined against her chest, his knees rising from the water like volcanic islands in front of him.

"Hmm?" he hummed absentmindedly, resting his muscular arms along the curved lip of the basin.

"My boss offered me a promotion." Her hands slid along his ribs in the warm water, tracing the definition between his abdominals. "It's a huge deal. Basically, my dream job, and I want to take it."

She could sense him tempering his response, and he cleared his throat, the sound amplified in the tiled room. "What does that mean?"

"They want me to move to Tokyo for a year."

"Tokyo, *Japan*?" Sitting up fast enough to send water sloshing over the sides of the tub, he twisted to face her, his expression blending remorse and profound reprobation.

"For a *year*. It wouldn't be forever." She drew him into her arms again, her feet draping between his thighs. "Listen, I know how it feels to have someone you care about pull the rug out from under you. That's not what's happening here."

The muscle at the corner of his jaw flexed, and the hard edge in his voice softened, taking on a bittersweet tone. "I really wish you'd told me before you let me fuck you."

"All right, Mr. Misery Guts, I know we both had a rough day, and we're tired. But I feel I should remind you that it was not a one-sided operation. I fucked you right back." She started kneading his bulky trap muscles. "What's your policy on completely insane ideas?"

Sam turned his head, as if he was trying to see her from the corner of his eye. The divot in his cheek deepened. "I'm listening."

# CHAPTER

*Twenty-Eight*

He registered the pleasure first, the heavy shroud of sleep lifting as he realized he was hard as hell, and there was something hot and slippery gliding over his length. There was a flutter of softness against his naked thighs, and his hand slid down to rest on something round, firm, and very much alive. He pried his eyes open, gazing down at Gretchen as she teased at the head of his cock with her tongue.

"What're you doin'?" He groaned, his voice sleep-drunk and craggy. A clever smirk hitched one side of her lips and she opened her mouth, swallowing him until he bumped against the back of her throat. His fingers reflexively tightened in her hair, and his eyes rolled back, a coarse gasp escaping his lips. "*Fuck*...marry me."

She hummed, keeping one hand wrapped around the base while moving her mouth over his shaft in long, rhythmic movements until he was panting, his hips lifting off the bed with every stroke. *Damn*, she was good. So good he was starting to wonder if he'd rescued a basket of drowning puppies in another life, and earth-shattering wake up head was his reward. Gretchen was a cruel little trickster, though. Just as he started to crest, she let him slip free of her mouth, giving him a kittenish smile from her place coiled between his legs. "You want to come?"

"I was fucking about to before you stopped!" He choked out a laugh, lifting his head to watch her feathering her fingertips over his cock, creating a vexing ticklish sensation over his stretched-tight skin.

"Oh. Okay." She dove back on, caressing him with her lips and tongue until he started murmuring hot nonsense under his breath. But just as he could feel the pressure topping out, rising higher than it had before, she pulled away again, giving him a cold-blooded grin. "Because I wasn't sure if you really *wanted* to."

Aggravation flared. "*Fuck*, you evil little—"

"What now?"

"Treasure," he self-corrected, fisting his hand in her hair and staring down at her. "Angel. *Goddess*. Now for the love of *fuck*, finish me."

Resting the head of his cock against her chin, she flicked the tip of her tongue against his frenulum. "Beg me."

"*Please*! " he thundered, gnashing his teeth like a madman. "Please, I'll give you *anything* you want, just please—" He groaned with relief as she sucked him down to the root, the hot nonsense returning. "Sweet *Christ*... you're amazing. *Fuck*, kill me. Just fucking kill me now."

She added a little twist of her head on the upstroke, sliding one hand up the inside of his thigh and gripping his balls. It was a light caress at first; then as they started to tighten and draw closer to his body, she gave him a slow, firm tug, sending him right over the edge. He roared, emptying everything he had down her silken throat. It was so good it sapped his strength and turned his legs to numb, ineffectual weights below his waist.

She sat up with a satisfied sparkle in her eye, dabbing at the corner of her mouth with the sleeve of his lucky hoodie. "Welcome back to the land of the living."

"Guh-hm..." He swallowed, resting one hand over his racing heart. "Good morning to you too, Trouble."

She sat cross-legged between his knees, propping her chin on an upturned fist. "Sleep okay?"

"Fuck off, you little succubus." He chuckled, taking in his surroundings now that his vision was starting to clear. He was in his room, with its trademark lack of furnishings and stacks of books lining the walls. There were bright bars of golden light slicing through the blinds and falling across the rumpled bedsheets. Everything was as it usually was, except she was there, hair mussed, cheeks flushed and with a self-satisfied twinkle in her eye. He checked the digital clock on the side table and grimaced, pressing his thumb and forefinger into his eye sockets. "Please tell me it's six twenty-seven in the morning, and I've only been asleep for five minutes."

"No joy. We slept through Saturday." She rolled off the bed and sauntered into the next room, stretching her arms over her head as she did. Her voice echoed through the apartment. "I was starting to think I should check your breathing."

"Still alive." He sat up as she trotted back into the room carrying a pair of mismatched hand-me-down mugs. Settling cross-legged onto the foot of the mattress facing him, she passed him the one with the pastel cartoon bunnies on the side. He blinked at the contents. "Did I have tea?"

"There was nothing good on TV, so I took a walk to the

grocery store while I waited for you to regain consciousness."

"How long have you been awake?"

"I dunno, a couple hours." She lounged sideways, propping herself up on one elbow. "I thought about leaving, but I could just picture the sad pretzel face you'd make if you woke up and I was gone."

"Sad pretzel?"

"Yeah, you know..." She tousled her hair over one shoulder. "Hot, twisted, and salty because I took off without saying goodbye."

He snorted, narrowly avoiding swallowing his tea down the wrong tube. Choking on his mirth, he coughed against his fist and leaned to one side to set the mug on the floor. He got up and trotted into the bathroom to empty his bladder, speaking to her over his shoulder. "I bet you think you're cute."

"As a matter of fact, I think I'm fucking adorable!" she called after him.

She was still out there when he reemerged, laying on her belly with her nose buried in *The Tao Te Ching*. He sat down behind her and ran his hand over the curve of her leg, admiring her in the tiger-striped light. "So, last night. That happened."

"I'd say so." She tugged open the collar of the hoodie to display the baseball-sized hickey darkening her shoulder.

"Shit, when did *that* happen?"

"Probably when you woke me up for round three," she murmured, flipping the page in front of her. "You latched on like a lamprey eel."

"Oh. Yeah." He shoved the pillows into a mound and leaned back. Was he really considering this? Packing up his meager possessions and relocating to another *conti-*

*nent* for a woman he'd known for less than three months? Sure, the sex was... Okay, the sex was fucking phenomenal, but did that really translate to a year in a foreign country? "Tell me again what I'm supposed to do in Tokyo?"

"Cook and give me orgasms, mainly." She shrugged, completely nonchalant. "You could teach English. Or take a stab at writing. Or, hey! You could dress up in an old-timey unitard and wander the streets bending lead pipes with your bare hands and charging tourists to take pictures with you."

"Now there's an idea." He smirked as she slapped the book closed and crawled up to drape herself between his legs. She laid her chin against his sternum and closed her eyes like a contented cat as he carded his fingers through her hair. "Would that make me a kept man?"

"I prefer the term 'designated piece.'"

"And what happens if it doesn't work out?" he murmured, admiring the way the sunlight warmed her features.

"I hear they have these things called airplanes." She lifted her eyebrows. "Rumor has it they fly through the air, and if you buy a ticket, you can take a sleeping pill and wake up in a whole different place."

"There you go, making things simple again." His phone buzzed. A fraction of a second later, hers sang out from the living room, and they exchanged a knowing look. He reached for it, frowning at the screen. "Murphy's back in surgery."

She sat up, looking pensive. "Did something happen?"

"No, looks like they took him in to put a few pins in his leg and handle some secondary stuff that they didn't want to mess with until they stabilized him." He lowered the phone and looked at her, his heart squeezing at the stricken expression on her face.

"Hey. Come here." He opened his arms, letting her curl into his chest, the weight of her body laying against one of his thighs. Pressing his lips to her temple, he murmured into her hair, "Until Monday, the world outside this apartment is lava."

---

GRETCHEN WAS SPRAWLED atop him when the pizza arrived, resting one cheek on his heart and enjoying a late night monster movie marathon. He peeled her free and rolled off the edge of the couch, grabbing his wallet from the table. She ducked into the bedroom and waited, listening to Sam pay for their dinner. The door closed, and his voice carried into the next room. "Come on out. He's gone."

He was already folding open the box as she crept out of her hiding place, and he turned his head, a trenchant edge in his voice. "You know, the neighbors already got an earful last night. It's only a matter of time before someone puts it together."

"I know. And I know we're gonna have to tell everyone anyway, if you want to come to Japan." She eased up next to him, her stomach gurgling at the scent of sausage and peppers. "I like that this is just for us right now."

He handed her a plate, giving her a subdued smile. Slipping his arms around her waist as she separated a slice from the pie, he bent to worry at her earlobe. "This will *always* be just for us, Trouble."

"Will it?" She hissed in pain, licking a dribble of scalding tomato sauce off the back of her hand. She shook red pepper flakes over her plate and carried it to the sofa, sitting down cross-legged. "There are no secrets in this town. Everyone knows everyone else's business."

"Well, I don't plan to fuck anyone else," he returned, dropping a couple slices onto a plate. "People talk, but no one will ever know what goes on here, unless you tell them."

She took a big bite of her pizza, watching the broad span of his shoulders as he reached for a napkin. "Sam?"

"Hmm?"

"Can I ask you to tie me up, or do you have to be in the mood for it?"

He half-turned, his inscrutable gaze tracking over her face. "Is that what you want?"

# CHAPTER
*Twenty-Nine*

"On your knees." Sam watched as Gretchen tried to maneuver her artfully trussed legs close to her body and roll onto her front without the use of her arms, already neatly box-tied behind her back. She wriggled like a worm on a hook, naked but for the slender cotton rope wound around her body. He felt a wistful pang behind his breastbone—one that had nothing to do with lust. Gretchen Clarke was a willful pain-in-the-ass, but when she chose to bend, she gave of herself with such unreserved generosity that it made him ache in a way that he didn't know was possible.

The bindings on her legs kept each one folded tight upon itself, making it impossible to push off and use her momentum. She conceded to her helplessness after a few minutes and laid in a wilted heap on the sheets, her glossy ringlets tumbling across her face. He smirked to himself, admiring the almost sculptural beauty of her in this helpless state. Then he bent, helping her push herself to her knees. "There. Good girl."

He was glad he went with the red rope instead of the

black. It set off the indignant flush in her cheeks perfectly. She huffed around the knotted fabric in her mouth, the obstinate glint in her eye damn near doing him in. Fuck, she knew how to play his heart like a squeezebox, letting him take his time, building up his anticipation with every nod of consent, then getting pissy the moment he started giving orders.

He folded his arms, ribbing her. "What? No thank you?"

She had to arch her back to glower up at him, demonic sparks crackling in her eyes. Her expression of wordless fury went straight to his groin, and he reached out to push a stray curl behind her ear. She jerked away from him, hissing like an enraged opossum, and he chuckled. "You want to be that way? Fine."

He let the smile fall away from his face. "Spread your legs."

She shifted her knees apart on the mattress, and he stood up, resting his hand on top of her head as if he was patting a dog. "Wider."

She did as she was told, pushing her toes into the mattress to steady herself, and he smirked, a bolt of satisfaction jagging through him. "You know what's great about the frog-tie position?"

He gave the top of her head a gentle downward shove, and she toppled forward with an incensed howl, the side of her face connecting with the mattress. Now she formed a tripod, ass in the air.

"Stay!" he barked as she tried to pull her knees together, giving her a sharp swat on the backside and enjoying the bloom of rosy pink that spread over her skin. She went still, anticipation hanging in the surrounding air. "Good. Don't move."

A shriek of protest rose from the bed as he strode out of

the room. Crossing to the fridge, he took out a beer and popped the cap off the bottle, leaning against the counter to take a long, unhurried drink. He found her right where he'd left her a few minutes later, those big doe eyes tracing his movements as he approached the side of the bed. He pressed the frosty bottle against her exposed sex, reveling in her muffled cry of dissent. "Have you ever been fucked while wearing a butt plug?"

Gretchen didn't respond for a beat, then she shook her head against the crumpled sheets, making a vaguely hesitant sound around the gag. He bent to run a soothing hand over the upthrust curve of her ass, like a horse trainer petting a skittish colt, and tilted his head to give her a reassuring smile. "Don't worry. That won't happen tonight."

She sighed, sounding relieved, and he set his beer on the floor, climbing onto the mattress behind her. He smoothed his palm over the knots of rope on her hairpin-bent leg, stopping to pluck at her clit. For all her protestations, this was clearly working for her. She was shaking, and he could see a bead of lubrication forming at her entrance. "I'd like to try it another night, though. You'd make such a pretty picture, wearing a fox tail plug while you took my cock."

He folded over her, running one hand down her spine as he pushed down the waist of his pajama pants with the other, pressing against her wet heat. "Would you like that? You want to be stuffed in both holes like a good little fuck doll?"

A shiver went through her, and she made a soft, pleading sound, turning her face into the mattress. Her curls fell forward to provide cover, and she nodded, grinding against him. He grinned in approval, reaching to the side table for the condoms. Perfect. She was fucking perfect.

---

Gretchen sucked in a sharp breath, the aching arousal in her core redoubling as Sam threaded his fingers through her hair and eased the blunt head of his cock into her body. She'd never been so close to finishing just from feeling a man inside her. In fact, she'd never come from penetration alone, but there was something so freeing about being tied up and used—as if he'd found a way to shut off all the stressors rattling around in her brain. That, coupled with the ravenous sound of his voice as he described all the filthy things he'd like to do to her, made ripples of pleasure shoot up her thighs as he pulled out by a few inches and drove into her again.

He held her fast, grasping her hip with his free hand, the other fisted in her hair and tugging sharply at her scalp with every thrust. "Fucking *hell*, Trouble. You've got to have the finest pussy on the *planet*."

*Hell yes. Talk that nasty shit to me.* She closed her eyes, lifting up to meet him as he reached under her to stroke her clit. There was nothing to do but bite down on the gag and give herself over to it.

"*Christ* Gretchen..." He released her hair, clasping her under the chin and lifted her against the heated wall of his chest, working his cock in and out in a steadily mounting rhythm. "Where'd you come from?"

His words cut off as he latched onto her shoulder with his teeth. He was pounding into her now, his fingers massaging her bud in time with every merciless thrust. She'd been waiting for this moment, when he became a wild, rutting thing galloping toward the sheer drop-off of climax, hell bent on taking her with him. There was no resistance. No second guessing. Just pure, unrelenting pleasure. She screamed against the gag as the thunderbolt of a sudden orgasm jolted through her, and Sam roared in response, hammering into her twice more before he let go, his arms cinching around her shoulders and chest like steel bands. He fell forward, stopping himself with one outstretched hand before he could bring his full weight down on her, and for a few breathless moments, they stayed like this, still connected, like eagles cartwheeling to earth.

"You okay?" he panted, his index finger hooking against her cheek, pulling the gag down her chin. She spat out a mouthful of damp fabric and nodded.

"Yeah, I'm..." She twisted against her bindings. "Can you untie me?"

"Of course." He pulled out, and she heard the quiet snap of the condom coming off. An instant later he was straddling her waist, loosening the intricate knots at her wrists. She relaxed against the bed, giving him time to work.

"I've never come like that before," she breathed, her brain swimming with happy-time chemicals.

"Like what?" he murmured, releasing the loops around her forearms. She let them fall to her sides as he worked his way up to the restraints on her biceps. He was so meticulous putting each knot in place, but now he loosened them like he was pulling the laces from the eyes of a boot, in a hurry to make her comfortable.

"Usually, I have to finish myself off or use a vibe." The ropes around her chest slid free, and she lifted her arms to fold them under her chin as he moved down to her legs.

"If I wasn't feeling good before..." he mused, a distinct smile in his voice.

She moaned with gratitude when she could finally unfold her legs. Sam lifted one of her feet and propped it on his shoulder, carefully kneading her muscles to work the blood flow through them. Seized by a sudden sense of exuberance, she laughed. "Orgasms *and* physical therapy? What do I get if I wear the fox tail?"

"What do you want?"

She considered for a moment. "A caviar omelet, a puppy, and world peace."

"Done." He crawled over her, sweeping her hair over her shoulder and pressing his lips to the nape of her neck. Rolling to the side, he collapsed next to her with a satisfied groan. "I might have to make some calls on the third thing."

"And the fox tail has to be faux," she added, staring at the wall. "Something about wearing a butt plug adorned with the tail of an animal put to death via anal electrocution feels especially perverse."

"I ah-ghree." She turned her head at the oddly distorted sound of his voice and caught him pulling the cap off a fine-point permanent marker with his teeth, staring with intent at her back. Spitting out the cap, he angled his body over hers.

"Where'd you get that?" She laughed as the marker touched down just below her left shoulder blade.

"Your skin is so perfect," he murmured, focused on his task. "It's like a blank piece of paper."

"So, naturally, you thought you'd write all over it." She lifted her head to glance at the ink decorating his body. "What are you writing?"

"You can look at it when I'm done. Stop moving around."

She sighed again, resting her chin on her folded arms. "If you're drawing a dick on my back, we're never having sex again."

"What are we, twelve?" He chuckled quietly, clicking the cap onto the marker. He swung his legs around, reaching for his cell phone. "Okay, stay just like that."

There was a muted electronic click, and he settled onto his belly next to her, his smile turning apprehensive as he passed her the phone. She looked down, prepared for a dirty limerick. Instead, she felt her eyes start to burn. Scrawled across her back in bold, three-inch-tall letters was the phrase YOU FEEL LIKE HOME.

# CHAPTER
## Thirty

Something changed last night. They were curled up on the couch watching *Creature from the Black Lagoon*. She was lying in her preferred cuddling position on top of him, her head resting in the hollow under his chin. He was toying with her hair, absentmindedly twisting the curls around his finger and unwinding them again, when she lifted her head and smiled at him in this sweet, serene way that filled him with a nameless yearning and damn near broke his heart. He kissed her, watching the way her lashes fanned across her cheek when she closed her eyes, and suddenly knew: This woman could be his everything if he let her.

He made love to her, without thinking about the outside world or what came next. It was the kind of hot-blooded impulse that came upon them with so little warning they didn't even undress completely. He pushed aside the crotch of her panties and slipped inside, her leg thrown over his hip, the springs creaking under them. He groaned into the soft cradle of her neck as he came, that tightly spooled feeling suddenly reversing itself, exploding outward and spreading through his whole body, and as always, physical relief was tempered with a creeping sense of vulnerability.

"*We okay?*" he'd murmured into her hair, his head spinning as they laid tangled up in the afterglow. They hadn't used anything this time, a decision made following a hasty monosyllabic conversation about birth control and testing status, the exchange held while grinding his erection between their bodies. It wasn't like him to be so cavalier about protection. In fact, to that point, he'd only had unprotected sex with one other woman in his life, and he was struck by how significant it felt.

"*We're good,*" she'd whispered, draping an arm over his chest. They'd gone to bed sometime later, lying face to face with her nestled into his chest. She rolled over sometime in the night, and when he woke, she was sleeping on her belly with her face turned to the window and the blankets falling off one sleek shoulder. He rolled over and took in the tranquility of her slumbering expression, an unheralded exhilaration clutching in his chest.

She stirred as he pushed back the covers and reached for his boxers, tugging them up his legs. Sitting up on one elbow, she gave him a drowsy smile, rubbing the sleep from her eyes. "What time is it?"

"Little after ten." He twisted to drop a kiss on her forehead before getting to his feet. "Stay in bed. I'll make breakfast."

"What service." She hummed, pulling the blankets up under her chin. "Don't forget to iron the newspaper."

He was standing over the stove making eggs in a basket when he heard the familiar chirp of her phone in the next room, followed in quick succession by his own. He waited, poised to react. There was a burst of jubilant laughter and a thump as she flung herself out of bed. The bathroom faucet ran, and she popped her head around the corner, her hair standing out around her face in a wild mass of curls. She jammed a toothbrush into her mouth, speaking carefully to avoid dribbling toothpaste foam on the floorboards. "Murp-hee op-hened hith eyesh!"

"Really?" He spun, brandishing the spatula as she dipped out of sight. He heard her spit and rinse, and then she was rushing around the bedroom, picking up her clothes.

"Yup!" She exploded into the living room, yanking on her sweater as she went. Grabbing her coat and bag, she spun like a dervish, locating one of her boots where it had gotten kicked under the television stand. "Cricket needs me to meet Paolo at her place. I guess she sent him home to pack a few things to take back to the hospital, but he doesn't know what half the stuff she's talking about actually is."

"Right." He grinned, watching her hopping around, trying to shove her foot into her boot without letting her bag slide off her shoulder. "Did she need me to do anything?"

"Why would I know that?" She toppled onto the sofa, forcing her foot into the boot, then bending to pull on the other one.

"My phone went off at the same time as yours. You could've checked it."

"Ha!" She gave him a sarcastic smirk. "I'm not about to fall into *that* tiger pit."

Leaping to her feet, she twirled to retrieve her bag from where it had fallen next to the sofa, throwing the strap over her head cross-body style. Taking a few quick steps in his direction, she hopped up on her toes and gave him a peck on the lips. "I have to run. Okay? Good. Love you, bye."

The door slammed behind her, and Sam chuckled, moving the frying pan off the heat. He leaned back against the counter and folded his arms, mentally counting down from *five. Four. Three. Two...* The door flew open, and she slunk inside, a sheepish smile on her face. "So, I worry that what you heard..." She pressed one hand to her forehead, resting the other on her hip. "What I meant to say was, I didn't mean—"

"Gretchen?" He suppressed a grin at the twin points of pink coloring her cheeks.

"Yeah?" She froze in place, her eyes brimming with trepidation.

"See, if it was up to me, we'd just leave this at 'I love you, too.' But this sounds like it'll take a lot longer than five minutes."

"Oh." Her hand fell away from her face, and she glanced at the door where it stood open to the hallway. "So, we're good?"

"We're great, as far as I can tell."

"Okay." She swung her arms, inching toward the door. "I should go. And you know...meet, uh..."

"Paolo?"

"Yeah."

He dipped his head, doing an abysmal job of concealing his amusement by scratching the side of his nose. "Better get on that."

"Right." She backed into the hallway, slowly drawing the door closed behind her until it hung open by an inch or two. "Sorry about breakfast."

"Not a problem."

The door clicked shut, and Sam released the laughter he'd been holding back.

---

"SHIT, FUCK, FUCKITY, SHIT, FUCK-FUCK-FUCK!" Gretchen spat out a long string of profanity as she walked down Main Street, earning a round of alarmed stares from a table of Sunday brunch-goers sitting outside Magdalena's, the little Tuscan trattoria on the corner. She kept moving, bundling her hair into a knot at the back of her head and securing it with an elastic from her bag.

Paolo had parked his olive green Wrangler at the curb in front of The Paper Frog, and as she reached for the door of the shop, she lifted the front of her sweater to her nose, giving it an exploratory sniff. She really should have taken a shower before she left the apartment. The smell of sex and Sam's sandalwood soap were all over her. She snatched a napkin dispenser off the closest table, inspecting her neck in the reflective chrome.

"God*damn* it, Sam." What kind of high school bullshit was this? She snarled under her breath and hurried to rearrange the folds of her scarf to conceal the eggplant-purple hickey darkening the side of her neck. Unfortunately, the lightweight fabric of the scarf was excellent for layering but didn't maintain enough loft to cover the mark. She folded her jacket collar up and futzed with the scarf for a moment longer, then slammed down the napkin holder, resolving to keep Paolo on her left side at all times.

She found him passed out on the rose-pink, velvet sofa upstairs, catching a few Zs while Cricket's psychotic calico, Barbara, gobbled chicken liver pâté from a china plate in the kitchen. Obviously, Cricket had asked him to look after the cat while he was there.

Creeping past the sleeping man, Gretchen found her way into Cricket's pink-on-pink bedroom where a half-packed duffle bag sat open on the bedspread. Locating the remaining items on Cricket's list, she tucked them into the bag and carried it into the living room, where Paolo continued to snooze, the cool morning sunlight adding a pallid cast to his skin and emphasizing the asymmetrical bent of his nose.

Truth be told, she'd never really understood the whole Cricket and Paolo *thing*. Compared to Cricket's unstoppable earth mother vibrance, Paolo seemed about as interesting as a bowl of plain oatmeal, and she hadn't heard the guy speak more than ten words since they met. But looking at him now, seeing the overgrowth of stubble shading his cheeks and the dark crescents under his eyes, it started making sense. He probably hadn't left Cricket's side for the last three days, except to fetch her coffee or something to eat. Paolo had *shown up* for her friend in his own unobtrusive way, and when he woke up in an hour or two, he would get right back into his car and drive straight to the hospital to keep on doing it. Paolo was a rock star.

Setting the duffle bag next to the sleeping man, she saw herself out and stood on the sidewalk, considering what to do next. She wasn't looking forward to finishing that conversation with Sam now that she'd seen the state of her neck. She was willing to own that she might be reading too deep into things, but in the last thirty or so hours, he'd managed to give her two *massive* hickeys, write on her back in permanent marker, and fuck her until she was sore. She needed to come up for air, if only to consider how best to address his latent possessiveness, because she sure as hell couldn't be showing up to the office in Tokyo with love bites decorating her neck.

Walking back to her bungalow in the cool mid-morning sunshine, she scuffed through drifts of fallen leaves, meditating on everything that had occurred since they left the hospital. She didn't regret sleeping with Sam. They'd both needed distraction, and release, and companionship, and it was so much better than she'd imagined. So good, in fact, that her mental faculties had temporarily rerouted through her lady bits. That was the only explanation she could find for blurting out that she *loved* him.

Seriously, what was that?

*Cut the shit, sunshine,* her lady bits chimed in, reminding her that this morning's little slip of the tongue was hardly the first shot across the bow. Hadn't she oh-so-casually invited the man to move to Japan with her? She'd settled on that plan of action before the pants even came off. Then, last night, when they were cuddled up on the couch watching another classic horror movie, she suddenly felt closer to him than anyone else. Closer than anyone she'd ever dated, at least. It was so random, and yet, before either of them knew what they were doing he was pressing his unsheathed cock against her and asking her if it was okay.

She said yes without a shred of doubt. Now in the present, her footsteps slowed, and she stood marooned on the side of the street, lost in her thoughts. There was something almost reverential about the way his eyes locked on hers as he pushed into her, telling her without speaking that this time was *different.*

*"Can I come inside you?"* She heard his ragged query echo in her memory, sending a tingle of arousal frizzling through her pelvis. That question, delivered between fevered kisses, was somehow both sweet and *incredibly* dirty. Crushed

between the unyielding wall of his body and the back of the couch, she felt him moving in her, just him with nothing between them, and the look of unguarded supplication in his eyes told her what she needed to know.

"Yes." She'd nodded without breaking eye contact. "Come inside me. Let me feel it."

His hands flattened between her shoulders, holding her tight against him, and he buried his face against her neck, his breathing growing more rapid until a shudder traveled through his body. He didn't shout like he had before; he *moaned*, his voice ringing with pure, stunning release that ran so much deeper than physical. She hadn't heard a man come that way since she was a teenager, when sex was something magical and new.

# CHAPTER
## Thirty-One

Sam opened the door and Gretchen swept past him, unwinding her scarf from around her neck. "All right, Mountain King. Let's get something very clear, shall we?"

"Sure thing, Trouble. Shoot." He smiled, closing the door.

She huffed, dropping her bag on the table and slipping off her jacket, tossing it over a chair. Yanking the collar of her sweater open, she displayed her purpling neck, fixing him with a murderous glare. "If you *ever* give me another hickey again, we're through. I'm not kidding."

"Done. Anything else?"

"This isn't a joke, Sam!" she insisted, her eyes flashing in fury. "I'm not your *property*. What you're doing is *not cool*."

"I'm sorry." He held up his hands, realizing the seriousness of what she was saying. "It wasn't intentional."

"Bullshit," she snapped, stomping her foot like a petulant child. *Fuck, that's cute.* "At this point, you've done everything short of pissing on my leg."

"You're right. I *know* you're right," he admitted. Even if

it wasn't a conscious choice, it was problematic, and not just because it ticked her off. He didn't want to be this guy. "Listen, I'm sorry, okay? This is my problem, not yours."

She cocked a hip, looking him over. Then she shrugged, flicking her eyes to the side. "Great. You can pay for my concealer."

"Did you eat yet? I can make you something."

"No." She snatched her coat off the chair. "I'm mad at you."

"Then why'd you come back here? You could have yelled at me over the phone," he asked, already knowing the answer. She was here for the same reason he'd been staring at his phone, wondering if it was too soon to text and ask how it was going at Cricket's. He watched her pull on her coat, his heart swelling at the adorable crinkle of exasperation between her brows. "I love you, Gretchen."

She froze, her hands on her lapels, and stared at his chin for a long, pensive moment. Taking a step toward him, she slid both arms around his neck, pulling him down to press her lips to his. "I love you too."

A tsunami of relief washed over him, and he stooped to wrap his arms around her hips, picking her up and burying his face in the softness between her breasts. She laid a cluster of kisses on the side of his face and leaned back to smile at him. "Can I go now?"

"Go?" He laughed in disbelief, letting her slide down the front of his body. "Gretchen, this is beginning to feel punitive."

"Oh, for fuck's sake. I'm not *punishing* you, Sam." She rolled her eyes, adjusting the strap of her bag over her shoulder. "We've been in each other's faces for two straight days and telling me you love me won't make me magically forget that I'm mad at you. This isn't going to work if you don't give me space to recalibrate sometimes."

"Well, if you're going to be an *adult* about it..." He reached for the doorknob, earning a grudging snort from the woman in front of him. "I guess I'll have to call you later."

"I guess so." She stood to the side as he opened the door for her, an appreciative smile bending her lips.

Another reason to love Gretchen Clarke. He was still smiling, even after she left his apartment angry. Closing the door behind her, he turned to survey the wreckage of his apartment, amazed that they'd made such a mess when they'd barely gotten out of bed. He was knotting the top of the garbage bag, preparing to make a run to the communal cans at the back of the building when he heard a knock and grinned broadly.

"Missing me alrea—" he greeted as he threw open the door, his smile instantly flatlining. "Christ. Why won't you go the fuck away?"

---

"HEY HON, YOU HOME?" Paige's lyrical feminine intonation echoed from the front porch.

"Come on in, it's open!" Gretchen called, without bothering to look up from her computer.

The door opened, and her friend shuffled inside, the top half of her body obscured by a barm of crinoline, organza, duchess satin and floral appliqués. "I hope one of these will work for you."

Gretchen sat back in her seat, a worried smile on her face. "In what context?"

"For the party!" Paige called, moving into the living room.

"I didn't realize that was still happening." Pushing back her chair, Gretchen got up and trotted after her, folding her cardigan across her chest. "I hadn't planned on going."

"Well, I talked to Cricket about it," Paige said, carefully draping each dress across the back of the couch. She ran her fingers over the gathered waist of a cantaloupe-orange abomination, then selected an aposematic electric blue and magenta mermaid gown, holding it under Gretchen's chin. "She's still not sure she'll make it, but now that Murphy's out of the woods, we agreed that we could all use a little levity right now."

"*Is* Murphy out of the woods?"

"He's not brain damaged, as far as they can tell. That's about as close to a cause for celebration as we're gonna get right now," Paige answered without looking up, choosing a ruffled emerald tulle number and draping it over Gretchen's shoulders. "I think this one would work best with your coloring."

"I thought the idea was to wear the ugliest bridesmaid dress you could find." Gretchen held the garment against her body, staring down at the frothy tea-length confection.

"Oh, you're still going to look like a contestant on *Star Search*. But at least you won't look jaundiced." Paige pinched the skirt of the dress and held it out to the side, her expression growing serious. "Have you spoken to Cricket?"

"Briefly. We texted this morning, but she's been so stressed. I didn't want to be up her ass about it."

"You and I are very different people." Paige sighed, lowering herself to the arm of the sofa. "I get really needy when I'm dealing with something. My mom got sick a few years ago and let's just say that Dane deserves to be canonized for the amount of water-carrying he had to do."

She stared at the floor, tucking her hands under her body. "I think that's why I get so smothering when I see my friends struggling. We all try to give the people we care about what we would want if we were in their shoes."

Sensing an oncoming shift in conversation, Gretchen pushed aside a dress and sat down. "Makes sense. I prefer to be left alone to decide how I feel about things. Maybe I should reach out to Cricket more."

Paige shrugged, avoiding her gaze. "Cricket's more like you. She's a compulsive fixer, so it's *killing* her that there's nothing she can do right now. Every time someone asks how she's doing, it just reminds her of how powerless she is."

"I know that feeling." Gretchen nodded. "It's easier focusing on the external, rather than thinking about your own problems."

"The thing is, Cricket's been raising Murphy since she was a kid herself. Their dad tried, but he wasn't in great shape. Everything fell to Cricket." Paige ran her fingers through her intricate braids, crossing her legs. "That's why it was so great to see her get out. She was finally doing something for herself, living in Paris and Miami and being a major *boss,* you know? Then their dad died, and she had to come home to take care of Murphy. It was like, *fuck,* this girl can't catch a break. And now this..."

"Jesus." Gretchen shook her head, suddenly feeling like a terrible friend. "I knew that their parents were gone. I should have realized—"

"Don't feel bad. Cricket isn't the type to wallow in her misfortune." Paige gave a sorrowful laugh. "I think I assumed you already knew all this, especially since you and Soren were getting close."

She must've looked scared shitless, because Paige's smile widened, taking on a Puckish glimmer. "Don't worry, I didn't hear it through the grapevine. You two were looking pretty cozy at the hospital, and I'm guessing you forgot about that hickey."

She cocked her head to the side. "Soren's a deceptively sweet guy, huh? I remember once when he and Cricket were still together—"

"*Whoa!*" Gretchen leapt to her feet, clapping one hand over her neck. Her mind reeled between embarrassment at forgetting to hide her stupid love bite to the sudden revelation that Sam and one of her best friends had carnal knowledge of each other. She slapped down a sudden surge of jealousy. "Sam? And Cricket?"

Paige's mouth dropped open, and she eased off the sofa, holding her hands out in front of her. "Oh. Oh no. I'm *so* sorry, it's such common knowledge that I thought you *knew*. I never would have—"

"Well, it's out there now!" Gretchen collapsed onto the sofa cushions, feeling lightheaded. "Just tell me."

"It was nothing." Paige settled onto the arm of the sofa again, looking mortified. "It was senior year of high school; you know? They broke up when she left to go to culinary school, and by the time she came back he was already with Trinity. The timing was bad."

Gretchen blinked. Did this mean Cricket was Sam's first? No, she reminded herself, he'd been statutory raped when he was sixteen. But that didn't mean he wasn't *Cricket's* first. She stared at the fireplace for a long moment, absorbing this information. "Sorry, this just...this explains so much."

"God, Gretchen." Paige's eyes swam with tears. "I'm so, *so* sorry. I shouldn't have said anything. It's just a small town, you know? Sometimes I forget you haven't been around since kindergarten."

She sucked in a breath and set her shoulders back. "If it makes you feel any better, I don't think they were ever even *tempted* to get back together, not even after he and Trinity broke up. The most I ever heard either of them say was that the relationship ran its course. I don't think there's anything there anymore; at least, nothing romantic."

"It's not that." Gretchen huffed out a stunned laugh, thinking back on all the times Cricket shipped Sam a little too hard. "She's always had this odd, proprietary attitude about him. She was *really* invested in getting me to not hate him."

"I'd be willing to bet that has something to do with how they broke up." Paige hazarded a restrained smile. "We all thought they were gonna be the couple that made it, and then she left so quickly... It was like she'd never considered the world outside as an option until she was given a chance to get out. Soren was a terrific partner, especially for a girl with the kind of problems she had, but he was never going to be enough to keep her here. I think she always felt bad about leaving him behind, even more so after Trinity and Justin screwed him over. He deserved so much better."

"But no pressure, right?" Gretchen snickered, pushing her bangs out of her eyes.

"I didn't mean it that way, but I'm not going to lie, that was my first thought when I saw him working so hard to not even *look* at you." Paige slid a hopeful smile in her direction. "It's been a long time since any of us saw him that flustered, and you really have your shit together. Soren gives so much of himself; he deserves someone who isn't gonna flake on him when they're feeling strong enough to leave."

"Is this your way of saying if I hurt your friend, you'll kick my ass?"

"I didn't want to have to go there, but..." Paige grinned, shrugging one shoulder.

"No, girl. *Respect.*" Gretchen shook her head, smiling with admiration. "And respect to Cricket. I can't stand to talk to any of my exes, let alone be their friend. Just hearing the last guy's voice gives me a raging yeast infection."

They shared a laugh as Gretchen rose, realizing she was still clutching the dress. She passed it to Paige with a regretful smile. "Listen, it's not that I don't appreciate the effort, but I'm not really a party person. I think I'll sit this one out."

"Cricket warned me you'd probably say that." Paige sighed, gathering the dresses into her arms. "You and Sam could still come to the thing at the house if you wanted to. We're keeping it pretty low key this year."

Gretchen paused, hearing Paige express their names as a unit in such a casual tone. Her face heated. "We haven't been fooling anyone, have we?"

# CHAPTER
## Thirty-Two

"Thank *Christ*," Sam breathed as a white Lincoln hatchback came jouncing down the unpaved drive, a familiar figure behind the wheel. Standing up from the rear steps of the apartment building, he cradled his wailing niece against his ribs, waiting for the car to come to a complete stop before he started toward it. His mother climbed out into the waning twilight and gave him a solemn frown, pushing one side of her smart sable-brown bob behind her ear. It comforted him how she always remained unchanged, right down to the white Mallen streak above her left eye.

"Jesus, Sam." She took Ellie from his arms, gathering the bawling child against her chest. "How did this happen?"

"I don't know," he said, shaking his head in bafflement. "Trin just showed up and shoved the kid at me."

"I can see that," his mother said, looking the toddler over. Lifting one finger, she booped Ellie's tiny nose, which appeared to work as an *off* switch. The baby hiccupped, seeming to forget what she'd been crying about, and stared in wonder at the benevolent fairy godmother who'd materialized just in time to save her from Uncle Ogreface. "Who *does* such a thing?"

Sam glowered. That little gremlin had been inconsolable for the last three hours, but the second his mother showed up, she fell right in line. Reaching for the door, he ushered them into the stairwell. "Thanks for coming. I didn't know what else to do."

"Did you get a hold of Justin?"

"He won't be here for a couple more hours," he explained, showing her into the apartment. "He was in New Haven for work."

"And Trinity didn't say where she was going?" His mother settled onto the couch, bouncing the baby on her knee. She pursed her lips in disgust. "Unbelievable. Some people shouldn't have children."

"Mom, come on." He nodded to the kid.

"What?" She widened her incisive brown eyes at him. "You think she's going to *forget* that her cheating tramp of a mother just up and *abandoned*—"

"*Mom!*" Sam barked, wincing as the baby started squalling again. His mother glared at him and got to her feet, bobbing Ellie on her hip until she settled again.

"Have you changed her since she got here?" his mother asked, patting the child's diapered bottom.

"Twice already. Do you think she's sick or something?"

"You have two little brothers, Samuel." His mother sighed, digging into the diaper bag. "You know how babies are."

"I was hoping to never be reminded." He leaned against the counter, watching his mother lay the baby down on the couch and peel the Velcro back on the diaper. He'd spent the first twenty minutes pacing back and forth, trying to calm the screaming creature while calling his brother again and again until he finally picked up. Shouting to be heard over Ellie's caterwauling, Sam explained to Justin that his wife had deserted their child at his place and ordered him to get his ass there before he lost his sanity. When an hour had elapsed and Ellie still hadn't stopped yowling, he panicked and did the only think he could think of: He called his mother.

"Not that I'm not touched you called me." His mother gave him a curious smile. "But isn't there anyone in town that you could've called?"

"You're the only mother I know." He ran his hand over his scalp, satisfied with the half-truth. In all honesty, his first instinct had been to call Cricket, but she was at the hospital in Burlington. As for Gretchen or Paige, what the hell did they know about kids? For all he knew, he'd done more babysitting than Gretchen, and he'd once seen Paige freeze like a deer in headlights when someone handed her a baby. She stood there looking terrified, holding the child under its armpits until the mother came to reclaim it.

"I never thought I'd see the day my eldest son would actually need me," his mother murmured, securing the straps on the fresh diaper and lifting Ellie again. "The only thing that would make this sweeter would be if this was my own grandchild."

"I'm sure Justin wouldn't object to you filling the role," Sam offered, mindfully side-stepping the dig about his refusal to breed and thinking instead of Justin's mother, who was unreliable at best.

"Speaking of, what happened to Trinity's parents? Couldn't you call them?"

"They moved to South Carolina a few years ago." Sam shook his head, hating that he was still privy to so much information about people who were, by all accounts, happy to see him go.

"So what happens now?" She got up to deposit the soiled diaper in the trash. "Is Justin planning to rebuild the pool hall? He really couldn't ask for a better place to bring up a baby than Halberd Peak."

Sam's head snapped up at the question, and she gave him a knowing smile. Of course, he'd called her after the fire just to let her know he'd gotten out okay. He wasn't *that* heartless. But he'd been planning to talk to her about signing over his shares at Thanksgiving, when he could explain his decision in person. "What? Did you think I wouldn't find out? Lyle told me."

"I didn't realize you and Dad were on speaking terms."

"We have lunch once or twice a decade," she explained, patting the baby's back in a steady rhythm. "Used to do it more when he was still living up here. You were such an uncommunicative kid. It was the only way to keep tabs on you."

"You and Dad have lunch," Sam repeated, feeling his entire world tilt on its axis. He'd been there for the fights. It seemed unimaginable that the two of them could share a meal without bloodshed.

"Just because I couldn't stand to stay married to him for a single second longer doesn't mean we couldn't be friends." She added a sagacious laugh. "That part of the relationship was never the problem."

"Oh."

The sound of an unfamiliar ringtone interrupted the moment, and his mother crossed the room, bunny-dipping to retrieve her cellphone from her purse without dislodging the moppet. She held up a finger, indicating that he should wait, and lifted it to her ear. "Hey Sweetie.

Yes, I'm here with your brother. She looks fine, but
—Right."

She held out the phone. "It's Liam. He needs to talk to
you."

"What? Why?" Sam straightened, accepting the proffered device. "Hello?"

"Hey man," his brother greeted him, his usual laid-back
timbre sounding bizarrely businesslike. "Mom thought,
and I agree, that it would be a helpful for Justin's case to get
all this documented for the record."

"Good idea." Sam sagged against the counter, awash
with an unexpected blend of gratitude and shock.

There was a pause on the other end of the line, and Sam
could hear rapid-fire typing in the background. "Are you
aware if Justin has already retained counsel?"

Sam sighed, gazing up at the ceiling. "No idea."

"Doesn't matter. I'd be happy to take this on."

Sam shifted his feet, watching his mother swaying from
side to side, slow dancing the baby to sleep. "I appreciate
that, man. I really do."

"Come on." Liam chuckled. "This is *family*, bro."

# CHAPTER
## Thirty-Three

"Here, let me," a voice spoke from behind her, a hand sailing over her head, plucking the cereal she was reaching for off the top shelf. She turned slowly, eyeballing the helpful stranger. He offered her the box. "Lucky Charms, huh? Used to love those."

"Life is a journey," she replied in a flat voice.

The stranger held out his hand, undeterred. "I'm Liam, by the way."

She clasped his hand, giving it a single pump. "I'm not interested."

He laughed, falling into step next to her. "And here I thought small towns were supposed to be friendly."

"Welcome to frigid North." She reached for a jar of Nutella and circled to the next aisle.

"Listen, I'm sorry. You should know I *never* do this." He was back again a few seconds later, a persistent mosquito buzzing in her ear. "I saw you earlier in the produce section, and I thought, that looks like a girl I'd like to get to know."

He leaned against the shelves next to her, giving her an

oddly familiar smile. There was a distinctive white stripe in his espresso-black hair, and she might've considered his laughing brown eyes kind, if he'd demonstrated even the most basic understanding of boundaries. He held up one hand, his expensive platinum wristwatch catching the light. "I'm only in town for the next couple days, dealing with some family stuff. I'd like to take you out for a drink or something. But if you already have a boyfriend or—"

"Oh, I see." She turned on him, giving him her most withering glare. "You would respect the claim of a man that isn't even *here*, rather than my stated preference to be left alone? Is that what you're saying?"

All his cocky self-assurance disappeared. He pushed away from the shelves and looked down, nodding to himself. She braced herself for the typical sour-grapes, *"whatever, you're ugly anyway"* response of a man scorned, but he simply lifted his head, giving her a tight-lipped smile. He started backing away, holding his hands open at his sides. "Sorry about that. My mistake."

---

"Well, it's official..." Liam called as he let himself into the cabin, his voice ringing off the pine-paneled walls. He strolled across the living room and leaned against the door-frame of Justin's old bedroom. "I just don't understand women. I saw this girl at the store, right? She was *gorgeous;* easily a ten. I tried to talk to her, and you'd think I whipped out my dick and slapped her on the ass with it."

"Have you considered not assigning a number value to them?" Sam suggested, holding his niece on one hip while studying the assembly instructions for her new crib. "This says you need the size B screws."

"There *are* no more B size screws," Justin snapped from his seat on the floor. "Are you sure you're reading the right step?"

"Yes, I'm sure!" Sam passed him the instructions and pointed at a spot on the page. This was absurd. He could take apart a car engine and put it back together blindfolded. It didn't seem plausible that a piece of baby furniture could present this kind of challenge. "Haven't you done this before? Who assembled the last one?"

"We paid extra. It came preassembled."

"Hey man," Dane addressed Liam from where he sat propped against the window sill. "You get the beer?"

"Yeah, it's in the fridge." Liam stepped to the side as Dane passed by, muttering something about needing more alcohol if he was going to be in the same room with both Soren brothers at the same time. Pushing his hands through his floppy teen idol hair, Liam frowned. "Seriously dude, I've never been told off like that before, just for trying to say hello."

"Sounds like she wasn't interested," Dane called, punctuating his statement with the *tink-kssh* of the cap popping free of a glass bottle.

"That's what I don't understand." Liam shrugged, his voice jumping an octave as he grew more defensive. "I was perfectly respectful!"

Sam snorted. "I'll bet."

"What?" Liam's mouth hung open in bafflement.

"She didn't bite your head off until you asked if she had a boyfriend, am I right?" Dane appeared in the doorway, squinting at the younger man over the upturned end of his beer.

Liam gaped at him. "How—"

"I live with a very hot, very liberated woman." Dane

grinned, holding up a hand at shoulder height. "Let me guess: Long braids, about yay tall?"

"No," came his perturbed answer. "Curly brown. Really cool eyes, though. Two different colors."

Sam pivoted so fast he elicited a squeal of excited laughter from the child in the crook of his arm, his eyes connecting with Dane's. A beat passed, and Dane laughed, tilting the beer to his lips again. "This fuckin' family, man."

---

"I REALIZE THIS ISN'T IDEAL." Cherie frowned into the computer camera, folding her hands on her desktop. "But with the timetable on production moving so far to the left, we're going to need someone in place before the end of the month."

"It's not that," Gretchen began, running her tongue over her lip. "It's just, with the holidays coming up and—"

"We understand the challenges; no one wants to be away from family this time of year." Cherie gave her a magnanimous nod. "Believe me, we didn't want to put you in this position, but we have to recalculate for moving expenses and the storage of your belongings as soon as possible, and the team in Tokyo needs time to make arrangements on their end. If you can't do it, we need to know by the end of the week."

"That's three days!"

"I know and I'm sorry." Cherie cocked her head to the side, demonstrating her contrition with a subtle widening of her eyes. "Is there anything we can do to help make this transition easier for you?"

"Thanks, but—" She jumped at the sound of Sam's

knock on the door. Closing her eyes, she sucked in a rheumatic breath and smiled. "I'll have an answer for you by the end of the week."

They said their goodbyes, and Gretchen folded the computer closed as Sam came through the door. "Safe to come in?"

"Yup, just got offline." She deflated into her chair, feeling gut-punched by the broad smile on his face. He walked into the kitchen and set two full bags of Chinese food on the counter. "How'd the thing with your brothers go? Everyone get out alive?"

"The crib got assembled. We'll leave it at that." He laughed, unpacking a collection of containers and upturning the bag, dumping an assortment of sauce packets onto the countertop. "They were out of Dragon and Phoenix, so I got you Eight Treasure Chicken."

"Sounds perfect." She took down two of the ugly stoneware plates that came with the house, passing him one.

"Were you at the grocery store this afternoon?" he asked, opening one of the cartons.

"Am I under surveillance?" She leaned a hip against the counter, watching him spoon Hunan pork onto his plate.

The dimple appeared in his cheek. "Talk to anyone?"

"I seem to recall having a conversation with someone." She traced her index finger and thumb over her top lip. "Creepy dude. Skinny porn star mustache. Tube socks and shower shoes."

He gave her a sideways smirk, his eyes shining in a way that would have seemed inconceivable a month ago. "Nobody else?"

"Tell the truth, is this a test?" She canted her head to

the side. "Did you ask some smarmy teenager to hit on me, just to see what I'd do?"

"You know I hate bullshit games." He laughed, carrying his plate over to the table. "But I'll be sure to tell my brother you called him a smarmy teenager. He'll hate that."

"Your brother?" She paused, holding a spoonful of rice suspended above her plate. "Seriously. What's up with the men in your family? Were you guys constantly forced to compete for your parents' love or something?"

"Justin and I were. I can't speak for Liam, though."

"I should have known." She sat down, pointing at him with her fork. "It was the smile. There was something familiar about his smile, and now I see it. I guess you can thank your mom for that dimple."

"I'll let her know at Thanksgiving."

*Shit.* Good feelings gone. She laid down her fork, tucking her hands between her knees. "We should talk."

"Okay, listen. I'm sorry about the hickeys. But what do you want me to say when every guy I share DNA with is apparently attracted to the same—"

"Stop, stop, stop." She laughed, laying her hand on his forearm. "That's not it. It's..."

There was no good segue into this one, so she took a deep breath and ripped off the Band-Aid. "I know I said you could take some time and think about it, but my boss called me today. There's been a change in the schedule for my project. Corporate wants me in Japan earlier than expected."

Sam pushed his plate away, folding his elbows on the edge of the table. "How much earlier?"

"End of the month."

He was silent for a long time, staring at the tabletop between them. Then he scrubbed one hand down his face, exhaling a harsh sigh. "Shit, Gretchen. That's way too soon."

"I know." She shrugged, dejection coursing through her. "I'm really sorry to do this now."

"Everything is so up in the air right now." He pushed back his chair and stood up to pace. "Justin has no idea what he's doing with the kid, and we don't even *know* when Murphy's coming home, but they're going to need—"

"Whoa. Wait a minute, Sam." She twisted in her seat. "Do you realize that when you were hurt, I got no less than six phone calls offering me a new place to stay? And do you know why? They all wanted you, a man they regularly call an *asshole*, to have the use of your cabin. Are you seriously telling me that there won't be other people willing to lend a hand?"

Sam stopped pacing and put his hands on his hips, staring down at her. "You don't understand."

"Yes, I do. I understand that you have a history with Cricket that I had to find out about from *Paige* of all people. And I understand you don't want to leave the people you care about in a tough spot." She gripped the top rung of her chair, searching his face. "What I don't understand is, why does it always have to be *you*?"

Sam looked away for a moment, his jaw flexing. "I'm sorry. I assumed Cricket told you, but I guess that's a sign that neither of us even thinks about it anymore. For me, that feels like a different lifetime."

"Sam." She blinked up at him, her voice wavering. "If you don't want to come, just tell me the truth. But don't pretend that they're all planning their lives around your availability."

"It's not that I don't want to come." He shook his head,

dragging his chair closer and sitting down to face her. "This is just a big decision to make in such a hurry."

He reached out to touch her face, running his knuckles down her cheek. "I love you, but this is the difference between us. I can't pick and choose my responsibilities."

She pushed his hand away, her brow crinkling. "That's incredibly unfair."

"I know it is."

"No." She took a deep breath, her stomach churning. This was it. They were really ending it right now. "I have responsibilities I can't get out of either. Isn't that why we're having this conversation? They have offered me an amazing opportunity, and I'm going to take it. For once I thought maybe I could have everything I wanted, but if I have to compromise, I'm going to choose myself."

"You *should*." He took her hands, running his thumbs over her palms. She fought the conflicting urges to scream at him to just *get out* and save her the pain, while also wanting to absorb a few seconds more of his touch. "I can't ask you to stay. You deserve to get everything you want."

"So do *you*, Sam," she beseeched, slipping her hand around the back of his neck and peering up at him. "You're not a doctor or a physical therapist, and the market for teenagers looking to pick up spare cash in this town is bullish as *hell*. If your brother needs help, he'll have babysitters coming out of his ass. You don't *have* to stay."

"I'm sorry." There was a subtle tightening around his eyes, and he swallowed, the corners of his mouth drawing down as if he'd just tasted poison. "If there'd been more time, if we'd been together longer—"

"Right." She let him go and sat up straight, brushing an errant tear off her cheek. This conversation was just prolonging the inevitable. If this was truly over, she needed him to be gone before she reached for him again, wanting the safety of his arms. Before they fell into bed together, telling each other it was the last time. Because when it was over, she'd still have to watch him put on his clothes and walk away, feeling like she was dying inside. "You should leave. Otherwise, we're just going to keep talking in circles."

# CHAPTER
## Thirty~Four

Tokyo was awash with the acid light of neon color, still thrumming with activity even at this late hour. Taxis honked in the congested streets, trumpeting above the muffled beats drifting out of the all-night karaoke bars and clubs. Talking billboards endorsing everything from sneakers to energy drinks battled to be heard above the din, while boozy businessmen brushed shoulders with fantasti-cally-equipped cosplayers in multicolored wigs. None of this chaos reached Gretchen, safely ensconced in the ivory tower of a company-appointed apartment. She pressed her hand to the cool glass of her floor-to-ceiling window and peered out at the dizzying spread of the Tokyo skyline. "So, what's up? How was Christmas?"

"It was really nice," Cricket said with cheer, the keen treble of the milk frother hissing the background. Gretchen could imagine her zipping around the café, filling orders with the phone propped between her ear and her shoulder. "But *oh my god*, twenty minutes after we finished putting up the tree, we heard this tremendous *crash* and we run into the living room to find it laying there like a beached whale.

Tinsel and broken ornaments *everywhere.* I don't know how I manage to forget Barb's love of tree murder every single year, but we ended up having to tether the thing to the wall with fishing line."

"Sounds about right." Gretchen scrounged up a smile, missing her friend's rescue kitty so much that it made her heart hurt, even though the antisocial bag of toxoplasmosis never spared her a single ankle rub when she was actually around.

She'd been so lonely since arriving in Japan that there were nights where she would start awake and sit up in bed, stunned to feel fresh tears drying on her face. Other times, she'd be standing in her kitchen making toast, or sitting at her desk at work, and a stabbing pain would go through her foot, the muscles spasming with such severity that her toes felt like they were in danger of dislocating themselves. Her assistant made her several doctor's appointments, but when all three physicians failed to find a somatic reason for the attacks, she'd walked away with a prescription for stress-relief tea and weekly acupuncture.

"I was thinking about you yesterday," Cricket said, unaware of Gretchen's troubled mindset. "I made a big batch of rosemary Linzer cookies with plum jam filling, and I thought I'd better put one aside for Gretch, because she'll be really disappointed if I run out before she comes in."

"Aww..." Gretchen sat down on the low-slung linen sofa facing the windows, running her fingers through her hair. If there was one crystalline moment after her arrival in the country, it was walking into her new apartment. Exhausted after fifteen hours on a plane, it took her breath away to see the sweeping view of Tokyo provided by these windows, the snow-capped peak of Mount Fuji rising in the distance. Then that spiteful little voice in her head piped up, reminding her that it would be nice to have someone to share this with, and she sat down and wept, crying so long and so hard that she fell asleep, her arms hugging her knees to her chest. "You could always mail them to me."

"I think I will. I always got my best feedback from you."

"And how's Murphy been doing?" Gretchen asked, running her hand over her leg. She'd missed the younger Bonhomme's homecoming from the hospital, but Cricket sent her several dozen photos—all cropped to remove a certain someone's potentially-triggering visage from the narrative of the day. Gretchen felt overjoyed to see Murphy's goofy smile again, but there was a bittersweet-ness to not being able to share in the celebration. Worse, she'd combed through each snapshot, desperate for any hint of a tattooed elbow or an alpine shoulder.

"He'll have to wait until next semester to finish his teaching certificate, but he's struggling less, which is great to see." Cricket sighed, the rustle and clatter falling away in the background, signaling that she'd stepped into the back room of the shop and away from the prying ears of the patrons. "The physical therapist is still coming every day, but she said he's been improving so fast that pretty soon he won't need the chair at all anymore. After that, she'll be coming by less, just to make sure he's keeping up with it on his own. And Paolo has been wonderful."

Gretchen felt a poignant tug at her heartstrings. "You've got a good one there."

"I know, I really do." Cricket's voice grew syrupy, and Gretchen could hear her dreamy smile. "He mentioned wanting to move in, but I said we should wait until Murphy doesn't need so much help. It might happen sooner rather than later though, because Murph is talking about taking the empty apartment that just opened up in Sor—"

She cut herself off with an audible click of her teeth, a conspicuous silence echoing between them. Gretchen sighed defeatedly, brushing away a tear. "It's okay. You can say his name."

Cricket cleared her throat. "I was just saying, there's a little one bedroom available and Murphy's getting sick of me fussing after him. At least if *he* was there, I wouldn't have to worry as much. I still have nightmares about Murph slipping in the shower."

"I get it." Gretchen slunk down against the pillows and curled up on her side, cradling the phone against her ear. "And, uh...how is *he* doing?"

More silence. "I thought you said you didn't want to know."

"I didn't. I don't. But—" Her voice wavered, and she gazed at the clock on the wall. The one she kept set to Halberd Peak time, because somehow knowing what time it was there made the distance easier to take. "Please, just tell me. Then I won't have to think about it."

"The truth? Not great."

---

CROUCHING in the one-car garage behind The Paper Frog under the watchful eyes of Murphy and Paolo, Sam squeezed the clutch on Murphy's bike, checking the slack on the cable. "It's not bad. But seriously, dude. How long has it been since you cleaned the chain?"

"What can I say?" Murphy grinned, tilting back in his chair and jerking the casters off the ground, executing a flawless wheelie. "Things got away from me."

*Still smiling.* Sam sighed, attacking the o-ring chain with a wire brush. It was supposed to be his day off, but here he was doing motorcycle maintenance in the middle of January—yet another pitiful attempt to keep his mind off the persistent stitch in his chest. It had increased in intensity over the last months, festering from a gentle tug to a wrenching pang that threatened to rip his still beating heart through his ribs. Every time he found some relief, another wave of anguish came on its heels, reminding him that it was a fool's errand to forget.

When he walked into the café that morning, he was greeted by the sight of Cricket holding an amiable chat on the bubblegum pink wall phone while making a double-shot cappuccino. One look at him and she dodged into the back room, leaving the counter unmanned. He stepped into the second-floor stairwell and listened to the quiet murmur of her voice, unable to make out her words, but understanding the tone and clinging to that sense of secondhand connection. Leaning against the wall, he drew a deep breath, fighting the strangling feeling of perdition that hung around his neck at all times, threatening to drag him under.

It'd been almost three months without her, and it wasn't getting any easier. His friends were looking at him like a wounded animal again, walking on eggshells the way they did when Trin skipped town. This time was worse though, because when his fiancée fucked him over, all they felt was bad for him. Now, there was an underlying contempt in the way they looked at him, and he could feel their judgments hanging over him like a dark cloud.

*Why does it always have to be you?* He closed his eyes, squatting in the musty garage, and tried to banish the sound of her voice in his head. It'd been like this since she left, replaying every moment with her in his head like a movie, until he came to the end, when he sat at her kitchen table, willing his feet to move. He pleaded with his brain to stop there, so he wouldn't have to feel her breath mingling with his as she leaned in to utter that last devastating *I love you*, but it seemed he was doomed to relive that final moment when she kissed him goodbye, her lips salted with tears.

Regret. So much regret. Some days, he regretted waiting as long as he did to kiss her. Other days, he regretted even meeting her. Most of the time, he regretted letting her leave his apartment that Sunday morning, letting her stay angry at him. He should have fallen down on his knees and pleaded with her to stay for just a little longer, but how was he to know that the last time was going to be the last time? That they only had those few precious hours when they could pretend the world outside didn't exist?

"*Whoop!*" Murphy let out a yelp as one of his wheels caught a crack in the cement and he toppled backwards, rolling free of the chair. Sam launched himself to his feet, prepared to vault over the motorcycle, but Murphy just laughed. Turning the chair upright again, he hoisted himself back into the seat, dusting off the legs of his jeans with a flustered chuckle.

"Jesus fucking *Christ,* Murphy!" Sam barked, hot rage blasting through his veins. "What the fuck is wrong with you?"

"Chill out, man." Murphy's smile faltered. "It was an accident."

"Yeah, well, you're gonna crack your stupid head open if you don't stop fucking around. Can't you stop acting like a selfish little shit for five fucking minutes?"

"It. Was. An. *ACCIDENT!*" Murphy screamed, eyes bulging. "You think I asked for any of this? I'm the one who has to get his fake knee replaced every fifteen years! I'm the one who has to spend the rest of his life on antibiotics because I lost a major organ! Stop acting like any of this is your problem because *NOBODY ASKED YOU TO BE HERE*!"

An uncomfortable silence descended on the garage, and Murphy snorted, his lip curling with disgust. Wheeling himself in a tight circle, he muttered a soft parting invective. "Asshole."

They'd spent an afternoon building ramps at every entrance to the café when he first came home, then they'd gone around to every other public building in town and done the same, because somehow it never occurred to anyone that Halberd Peak was not handicap accessible. Now, Murphy rolled out of the garage and up the ramp at the back of the building, disappearing inside. Sam stared after him, dumbstruck.

Sitting on the workbench against the wall, Paolo sighed and reached into his pocket, shaking out a little baggy of pot. Taking a rolling paper out of the breast pocket of his heavyweight plaid jacket, he pinched a little bud and crumbled it into the crease of the paper, going through the delicate motions of rolling a blunt. Tucking it between his lips, he lit it and inhaled, letting the air settle for a few seconds longer.

"You know, Soren..." He squinted, his heavy brows gathering, and exhaled a breath of skunky smoke into the tattered cobwebs festooning the rafters. "I don't know where you got this impression that you constantly have to prove your value to people but turning yourself inside out to be useful isn't love. It's codependency."

"The hell you say?" Sam gaped, caught off guard.

"No judgment, dude." Paolo reclined back against the pegboard wall and chuckled, taking another hit. "It all comes down to this: I know you mean well, but you put so much pressure on people to be appreciative that you're only setting yourself up for disappointment."

"Paolo..." Sam took a deep breath, feeling his jaw tick with the effort of keeping his temper in check. "You don't know shit about me, so please shut the fuck up."

"Whatever you say." Paolo chuckled, squaring his ankle over the opposite knee and snuffing the blunt on the heel of his boot before tucking the roach into his pocket. "You stay here and keep bleeding yourself dry for people who will only take you for granted. I'm sure that's much safer than finding the person who doesn't need a damn thing from you but keeps you around anyway."

# CHAPTER
## Thirty~Five

"Good morning, Ms. Clarke." Gretchen's assistant met her in the lobby as usual, the ruffles on the front of her neat white button-down shirt fluttering as she fell into step next to her, passing over the black folio containing the day's agenda. Hiroko was younger than any of the other assistants on this level, but they'd chosen her more for her proficiency in the English language than for her quantified experience.

They made quite a pair: the painfully out-of-place American and her nineteen-year-old assistant, a girl they'd dredged up out of the administrative pool in the Nagoya office. Youth and lack of experience aside, though, she was efficient and unfailingly loyal, which was more valuable to Gretchen than a thousand battle-scarred war horses like the lady guarding Director Sakai's office.

"Industrial Design called; they wanted your take on the final prototype." Hiroko trotted beside her as they walked down the long, sterile hallway to her office. "And you still need to sign off on the packaging proofs before we send them to the California office for approval."

"All right, can you resend me the proofs for review? And schedule an in-person meeting with Industrial Design for early next week." Gretchen took a stack of message slips out of Hiroko's hands. There were two more that had come through the night answering service from her mother, who still couldn't seem to wrap her head around the time difference. "And set up a video call with my parents as soon as possible, please."

"Yes, Ms. Clarke." Hiroko drew her office door closed, and Gretchen sat down behind her desk, kicking off her shoes with a grateful sigh. If she could get away with wearing sneakers to the office every day, she would, but office decorum demanded business drag.

The flat screen on her wall flickered to life, her mother's freckled décolletage filling the foreground as she adjusted the angle on the computer screen and smiled wide. "There you are, Sweet Girl! We've missed you so much!"

"Good yesterday night!" She waved as her mother sat back and her father spread his lanky arms over the top of the sofa. Between his cornea-scarring Hawaiian shirt and her giant square-framed glasses, they looked like the breed standard for retirement. "Did you get the package I sent you?"

"We did!" Her mother threw up her hands, her fingers bursting open like fireworks on either side of her shoulders. The clatter of her stacked acetate bangles was audible through the speakers, tweaking at another comforting sensory memory. Her mother wore her bracelets like armor during her waking hours, shedding them only when she prepared for sleep at the end of the evening. "The Japanese really love their freeze-dried seafood, huh?"

"Did you try the squid?" Gretchen smiled, recalling the sheer terror that gripped her the first time she stepped into the grocery store. Following that first disastrous attempt, she'd pressed Hiroko into accompanying her for her weekly food shopping excursions.

"No, I wasn't feeling brave enough for that one, but the orange roll cakes were very tasty. And what were the potato chips?" Her mother looked to the side, giving her husband's knobby mahogany-toned knee a coaxing love tap. "The ones you liked?"

Her father thought for an instant, then an easygoing smile spread over his lips. His voice emerged as a dulcet baritone; his inflection laced with warm Bajan sun. "Spicy salted egg yolk."

"Always with the spicy, you two." Her mother shook her head and smiled into the camera again, her eyes glittering with intrigue. "I was out with Vicky Barone yesterday, and we happened across Pam Clew in the formal department at Macy's. You remember her? Her daughter Jenny was in your class in elementary school? Well, she says Jenny just got engaged, and you'll never *believe* who the boy is."

Gretchen rolled her eyes. "Brian Harris."

"That's right!" Her mother affected an exaggerated grimace. "All I can say is, good luck to that girl. She's gonna need it with a schmuck like that."

"You know, Mom..." Gretchen pardoned her mother with a smile. Bless the woman for her loyalty, but she was about as subtle as a brick to the face. "I never even think about Brian unless you bring him up. And to be honest, I'm happier that way."

"If that's how you want it!" Her mother waved her hands again, her bracelets clacking like castanets. "My lips will remain sealed from this moment on."

The door to her office opened, and Hiroko minced into the room atop her syringe-thin high heels. She leaned into the frame to direct a respectful nod to the couple on the screen, then handed Gretchen another file folder, tapping her wrist. "Your next meeting is in fifteen minutes."

Gretchen nodded, returning her attention to her parents. "Well folks, we'll have to pick this up another time, because I have to run. Dad, I'll send you that crispy-fried chili garlic oil in the next care package."

Her father gave her an affable nod, ever the strong, stoic type. Her mother sat forward. "And we'll send you some taco seasoning and a few jars of that peanut butter you like so much."

"And a *case* of Texas Pete's, please?" Gretchen pressed her palms together pleadingly. "I'm down to my last bottle and I'm starting to panic."

"Right, and a case of Texas Pete's." Her mother leaned to the side and wriggled her fingers in acknowledgement of Gretchen's assistant. "Hiroko, sweetie, you look adorable as always."

Put on the spot, Hiroko's cheeks flamed, and she turned to the screen, bending from the waist. "Hello, Mrs. Clarke. Mr. Clarke."

"All right..." Gretchen snickered at her assistant's proper Japanese manners in the face of her mother's indomitable friendliness. She arched a brow at the screen. "I'm gonna let you go. Talk later."

"Byeeee!" her mother trilled, waving at the camera before the screen blanked. Gretchen sighed, feeling some-what rejuvenated, and glanced up at her assistant just in time to catch the gentle smile gracing the girl's lips.

"My mother will probably try to stuff you into her carry on when they come to visit."

"I would not mind." Hiroko's smile widened, revealing the snaggled eye-tooth on one side of her mouth. She demurred, covering her lips with her hand. "I like her very much, and your father is so tall and good-natured."

"Yeah, I think I'll keep them," Gretchen quipped, fitting her shoes onto her feet and squelching the urge to inform her assistant that she found the slight imperfection in her smile charming. The girl could only take so much embarrassment in a single morning.

"There is something else." Hiroko hurried after her as she started for the door. "Many of the women from the office go out for drinks on Fridays. Please join us."

"This is one of those 'new boss pays' deals, am I right?" Gretchen cast a sidelong smile at her assistant as she pressed the button to summon the elevator. It was a racket, but she could certainly use the company tonight. Otherwise, she'd just go home and waste the weekend reading romance novels, sinking deeper into her solitude. Stepping into the elevator, she gave the girl an indulgent grin. "All right. I'm not a big drinker, but how about a round of tsukemen on me?"

---

AH, the antiseptic aroma of a tattoo parlor. Was there anything more comforting in this world? Reclining in a chair at DelINKuent Body Art & Piercing, Sam stared up at the ceiling as Doyle "Gargoyle" Garrett, the artist who'd been systematically grinding ink into his skin for the last two decades, put the final touches on the new piece over his heart. The bells at the front of the shop jingled, and the squawk box on the wall of Doyle's cubby crackled to life. "Someone here to see Sam."

Doyle lifted the needle from Sam's skin as the door cracked open and Cricket's Easter egg-painted noggin popped into view. "'Sup Soren. Safe to come in, or do you want to put the guns away?"

"You need something?" Sam asked in a gruff retort. Doyle returned to his work, ignoring the strange girl who'd intruded on the session.

"Actually, I came to bring you something. But it can wait until you're done here," Cricket explained, making herself comfortable on the cracked leather chaise against the wall. Sitting back, she nibbled a thumbnail. "Is that the Gill-man from the Black Lagoon?"

"Yup," Sam grunted, consciously separating himself from the pain. Another quarter hour passed, with only the whine of the tattoo gun and the thumping heavy metal coming from Doyle's stereo to fill the silence between them. Finally, Doyle killed the machine, wiped the blood and ink from the left side of Sam's chest, dressed it, and declared his latest masterpiece complete.

"You know the drill." Doyle sat back, peeling off his nitrile gloves and stuffing them into the biohazard can next to his stool. "Take the wrap off when you get home and keep it shiny."

Sam tipped the artist and reached for his shirt without sparing a glance at the sheet of cling wrap taped to his chest. He didn't know why he did this to himself, because this one was going to keep hurting for a *long* time after it healed. It would be so much easier if he could put her out of his thoughts and move on, but as time stretched between that night to this one, a new fear took shape: that he might wake up one day and think that final night with her wasn't as perfect as it looked in hindsight, and he should just let it go. Pulling his shirt over his head, he addressed Cricket without looking at her. "How'd you know where to find me?"

"Frank told me when I called the garage this afternoon." She shrugged, a distinct sound of amusement in her voice. "He said you lit out early to get a new tat. I figured this was as good a place as any."

"So, what is it?" he asked, pulling on his coat.

"Oh, right. I've been looking forward to this." She passed him a flat manila envelope and stuffed her hands into her pockets, waiting for him to open it before giggling in triumph. "It's a petition. Congratulations! You've been voted out of Halberd Peak."

"Have I?" He flipped through the pages, counting line after line of signatures until he came to the end and barked out a surprised laugh. "Did you actually get my *mother* to sign this?"

"Oh yeah." She grinned, reaching out to tap the foot of the page, next to an embossed stamp. "And Liam had it notarized."

Clearing his throat, Sam scanned the lines again and stopped next to another name, the shy, downward sloping letters of Justin's signature jumping out at him. The next line had a messy squiggle of orange crayon which someone had taken the time to annotate as "Elliot Soren." He laughed, impressed by the thoroughness of the jest. "Wow, you really put in the hours on this one, Cricket. This is funny."

"Ha. About that," Cricket began, a hint of exigency coloring her amusement. "This isn't a joke. If you attempt to reenter Halberd Peak, there *will* be people waiting with pitchforks and torches, fully prepared to chase you out again."

Sam paused, lifting his gaze to hers, and finally recognized the candor behind her lopsided smile. He scoffed, brandishing the papers in his hand. "You can't just kick someone out of town."

"That's true." She shrugged, conceding the point. "But try finding a place to live."

She held out her hand. "Which reminds me, I'm going to need your keys."

Sam turned and marched past her, shoving through the front door of the parlor just in time to catch Charlie Scarver activating the arm on his tow truck, lifting the front end of Sam's SUV off the ground. He waved, shouting above the squeal of the winch. "Hey, don't worry! I'll be out of here in a tick!"

"Thanks Charlie!" Cricket called, appearing at Sam's shoulder. "Give me the keys, Soren. If you don't, they'll have to rekey the locks at the apartment."

"All right, you win," Sam capitulated, reaching into his pocket and slapping the keys into her hand. "Now, joke's over. This isn't funny anymore."

"I keep telling you, Soren," Cricket insisted, tossing the keys to Charlie. She grinned, rumpling her fingers through the front of her hair, setting it on end. "It's not a joke."

Sam held his hands out at his sides. "Why are you doing this?"

"Because you've been a miserable prick for months, and we're all sick of you." She smiled with a breeziness unbefitting the situation. "Also, you're ugly and you smell bad."

Reaching into her jacket pocket, she passed him another envelope, this one letter sized. "The good news is that the vote came with some prize money. We were concerned you might spend it all on hookers and blow, so we reinvested it for you."

Sam opened the flap on the envelope and felt his jaw go

slack. She put her hands on her hips, lifting her shoulders to her ears. "You're some other country's problem now."

"Wait a minute," he protested as she led him to her car. "I can't just leave! I need to pack! I need my *passport*!"

"Fun fact: did you know Paige took up lock-picking a while back?" Cricket climbed behind the wheel, holding the door ajar. "We took the liberty of breaking into your place and packing all your clothes, and I had Paolo bore the lock on your fire safe. Everything you need is in the trunk."

"But..." Sam's feet felt like they were bolted in place, stranding him in the center of the lot as all the shit he'd been struggling to keep at bay crashed down on him. He thought he'd been doing the right thing, the smart thing, but hadn't that always been his problem? He overthought every stupid fucking turn of the worm, needing to rationalize the horrible desolation he'd condemned himself to, even though he missed her more every day, and he knew it was sucking the life out of him.

"Damn it, Soren!" Cricket shouted with impatience. "We only have five hours to get to the airport, so stop dragging your ass and get in!"

Sam blinked in wonderment as a sense of amnesty unfurled in his chest, the sudden realization that *he didn't have to live this way* making the weight lift off his shoulders so fast that his knees almost buckled. He reached for the door, barely feeling his fingers as they curled around the handle. Cricket glowered, waiting for him to climb into the passenger seat before she slammed her door and started the engine. Throwing the car into drive, she muttered in exasperation. "I can't believe you've made me party to a rushing to the airport scene. This is such a cliché."

# CHAPTER
## Thirty-Six

"They are predicting snow for tonight." Hiroko stared out the window of their chartered car at the ominous blue-black clouds rolling in over the eastern horizon. They were passing over the Rainbow Bridge from Yokohama, and there were towering whitecaps stacked up all the way to the mouth of the bay.

Glancing up from her tablet, Gretchen followed the girl's stare and nodded with practiced detachment. "I hope you got your bread and milk."

"I do not believe so." Hiroko cocked her head to the side, looking confused. "Would you like to stop for some?"

"No, that's just something we say where I'm from." Gretchen sighed, returning to her reading. *As if I needed another reason to feel homesick.* "I'm being silly."

"I would like to see America someday," Hiroko said, her expression wistful. "Especially Yellowstone National Park. And Maine!"

"Stick with me, kid, and you will."

The driver pulled the car to a stop in front of Gretchen's apartment building and uttered a few brusque words to

Hiroko before he climbed out to open the rear door. Her assistant made a worried noise as the building's daytime concierge scurried out to meet them, speaking at a brisk clip.

"She says," Hiroko explained, pausing to parse the woman's austere cadence. "They did not wish to be discourteous to your guest, but it is not acceptable to have men sleeping in the hallways like beggars."

"My guest?" Gretchen stared in confusion at her assistant. "I know *three* people in this city."

Hiroko conferred with the attendant for a moment longer, then pivoted to translate. "She says he asked for you when he arrived, and a staff member directed him to your apartment. Several hours later, one of your neighbors came downstairs to complain that he had fallen asleep in the hallway."

The concierge gestured for them to follow, hastening to the elevators at the back of the lobby. Several minutes later, Gretchen disembarked to the sight of a slumbering giant slumped against her door. The front desk attendant spoke again, clasping her hands in genteel vexation. Hiroko continued from her other side, "She says if you do not know him, they can request for the police to remove him."

Gretchen sighed, smiling helplessly. "No. He's...*watashi no*. He's mine."

---

Two solid days of airport hopping, an overnight layover in Frankfurt, a full day spent napping in the terminal in Seoul, and just when it seemed like the odyssey was ending, he found himself stranded at the airport in Narita with zero idea how he was going to make the final journey to the city.

Finally, a kind grandma stopped to help the wayward American man buy a rail pass. Relying on hand gestures and gentle smiles, she led him to the platform, force-fed him a triangle of cold rice stuffed with some kind of salty dried fruit, and instructed the conductor to kick him off at his station. He'd hailed a taxi on the other end, and when he arrived at the address Cricket had given him, Sam stared up at the opulent high-rise and asked the driver if he was sure this was the right place. The driver barked a string of terse syllables at him, shooing him away from his car and probably cursing him in the process, then sped away before the clueless foreigner could hold him up any further.

He remembered being intercepted by a gracious, smiling woman and being asked in halting English if he was there to visit someone. She directed him to a bank of elevators, but when he got to the right door, no one was there. Checking his watch, he realized that she probably wouldn't be home for at least another two hours, so he sat down to wait. The next thing he knew, he was being shaken awake by an angel, her beautiful face swimming in front of his eyes like the hazy remnants of a dream.

"Sam?" Her sweet voice wound its way into his fatigued brain, tinged with amusement. "Hey, Mountain King. You trying to get me evicted?"

He blinked up at her for an instant, and then pulled her into his chest so fast that she tipped forward, the toes of her shoes scuffing the tile floor. Burying his face in her hair, he inhaled her green apple and fresh laundry scent deep into his lungs and closed his eyes. "God, I've missed your smell."

"What are you *doing* here?" She laughed against his shoulder. Leaning back, she reached up to touch the stubble on his chin. "You look *awful*."

"Really?" He smiled for what felt like the first time in

months, framing his hands on both sides of her face. "Because I feel fucking fantastic."

Sweeping his eyes over her, he shook his head at his own stupidity and swallowed around the lump in his throat. "I'm so sorry, I'm so, so sorry. I was such an asshole. I fucked up—"

"Ms. Clarke?" a tiny voice interjected, alerting him to the presence of a stranger. A delicate young woman, barely out of school by the looks of her, stood to one side, twisting her fingers together. "Do you require assistance?"

"No, Hiroko." Gretchen giggled, taking hold of his elbows and tugging him to his feet. "He's not drunk, just jet lagged."

The girl's eyes widened as he climbed to his full height, but she stepped back and bowed, excusing herself. Gretchen tapped a code into the keypad on the door, pulling him inside. "They don't do PDA in Japan, Sam. You've probably scarred that poor girl for li—"

Her admonition came to an abrupt end as he dragged her against him, needing her like air. Plaiting the fingers of both hands together at the back of her neck, he pressed his forehead to hers. "I missed you so goddamn much."

"I missed you too, Sam." She clutched his wrists, pulling away from him. "And it hurt like hell, but you can't just show up like this. Not when I'm finally starting to—"

"Don't," he said, gulping down the thick feeling in his throat. Fuck it, what was pride? What was *anything* without her? "I know I don't deserve this. I know I'm not the first person to ask for another chance, but I swear to God, this is not the same."

She shook her head, exhaling a long, shuddering sob. "I want to believe you, Sam, but..."

"Then believe me," he pleaded, his voice starting to

break. "*Please*, Gretchen. I missed you so much I thought I was going to die. I couldn't breathe. I couldn't eat. I just walked around feeling sick all the time, making everyone so miserable that they couldn't stand to be around me anymore. And the worst part was hearing your voice in my head, telling me I was going to be okay, because I wasn't. I was wrong, so wrong, and I'm sorry. Please, *please* tell me it's not too late."

Her chin crumpled, and he held his breath, watching a single tear trail down her cheek. An eternity seemed to pass, and then she was nodding and leaning in to pepper his jaw with kisses. Before he knew what was happening, their mouths were crushing together. They spun once, clinging to one another, and made it another step into the room before toppling to the floor and falling upon each other in a love-starved frenzy.

Pushing her skirt up to her waist, he heard the elastic of her panties rend as he pulled them down her legs with a little too much violence. Finding her wet and ready for him, he ripped open the front of his jeans and fit himself against her opening. He was inside her in a single motion, letting out a deep sigh of pure contentment at the feeling of her tight walls rippling around him. He hadn't imagined it. They fit together just as he remembered, *better* than he remembered, so perfectly that he didn't know what the fuck he'd been doing with his life until this moment. She closed her eyes as he started to move in her, digging her nails into his arms, and he pushed her hair away from her face. "Look at me, Gretchen."

Her eyes drifted open, the tears shimmering there hitting him like a knee to the gut. "You okay?"

"Yes," she whispered, hitching one leg behind his as he started to pull out. "Please stay."

He wrapped his arms under her shoulders, all the furious, brutal need he'd been carrying around for months disappearing like a puff of smoke. This was not that kind of night. Not anymore. "Tell me what's wrong."

"I thought I'd never have this again." Her voice shook, and she kissed him, a kiss that conveyed raw hunger, a need that could only be fed by another person.

"I know." He held himself over her, filling her because it was the only way he could get close enough, and took her hand, slipping it between their bodies. "I'm here now."

"Don't stop." She gasped as she strummed herself. "Please don't stop."

He quickened his pace, their bodies rocking together until she stiffened under him, a stunned expression lighting her eyes. She yelped, tightened around him so hard that he slammed his palm against the floor and fought to stay inside her. She wept in earnest, tears trailing down the sides of her face as her body clutched and released hard enough to send a river of magmatic joy gushing down his spine. He was taken an instant later, dragged under by a riptide so violent that it pummeled the air from his lungs. Seconds passed before he picked up his head and gave her a rapturous smile, smoothing his hand through her damp hair. "I love you."

---

"Wow, you weren't kidding." Gretchen sat on the edge of the bathtub, paging through the petition as Sam climbed out of the shower, wrapping a towel around his waist. "They *really* hate your ass."

"They were trying to help me." He started the faucet to fill the sink and swept a hand over the steamy mirror, gazing at his reflection as he swirled his shaving brush in one of her streaky blue Agano bowls.

"This person didn't even sign their name. It just says, 'Burn in hell Soren.'"

"Probably Chet Rice. I drove my motorcycle over his lawn when I was nineteen. He never got past it."

"That checks out." Gretchen smirked, bending to retrieve her skirt from the tile. She sucked her teeth when she noticed a conspicuous white stain on the front, tossing it into the hamper. "Fantastic. I've been looking for a way to get Hiroko to quit. Now, all I have to do is make her explain to the nice old man at the dry cleaners what this stain is."

"All that power is going to your head." He grinned as she hopped up onto the counter in front of him, taking the bowl from his hands. Raising his chin, he stared down his nose at her as she daubed a layer of piney shaving soap over the stubble on his face. "You sure you want to do this?"

"Oh, hell yes." She unfolded his straight razor, testing its sharpness against the pad of her thumb. "You know, Queen Victoria used to watch Albert shave every morning."

"No." He waved a hand between them, locking his eyes on hers. "I meant *this*. Us."

"I'm holding a sharp instrument, Sam," she teased, swirling the razor in the sink to wet the blade.

He bent closer and rested his hands on either side of her knees, tipping his chin back to give her better access. "I'm not trying to talk you out of it, Trouble. I just want you to understand, I'm going to be around a lot. Touching you. Kissing you. Doing all sorts of unspeakable things to you."

"We'll figure it out." Gretchen pressed two fingers below his temple, pulling his skin taut before she applied the blade. "Now shush. You don't stop moving, you're going to get cut."

"Oh, I already know I'll be bleeding by the end of this," he murmured, watching her from the corner of his eye. His brow arched. "But when you get good, we can invest in a barber's chair."

She started to draw the razor down his cheek, wicked delight dancing in her eyes. "Yes, please."

# CHAPTER
## Thirty-Seven

Gretchen gathered her soft cashmere wrap around her shoulders and clutched a cup of steaming ginger tea under her nose, watching the snow swirling outside the living room windows. It felt like the whole world was standing still, the discordant chaos of the city smothered under a thick blanket of white, and for once, she had nowhere to be but right here, warming her feet under the kotatsu.

A thump echoed from the next room, and Gretchen smiled, listening to the sounds of Sam navigating his large frame around the small, unfamiliar space. The panel dividing the bedroom from the rest of the apartment slid open, releasing a flood of warm, dry air into the main living space, and Sam shuffled into the room wearing flannel pajama bottoms, arctic-weight socks, and his favorite hoodie. "It's freezing in here."

"Regretting coming to find me yet?" Gretchen smiled, saluting him with her tea. As a general rule, apartments in Japan didn't have central heating. Even in luxury buildings like this one, the floors were heated, but there was no forced air, which meant they had several more months of kotatsu and space heaters to look forward to.

"Nope." Collapsing onto the sofa next to her, he lifted the edge of the comforter and slid his feet under the table. Slinging his arm around her shoulders, he pulled her against his side, scuffing his hand over her arm. "How long was I out?"

"Sixteen hours."

He hucked out a stunned laugh, scrubbing one hand down his face. "Shit. I guess I was more tired than I realized."

"You feel better now?" She sipped her tea. Last night they'd slept curled together in her woefully undersized bed, her face pressed to his chest. He was out as soon as his head hit the pillow, but she'd fought sleep, not wanting to waste a single moment spent in the shelter of his arms, feeling the steady rhythm of his heartbeat against her ear.

His lips pressed to the top of her head, and he breathed deeply, his chest swelling against her shoulder. "As long as I have you."

The wind whistled against the side of the building, and she almost imagined she could feel the structure shimmy like a tuning fork. She sighed, relaxing into him. "I'm not going anywhere."

———

THERE WAS A MOMENT, just as he was waking up and his thoughts were still fuzzy, when he was afraid it was all a dream. He felt that hateful pang of withdrawal in his chest and pinched his eyes closed, afraid to open them and start another day without her. Then, a miracle happened; he realized that the light was wrong. The windows in his bedroom faced southeast, making the bright morning sun an unavoidable adversary, but this light was cool and subdued, gently coaxing him to consciousness.

The smell of her was everywhere, and as his mind cleared, he looked around at the blank walls and paper room divider. The little electric space heater was humming away in the corner, and he felt a new sensation spreading outward from his heart, inching along his limbs until it reached all the way to his toes. He was *happy*. It wasn't a cruel hallucination; he was really here. And that meant...

He found her huddled under the heated table thing with a cup of tea, wearing fingerless gloves and a fuzzy green hat. She pushed those big tortoise shell glasses up her nose and smiled at him, looking like the first sunny day after a nuclear winter, and he couldn't believe he ever let something as inconsequential as six thousand miles get between them. Looking at her now, he knew that he would have gone to *Neptune* to see that smile again.

Serenity settled around him when he felt her nestle into the hollow under his arm. She exhaled a soft sigh of contentment that he felt all the way down to his bones, and for a few minutes they just talked, passing a few unhurried sentences as the storm raged outside. He caught one of her curls and wound it around the first knuckle of his index finger. "You have to go to work today?"

"Nope." She shook her head, tightening her arms around his waist. "Hiroko can cover for me today, but I'll have to break a bone if I want to miss any more time after that."

"I can keep myself amused tomorrow," Sam murmured. It was the days after the amusement ran out that he couldn't account for. It wasn't that he needed a *job*. The check from the insurance company arrived three days after

Gretchen left, and he had more than enough money to last for a couple years, provided he didn't develop any extravagant habits. He just didn't relish the idea of having nothing to *do*. With the exception of the handful of days after the pool hall burned down, Sam had never been without an occupation. Then, he thought about all the hours he spent confined to his plane seat, with nothing to do but meditate on the inertia that governed his life to this point and what he wanted now that he'd finally broken free. "Hey. What do you think about me taking some classes?"

She tipped her face up to give him a curious smile. "What kind of classes?"

"Whatever looks good." He shrugged, recalling all the times he stood on his side of the bar and poured another round of shots for a friend leaving for college. "Probably something related to literature."

She slid her hand over his chest, her smile widening. "I think that's a fucking fantastic idea."

———

"I CAN'T BELIEVE I had to come all the way to Japan to try something called 'Vermont Curry.'" Sam chuckled, watching her melt bricks of roux into a pot of simmering vegetables. They were standing shoulder to shoulder in her tiny kitchen, making dinner together as if this was the end of any other day, and not the first they'd spent without a dark cloud hanging over their heads.

"If I'm honest, I was just excited to find a package I could read at the grocery store. Then I got hooked on it." She set the lid on top of the pot, leaning into him when his arms snaked around her waist, and he bent to press his lips to the back of her neck.

"How long does that have to go for?" he asked, his lips brushing her ear.

"Twenty minutes?" She tipped her head back against his shoulder as one big hand slid under her sweater to cover her breast.

"Good." Fitting the other hand under her jaw, he turned her face to his and gave her a deep, languorous kiss, a growl welling up in his throat. He spun her without warning and hoisted her over his shoulder with such speed that she yelped out a laugh. Delivering a quick slap to her ass, his feet ate up the distance to the bedroom. "We've got time."

# *Epilogue*

Gretchen was forest bathing again. She wasn't supposed to be home until tomorrow, yet here she was, stretched out on the sun-dappled riverbank letting the temperate breath of the Vermont summer wash over her skin. Peering through his windshield at the brazen, nude form of his slumbering girlfriend, he forgot for a moment that her being here threw a giant wrench into his plans. How the *fuck* was he going to get away with this now?

He killed the engine and slowly opened the door, lowering his feet to the packed clay drive. Easing the door closed, he crept up the makeshift stairs at the back of the unfinished A-frame house with both arms clutched around the front of his body.

The scent of fresh lumber greeted him as he entered the echoing front room. When Gretch first started doing these little doodles back in Japan, he didn't know where it would go, but as the idea began taking shape and she got serious about it, he started seeing it too. They broke ground on the project two weeks after getting back to the country, and now it was really coming together. It was a good feeling, bringing her dreams to life.

Sam shut himself in the bathroom and removed a wriggling ball of fur from his shirt. "All right, bud. Are you gonna be cool if I leave you in here for a few minutes?"

The puppy blinked his liquid copper eyes and let out a tiny whimper, already missing his protective cocoon. *Great, now I'm trying to reason with a dog.* It was a futile effort anyway. The little whiner had fussed nonstop on the way back from the rescue in Rochester until Sam surrendered and shoved him under his shirt in an effort to shut him up. The pup promptly fell asleep, exhaling tiny snores against Sam's breadbasket.

He set the puppy in the bathtub and glanced around for something to repurpose as a bed, but there was nothing but remnants of torn cardboard from when Paolo came over to help him install the toilet. Shit, he really should have considered the logistics *beforehand*. Putting his hands on his hips, he sighed. "Sorry about this, little man."

The puppy put two plunger-sized paws on the side of the tub and stood up, perking his funny *Flying Nun* ears in wordless discombobulation. Sam turned and opened the door, addressing the little dog for a final time. "Don't look at me that way."

A breeze rustled through the trees as Sam walked up to the sandy shoulder of the riverbank and paused, looking her over. She probably didn't realize this, but four days from now would mark two years from the night when she blew into his life and turned everything upside down. He still wondered what might've happened if her car hadn't died, and she'd driven past the Halberd Peak exit. If she'd started walking in the opposite direction, or there was another rental available, or if he'd succeeded in running her off. He canted his head, observing the slow rise and fall of her breasts in the leafy quiet of the clearing, and smiled at the million little ways that everything had to go so spectacularly wrong to bring them to this place. "I am the luckiest man alive."

Opening her eyes, she gave him a radiant smile. "Well, hey there, Mountain King. If I'd known you weren't gonna be here to give me a proper welcome, I'd have stopped at Cricket's for a coffee."

"I do have a life outside of *this house,* you know." He grinned, crouching down to kiss her, craving the taste of her after their time apart. "How was the launch?"

"Meh. Once you've seen one adult products expo, you've seen them all." She sat up, sounding underwhelmed by the hedonistic wonderland where she'd spent the last four days. "I had Hiroko book me an earlier flight back as soon as my portion of the presentation was over. But *oh!*" She swatted at his arm as he lowered himself to the blanket next to her. "I almost forgot! The booth across from ours was showcasing a new line of horror-themed toys."

She struck a relaxed pose next to him, reclining on her side with her head propped against her fist. She swept the edge of her foot over his leg. "Monster cocks are having quite a moment right now. Naturally, I thought of you."

"Ah, Trouble..." Slipping his arm around her, he rolled her under him and kissed her again, this time deep and slow. Smoothing a tendril of hair away from her eyes, he gazed down at her, admiring the play of light and shadow across her face. "When my mother asks me what you do, I tell her you're a web designer."

She ran her fingers along the stubble on his jaw, giving him a heated smile. "Is this for me?"

"Yup, grew it just for you."

"So *thoughtful.*" She giggled, crinkling her nose in that knee-weakening way that always put him in mind of forever. "And good job on the house."

"We had to push hard, but I wanted to get the bathroom done before you got back." He dipped his head to lay a kiss on her collarbone, feeling her pulse leap against his lips. "We should throw a couple sleeping bags down in the loft and camp out tonight. See how it feels."

"After three days in Vegas, a camp out sounds *perfect.* But first..." She slid out from under him, reaching for her little green sundress. Slipping it over her head, she twisted to drape her body over his chest. "I really don't have to pee in the woods anymore?"

"Nope." He folded his hands behind his head and grinned. Maybe he hadn't put the big red bow on the puppy's collar, but this was still a damn good surprise. "Knock yourself out."

He closed his eyes and listened to the soft rubber soles of her sneakers traveling up the stairs and into the house. The door creaked open, and he waited a few seconds more, until an ecstatic feminine squeal rang through the clearing, followed by a barrage of shrill puppy barks. He pushed himself up onto one elbow and laughed, watching the back of the house until she burst into the open air with the puppy held tight against her heart, her cheeks flushed with joy. "Can we call him Kaiju?"

*About the Author*

After two *long* years of exile, Rowan Helaine and her trusty copilot, Filburt the rescue hound, are returning to New England. She's wicked excited to be home.

Made in the USA
Columbia, SC
07 June 2022

61335534R00174